A Watery Grave

Joan Druett

A Watery Grave

ST. MARTIN'S MINOTAUR ❧ NEW YORK

www.minotaurbooks.com

Library of Congress Cataloging-in-Publication Data

Druett, Joan.
    A watery grave / Joan Druett.—1st St. Martin's Minotaur ed.
        p. cm.
    ISBN 0-312-33441-9
    EAN 978-0312-33441-3
    1. United States Exploring Expedition (1838–1842)—Fiction. 2. Americans—Foreign countries—Fiction. 3. Scientific expeditions—Fiction. 4. Explorers—Fiction. 5. Linguists—Fiction. I. Title.

PR9639.3.D68W37 2004
823'.914—dc22

                                                              2004049572

10   9   8   7   6   5   4   3   2

For Gillian (who knows who she is)

Author's Note

On Sunday, August 18, 1838, the six ships of the first, great United States South Seas Exploring Expedition, commanded by Lieutenant Charles Wilkes, crewed by 246 officers and men, and with seven scientists and two artists on board, set sail from the Hampton Roads, Virginia, headed for the far side of the world. Almost four years later, in June 1842, the remnants of the expedition straggled into New York. One vessel had been sent back in disgrace; one had been lost with all hands; another had been wrecked at the Columbia River; and a fourth had been sold into the opium-running trade on the coast of China. Much had been accomplished—huge tracts of the ocean had been charted, plus 800 miles of scarcely known Oregon shore and 1,500 miles of entirely unknown Antarctic coast. The Stars and Stripes had fluttered off the lagoons of well over 200 tropical islands, and more than 4,000 artifacts and 2,000 scientific specimens had been collected, an enormously rich fund that became the foundation of the collection of the new Smithsonian Institution. For uncounted thousands of Pacific Islanders the Exploring Expedition had been their first introduction to the official face of the USA. Yet, instead of returning home in triumph, Lieutenant Wilkes chose to slink on shore by hitching a ride on the pilot boat.

The strange voyage of the U.S. Exploring Expedition is the setting of the Wiki Coffin mystery series. While the novels are based on true events, and many of the participants in the stories are real, the mysteries and the people most intimately involved with them are figments of the author's overactive imagination— as is the brig *Swallow,* the seventh ship upon which most of the action takes place.

A Watery Grave

One

The man who was about to be wrongfully arrested waited in the black shadow of a tree by the Elizabeth River. His name was Wiki Coffin, and he had been waiting without moving for more than two hours. Thinking that it was surely time the appointment was kept, he restlessly touched the pistols in his belt. Stilling again, he listened intently for the sounds of people approaching—the rhythmic swish of oars or the rattle of harness and beat of hooves—but heard nothing.

When Wiki had taken up his station the moon had been high, glinting on the leaves above his head, its face occasionally obscured by high clouds. The soft breeze was redolent with the smells of cypress and swamp, warm growth, and salt sea; and the night was filled with the quiet rush and lap of the river, along with the almost inaudible chuckle of one of the creeks that fed the great stream somewhere beyond an upriver headland. Closer, crabs scuttled and shellfish plopped. Too, Wiki had heard small creatures prowl the thicket behind him, owls calling in distant trees, and faint ghostly cries from the Great Dismal Swamp, *Whip poor Willy, whip poor Willy whip* . . . Now the graying sky rang with the harsh call of hunting ospreys, while gulls swooped and squalled over the harbor. The moon and stars had faded.

Across the river the far shore was becoming distinct. The waters were a clear brown like strong tea, streaked with veins of mud, shimmering as the sun nudged the low horizon, waves rising and falling so that the seven ships of the United States Exploring Expedition rocked gently at their anchors. The flagship *Vincennes*, her massive hull painted black save for the white streak regularly interrupted with square black gun ports, was lit up by the first long rays; and the intricate rigging of the second-in-command, the sloop of war *Peacock*, became silhouetted against the sky. Then the chunky hull of the expedition's storeship *Relief* came into view. The smaller ships of the discovery fleet—*Porpoise, Flying Fish, Sea Gull,* and *Swallow*—were veiled in the mists that rose off the water, but Wiki could hear faint piping and drums as the watches were summoned to swab decks.

He thought that soon there would be antlike figures in the yards and masts, reminding all of Norfolk and Portsmouth that after years of dissention and controversy the great United States Exploring Expedition was truly bound for exotic shores and distant seas, and heard the distant sound of a trumpet, echoed by trilling calls from all the ships. It was the order to get ready to make sail and trip the anchor, and he realized with a lurch in his chest that the fleet was readying for departure. Boats were putting out hastily from shore, heading for the ships. He thought urgently that he should be on board the *Swallow*; soon he would be missed. Wiki shifted from one foot to the other, a knot in his gut, on the verge of abandoning his vigil.

With a queer mixture of foreboding and relief, he saw a small boat heading his way. Unexpectedly, however, it was coming from an upriver direction, not from across the harbor, so that it was only about forty or fifty feet away when he first saw it. It was a curiously derelict craft, too, but he stepped out of the shelter of the tree, raising his palm in a signal. Then, from the corner of his eye, Wiki glimpsed movement—not on the river, but in the thicket on the low slope behind him. He whirled around, heard the utterly unexpected crack of a rifle, and felt the wind of a bullet as it whined close by.

Ambush! Wiki dived full length, rolling in the mud to keep a low profile as he discarded his pistols, spinning them into the cover of a bush. The rifle cracked a second time as he hit the water, and he dug his head into the first wave and struck out strongly for the boat.

When he lifted his face to suck in a breath the gun was silent. He had no way of telling how many shots had been fired in the meantime. There was no movement in the thicket, but the feeling of being watched persisted. Then he looked for the boat. It was just a few yards away, revolving with the current. There was no sign of any oarsmen. To all appearances, it was empty. Perplexed, Wiki paused, kicking slowly to keep still in the water.

Something white lifted up from inside the boat. It was just a flicker, but looked like a woman's arm gesturing for help. A superstitious shiver lifted the wet hairs on his neck. A man in a Norfolk tavern had told him the story of the Lady of the Lake—the ghost of an Indian girl who had died in the Great Dismal Swamp on the way to a tryst with her lover. The sight of her canoe always came as a dire warning, the man had said. However, Wiki ducked his head down and swam for the boat because he reckoned he had no choice.

Another dozen strokes and he was there. Wiki gripped the rough wooden gunwale on the side away from the beach, shaking his head vigorously to flap his long hair away from his face and blinking water from his eyes. Then he froze, his grasp convulsive. There was a dead woman lying in the bottom of the boat.

She was laid out formally, as if in a coffin, stretched out on her back beneath the single thwart with her gown spread neatly all the way to the toes of her satin slippers, her hands clasped together on her breast. A paddle lay tidily beside her, its blade still wet. Wiki knew something of boat burials. In the remote Pacific he had visited atolls where it was the custom for a funeral canoe to be pushed out to sea with the corpse inside. Too, he had read about Viking funerals, where important cadavers were placed in longships and buried or burned or set adrift; but this was definitely his first personal experience of any such thing. He was also certain boat burial was not the custom in Virginia.

The dead woman appeared to be quite young, not much older than himself. Her muslin gown was white, and he saw that a fold of this, catching the breeze, had tricked him into thinking it was a beckoning arm. Realizing that she had not been dead many hours, he shivered again. The yellow curls that escaped from her lace cap still held some of the shine of life. Then, as the boat bobbed with his weight on the gunwale, the woman's head fell to one side, and her mouth gaped. She had been beautiful, but now she looked grotesque.

He heard shouts and the thump of hooves and looked up to see that people had burst out onto the riverbank, followed by a

4

big man on a horse, who held himself as if he was someone official. The low sun caught the glitter of the badge he wore on his coat. The law, Wiki realized, or maybe even the sheriff, which meant there was a good chance it was safe to return to the beach. Perhaps they had arrested the rifleman. He slid hand over hand along the side until he came to the trailing painter, and then, drawing the rope over his shoulder, he gripped the cut end between his teeth and began to swim, lugging the boat with its macabre burden behind him.

He swam slowly because the going was much harder than he had expected. The boat was getting heavier by the moment, and when he turned his head he saw it was lower in the water, sinking visibly. Then he saw that water was pouring in from two holes bored into the hull just below the waterline. The loose fold of the woman's white gown was now too sodden to lift with the breeze. Another ten minutes and the body would have disappeared forever. The boat would have sunk, the current dragging it along the river bottom toward the waiting sea, and the thwart would have prevented the decomposing corpse from floating free.

Wiki swam hard to get the boat to the beach before it foundered, thinking it was going to be a close call. As it was, if people had not dashed into the water to help, he would have been forced to give up. When they finally got hold of the boat, Wiki crawled up onto the grass with what felt like the last of his strength. He sat slumped, waiting for his breathing to settle. The sound of the hull grating on mud and sand and people shouting was muted in his thundering ears. Then he heard the rattle of leathers as the horseman dismounted. Wiki slowly clambered to his feet.

However, the officer was paying him no attention. Instead, he was hunkered down by the beached boat, so Wiki took the opportunity to look about for his pistols but without success. Then, when the man finally stood up and turned to face him, Wiki saw he had the two heavy weapons held by the barrels in one massive hand.

The officer was a middle-aged, burly fellow, his face mottled red with good living and creased with years of sun. His coat and riding breeches were well-tailored and fashionable, so that despite the five-pointed nickel star on his lapel he looked a lot more like a prosperous landholder than an agent of law, order, and the collection of taxes. For a moment there was silence while this individual looked from one muddy pistol to the other, balancing them on his broad palms; then he lifted his head to stare at Wiki from under the brim of his wide planter's hat, saying, "These folks tell me they heard you firing these here pistols. What did you think you were shooting at, son?"

Wiki paused, disliking the word "son"—though, as he admitted privately, he had been called a great deal worse of late. Then he agreed. "They're right. Those pistols are mine. But I wasn't firing them. I was the one being shot at."

"Wa'al, is that so?" said the officer, sounding as if he did not believe a word of it. "And jes' who was this feller you reckon was taking potshots at your carcass, huh?"

"I haven't a notion."

"And you can't think of a reason?"

"No, I can't. He jumped out of the bush and fired without warning."

"And your name?"

"William Coffin Jr. I'm with the exploring expedition." Even as he spoke, Wiki could hear distant piping and the shouts of officers echoing across the water as the preparations to sail became more urgent.

The officer's thick eyebrows shot up. "You're a navy lad?"

"I'm a civilian—with the brig *Swallow*."

"Dod dog it, he ain't no civilian!" a voice hollered from the midst of the crowd. "He's a seaman jes' like meself—and his name ain't William Coffin, neither."

Everyone turned to gape at a scruffy old salt with an unshaven face and a dirty bandanna tied about his head. Wiki did not recognize the fellow at all, but it was all too obvious that the speaker remembered him. "Don't you be fooled by them blue eyes, Sheriff," this sailor declared with a smirk. "He's a Kanaka—a native from one of them savage islands in the Pacific. I sailed wiv 'im onct and not for long, but I know it for a fact. His Kanaka name be Wiki Kehua, which folks say means 'Willy-the-Ghost.' I reckon he's a runaway, sir!"

"Kanaka?" echoed the sheriff, pronouncing it "kernacker" in his long southern drawl. Turning back, he tipped up his hat with the barrel of one of the pistols to study Wiki at leisure, all the way from his long black hair to his flat broad feet planted strongly in the mud.

Wiki withstood the scrutiny in silence, knowing from experience that it was a bad idea to point out that though he was half New Zealand Maori, since the age of twelve he had been raised as an American and was probably better educated than any of these *pakeha* who were gawking at him now. It would not help, either, to inform them that though he was the direct descendant of famous warriors and powerful chiefs, he was also the son of a Salem sea captain—a man who had christened him "William Coffin" after himself. And it was certainly risky to mention that his Maori nickname, "kehua"—which did indeed mean "ghost"—was a mocking play on the name "Coffin," plus his chameleonlike ability to talk and behave like a true-blue American one moment and a beach-bred native of the Pacific the next.

The joke would be quite beyond them, he was certain, the *pakeha* understanding of the Polynesian sense of humor being so unreliable; and he certainly did not feel like laughing himself. Wiki was overwhelmingly conscious of the sounds echoing across the river from the fleet—the rattle of chains and the increasingly urgent shouting. Seagulls whirled and screamed above the sails that were unfurling in jerky succession.

The sheriff said meditatively, "Kernacker, huh? Up to this minute, I thought you were an Indian. How long you been here, son?"

"In Norfolk? A week."

"On this riverbank, I mean."

Wiki shrugged. "A couple of hours or more, judging by the stars. I don't have any kind of timepiece."

"You were here during nighttime, huh? You got your pass to show me?"

"My . . . ?"

"Your pass. All darkies got to carry a pass after curfew."

Wiki stiffened with rage. Then he reined in his temper. There was a corpse in that derelict boat, and he'd already been accused of firing the shots that had drawn this crowd. If it turned out this woman had been done to death, he would be the obvious scapegoat—and this was territory where lynch law once reigned. He thought of a gravestone he'd seen under a tree in a field the other day that read: JEB JOHNSON HANGED BY MISTAKE.

He said with forced calmness, schooling himself not to look at the ships making sail on the far side of the harbor, "I do not need a pass, and I knew nothing about a curfew. I was simply standing under that tree there minding my own business when I saw the boat come drifting downriver—from beyond that headland. I stepped out to see better, and I glimpsed a man behind me—he had a rifle, lifted it, fired. Once, twice, maybe more times, I don't know how many."

"How far off was he?"

"Not far. Back there." Wiki pointed at the thicket, thinking the marksman must have made a very quick escape since none of this mob had spied him.

"Yet he didn't manage to hit you, even though you was so close?" This time the tone was openly derisive.

Wiki was beginning to feel desperate. The *Vincennes* had now set her square sails, the broad canvas sheets luminous in the early sunlight. He tore his gaze away and said, "I shucked my pistols because of the weight and dived for the water. I was moving fast."

"But by your own accounting, he took you by surprise, and he had at least two chances to shoot you dead. And, what's more, you can't think of any reason he would want to do that. You're certain sure he was firing at you and not at somethin' else?"

"Aye," said Wiki. Then he paused, his mind suddenly filled with an altered picture of what had happened. He remembered the sounds of the first two shots, the double crack, the almost inaudible whine of the bullets—but suddenly he recollected, too, faint *thunks* in the distance as bullets hit something wooden.

The officer was watching him closely. Then he said, "So how come he hit that there boat instead of you, huh?"

Wiki frowned, remembering the two holes that had leaked so fast once the water reached them. It was certainly possible they were shot holes. Had the rifleman been firing at the boat? It had been higher in the water then, presenting a good target. He wondered with a grimace where the bullets had finished up. They were lodged in the corpse, he supposed.

The sheriff snapped, "I reckon those shots were fired in the wild hope of sinking the boat. What d'you think of that theory, huh?"

Wiki was silent a moment, thinking about it, and then said, "It's possible."

"So how long have you known the victim?"

Wiki said, aghast, "She's a total stranger to me!"

"You don't know who she is?"

"Of course I don't!"

The crowd was growing as more people streamed down through the trees. "Mrs. Tristram T. Stanton, she," an ancient beldame volunteered. "Richest woman in the whole of ole Virginny, married to the son of old man Stanton hisself. *Not* a happy situation. Threatened to do away wiv herself often. Looks like she done it. Poison, I 'spect," she added, with an air of omnipotence.

"You think she committed suicide?" Wiki turned to stare at the corpse, which somehow looked more lifeless. The head was awry, the jaw sagging open. The muslin dress was sodden and sullied. The yellow hair looked as dead as wet hay. In many parts of the Pacific this would be considered a time of great danger, when the potentially malevolent spirit was loosed. The Polynesian side of Wiki's nature craved some kind of ritual to send the hungry ghost on its proper path to the realm of darkness—*te po*, the place of departed spirits. The *pakeha* part of his mind dismissed the idea, but the hairs on his forearms kept on rising.

Then he thought about the manner of the woman's death. He felt certain that the old crone was wrong, but was not sure why he was so convinced that Mrs. Tristram T. Stanton had not done away with herself. The body was reposed in such a consciously artistic fashion that it was easy to envisage Mrs. Stanton pushing the boat out, wielding the paddle until she felt the poison take effect, and then sliding under the thwart and taking up this pose, preparing herself for a melodramatic end. But still the image was unconvincing. Something about her dress . . .

"Hysterical sort she were, the poor mad creature," the old crone nattered on. "I know it," she claimed, "on account of my granddaughter is help at the Stanton plantation house. Mistress was so 'ysterical at the very notion of 'im bein' gone for three or more years, there were strong doubts he'd get away."

This made no sense at all to Wiki. Then, as everyone stared at the old besom, the rapt silence was broken by the rolling thunder of a single cannon, setting the seabirds to wheeling and shrieking. It was the signal that the fleet was ready to drop down the river.

The sheriff didn't even bother to look at the source of the commotion. Instead, he turned his head to watch as two more horsemen came galloping through the thicket, reined in beside the beached boat, and leaped to the ground. Because they also wore nickel stars on their coat lapels, Wiki deduced they were the sheriff's men—his deputies, his *comitatus posse*. They knew their job, he saw, because after nothing more than a nod from the boss they embarked on a businesslike examination of the boat.

First, they picked up the paddle and studied it as if the damp blade could tell them something. Then, putting it aside, they set to poking fingers through the two holes in the hull. An animated but muttered conversation ensued. One produced a pad and pencil, and laboriously recorded the details of this discovery, along with the name of the victim.

Then they started in on the corpse. The head with its bedraggled lace and ribbon cap was pushed back—rather too easily, Wiki thought with a preternatural shiver—and the mouth pried farther open. "No signs of poison," the sheriff said sharply, as if this confirmed his suspicions. "No blistering of the mouth."

The hands got the same treatment. "No burns, no gunpowder marks, no blood. Wa-al," he said, straightening as this was noted, "let's get her out of the boat."

"Give way," said one of the deputies, and the crowd obediently shuffled backward, Wiki with them. Mud squirted around his feet—the riverbank was becoming very trampled. He expected the sheriff to give the order to break the thwart so the body could be lifted straight upward, but apparently he didn't think it necessary. The deputies, one on each side of the dead woman, gripped her stiff arms to pull her out from under the thwart. For a moment it looked as if the boat would refuse to yield its burden, but all at once with a ripping of cloth the body came up—with such a jerk that it arrived at a standing position before the officers could stop their hauling. When they staggered to a halt it dangled from their fists like a monstrous puppet, the head lying on the shoulder in a parody of life that was horribly grotesque. "Jee-rusalem," someone in the crowd muttered sickly—and yet another rider came galloping down from the thicket.

The deputies hastily laid the body on the grass and stepped back, brushing their palms against their sides and looking sheepish. The horseman vaulted to the ground and ran over to the corpse, crying in a low voice, "Oh my God, so she did it." Then he whirled on his heel and stared at the sheriff. "Who found her?"

Wiki saw that he was another big man, as brawny as the sheriff. Despite his wrestlerlike build, though, the newcomer had every appearance of a fine gentleman—albeit a most disheveled one. He wore a top-quality tailored coat, its black velvet collar turned down to display the lapels of his white vest, the high wing collar of his shirt, and the elaborate folds of his white silk cravat, but everything was spattered with mud. His knee-high boots were water stained after what had evidently been a wild gallop. He had lost or discarded his hat, and brown hair flopped over his broad, meaty forehead and heavy eyebrows. His ears were low down on his head and as protuberant as an ape's, sticking out from behind thick sideburns, and his small, alert eyes were set far back in the sockets.

This, Wiki had no doubt, was Tristram T. Stanton himself. Several of the men in the crowd had taken off their hats, presumably as a mark of respect to the bereaved. The sheriff, however, was unmoving, impassively waiting for Stanton to go on.

Stanton muttered, "I shouldn't have done it."

"Done what, Mr. Stanton?" asked the sheriff.

"I've been invited to sail with the expedition as an astronomer. She did not want me to go, and we quarreled about it. Last night I sent her a note, telling her I was determined to go. But I did not believe she would carry out her threat."

"Threat?"

"To put an end to her life."

The sheriff pursed his lips judiciously and then said, "She didn't."

"*What?*" The tone was astonished.

"I don't believe she committed suicide."

"Not suicide?" Stanton's face had gone scarlet. "But surely . . ."

"I regret to inform you that I reckon your wife was murdered."

"Murdered?" Stanton cried.

"I figure she was killed, put in the boat, and then set adrift.

When it was floating down the river, the murderer shot two holes into the waterline—two shots in quick succession, as many of the fine folks here have testified. His vain hope was to sink both boat and body without a trace, but people responded to the sound of the shots before the boat could founder."

"But that's insane!"

"A nasty business," the sheriff agreed. "The product of a savage mind."

Savage. Wiki's mouth was abruptly dry. Every eye in the mob was on him.

Stanton said blankly, "You've found the murderer?"

"I believe so," said the sheriff, and again looked deliberately at Wiki, who took a backward step, saying hastily, "Now then, just a moment—"

It was not the sheriff who seized him, however. Instead, it was the two deputies who sprang forward and gripped his arms. The sheriff was busily contemplating Wiki's pistols, back to bouncing and balancing them in his broad palms. "Two shots," he said reflectively. "Close together, which don't seem to allow much chance to reload. It appears to me a pair of pistols was exactly what the murderer needed—and that makes a lot more sense than an invisible fellow with a rifle."

Then, with ponderous deliberation, he thrust the guns into the wide leather belt that encompassed his massive waist and said, "Willy Kernacker, or whatever you call yourself, I am taking you into custody on suspicion of the murder of Mrs. Tristram T. Stanton and the desecration of her corpse."

As they escorted Wiki Coffin away, over his shoulder he could see the seven ships of the expedition taking their departure. They were sailing in order of rank with their canvas billowing straight and the yards manned, the *Vincennes* in the lead, and the others following, while cannon thundered over and over in a rolling salute from the Gosport Navy Yard. With a terrible sense of desperation, he realized that the fleet was sailing, and had left him behind.

Two

They confined Wiki in the old Portsmouth Sugar House at the south end of Crawford Street. The cell was made of stone; but though it was pleasantly cool, it smelled bad because of the miasmas wafting in from the privy in the yard outside. There was a view of the waterfront from the barred window, but Wiki sank to the side of the narrow berth, his head in his hands.

At this moment it was impossible to believe he had been reluctant about joining the expedition—that he had agreed only because he did not want to offend an old comrade. Now he would have given a great deal to be on board the brig *Swallow*, the deck dipping and swaying beneath his feet, a sticky salt tang in the air he breathed, on the verge of sailing off to the southern polar regions of the Antarctic. Instead, here he was incarcerated in a Virginian cell. When the sheriff and his men returned a half-dozen hours later, he stood up with every expectation of the worst. Then, with relief so intense that his face creased up into triangles of delight, Wiki recognized the man who was with them.

"George!" he exclaimed, and then recollected himself. "Captain Rochester!" George Rochester might have been a mere midshipman, but—as Wiki knew very well indeed—he was a midshipman who commanded a ship of his own, the *Swallow*.

George looked every inch a captain, too, dressed to the nines in a lieutenant's blue claw-hammer coat, its broad lapels embellished with gold buttons and lace, and a gold epaulette on the right shoulder, which announced to the world that he was the master of a ship. His long neck was encompassed by a stand-up collar lavishly embroidered with gold oak leaves and acorns and fouled anchors, and three more buttons decorated the cuff of each sleeve, laced with still more gold. His trousers were white, and because of the way he stood with his bottom and his knees tucked in, his muscular calves shoved out at the back.

Normally, George Rochester wore the benign expression of a sheep, the impression helped out by his long nose and fluffy fair sideburns, but at this moment he was extremely severe. "Mr. Coffin," he pronounced, "you failed to report on board the brig."

"I apologize, Captain Rochester," said Wiki humbly. "Events were out of my control. It's very good to see you—I thought you'd taken your departure."

"Then you were mistaken, sir! The squadron's lying abreast of Fort Munroe, ready to sail on the first fair wind, everything in a state of forwardness—it's a great day for America! However, when the sheriff informed me that he was taking you to revisit the scene of the crime, I insisted on coming along as your representative."

So things were not looking up at all. His optimism dashed, Wiki silently followed the sheriff out of the cell and along a bricked corridor to a yard where five saddled horses were waiting. As they trotted along Crawford Street, a deputy rode on either side of him, and he was very conscious of the stares and whispers of onlookers.

Then the town was left behind, and they were riding along the bridle path beside the river toward the place where he had retrieved the boat. Wiki could see the big tree that had sheltered him as he had waited from midnight to dawn. The strong, lower branches spread out horizontally, reminding him of a gallows tree. The boat had been taken away, along with the body, but a big muddy scar in the grass marked the place where the crowd had dragged it out of the river. Wiki glanced around, thinking that the place looked remarkably ordinary, considering the things that had happened here.

The sheriff reined in. He said to Wiki, "You still reckon it was suicide?"

"I never said it was suicide," Wiki retorted. Then he added soberly, "As it happens, I'm certain you are right. Someone killed her, and then laid her out the way I found her in that boat."

"You think so, huh?" The sheriff looked interested. "And are you going to tell us what led you to that conclusion?"

"Her skirt," said Wiki. He had thought about it deeply during the hours of imprisonment. "When I first saw the corpse, her dress was spread all the way to her feet. If she had laid herself out that way, she would have had to sit up and reach over the thwart to smooth down her skirt. Then, when she lay down again, the hem would have ridden up to her ankles with the movement. So, by logic, it was someone else who arranged her—after she was dead."

"Clever," said the sheriff. His eyebrows were hoisted high; it was the most complicated expression Wiki had seen on his face—surprise and curiosity mixed with a touch of admiration. "But you're sticking to your story of the mysterious man with a rifle?"

"He must have been the murderer. I presume he set up the scene to look like suicide, but when the boat was floating down the river he changed his mind and tried to get rid of the evidence."

The sheriff sat still a moment, gazing at Wiki in contemplative fashion. Then, moving abruptly, he wheeled his horse, leading the way up the slope to the thicket. When the brush surrounded them, it was suddenly warmer. Clouds of insects whined. Where the crowds had pushed through, the ground underfoot was heavily trampled. The sheriff looked over his shoulder. "You want to find the tracks of your rifleman, Mr. Kernacker-Indian?"

"I'm not that kind of Indian," Wiki said dryly.

The sheriff shrugged and nudged his horse along. They followed him in single file upriver through the brush, their horses walking a narrow track where others had come before. The air was filled with the sounds of unseen rushing water, the hum of insects, the rustle of twigs and reeds as the horses pushed through them, and the steady, slow thump of hooves. The late afternoon sun was hot, and a mixture of sweat and dust prickled Wiki's neck and arms. He watched Rochester's uniform-clad back bob along ahead of him and thought his friend must be very uncomfortable. However, the long torso was ramrod straight. Wiki himself was riding native fashion, slumped on his jogging horse with his knees well bent and his feet high up the withers. It was comfortable—almost relaxing. Then the little cavalcade emerged from the undergrowth, arriving at the top of a cliff that overlooked a creek.

The steep path that descended to the rivulet was overhung by trees. At the bottom was a backwater, where the stream formed a quiet lagoon. The surface of this pool was edged with reeds and dusted with pollen, and the water was dark with rotting vegetation. The air was cool, but the smell was unpleasant. This was the place where the boat with the dead body had been launched, Wiki realized. He could see the deep mark on the verge where the derelict had lain for a long time before being sent on its grisly last cruise and the dragging smear where it had been pushed into the creek. He slid off his horse—and was hit by a blast of overwhelming terror.

Wiki stumbled and fell, tearing one knee of his dungaree pants—he could *feel* the violence that had been done here, and the shocking abruptness of the release of the woman's spirit. *Haere e te hoa, ko te tatou kainga nui kena,* he cried in the back of his mind—"Go, friend, to the great abode that awaits us all," commanding the tortured ghost to take *te ara whanui a Tane,* the broad path of Tane, to join her ancestors and abandon this world of life to the living. He was aware of the *pakeha* staring and wondering at his distress, but he was incapable of hiding it.

When the inner panic had subsided, he clambered shakily to his feet, looked at the sheriff, and asked as calmly as he could, "How was she killed?"

"Neck broken," the sheriff said succinctly.

Wiki winced, remembering how the dead head had flopped. Now the progression of events was obvious to him—after the woman was killed, the murderer had laid out the corpse and had waded into the water to push the boat into the stream, using the paddle as a crutch. Then he had returned to the bank, mounted his horse, and from this vantage point had watched the craft float off on its way to the Elizabeth River. Changing his mind for some unknown reason, he had ridden along the riverbank with a rifle, chasing the boat in a doomed attempt to sink it with a couple of well-placed shots.

The sheriff seemed quite uninterested in dismounting to study the scene in detail, turning his horse to lead the way inland. The group followed. Within minutes the trail broke out of the brush and became a road that slashed through a patchwork of cultivated fields toward a mansion set among gardens and trees. This, it soon became obvious, was the sheriff's objective. The white marble columns of the wide portico gleamed magnificently in the late afternoon sun as they trotted toward it. For a long time they did not seem to be getting any closer, but then suddenly the dense shadow of the overhanging entranceway enveloped them.

While there had been no apparent movement inside the mansion, their approach had been watched, it seemed, as stable hands silently materialized to take their bridles. Wiki slid down from the saddle, feeling very much at a disadvantage in his crumpled shirt and dungaree trousers. Since dawn his clothes had soaked in the river, had dried on his body, and had become sweaty and dusty with the ride. George might have been hot and uncomfortable in his fine tailored uniform, but Wiki now envied him his smart appearance.

The entrance doors to this magnificent mansion were tall, with finely wrought glass panes. One of them opened to reveal a young black housemaid, the whites of her staring eyes matching the color of her mobcap. She looked terrified.

The sheriff said, "Mr. Stanton is expecting us."

The girl's gaze darted from one man to the other and then fixed on Wiki's face. She pointed at his chest and said, "I don't know that I oughter let *him* in, sir."

"Why not?" said the sheriff.

"I don't know about letting in Injuns."

An impatient male voice echoed from behind her. "Bring them in, Em, goddammit. Don't you ever listen to orders? Bring them in!"

The harsh resonance of the voice seemed familiar, but when Wiki arrived in the huge marbled hallway and looked up the curved stairway to where the speaker was standing, it was a man he had never seen before. However, the resemblance was so striking, it was obvious this was the father of Tristram T. Stanton. The hair was thick gray instead of brown but flopped over the same kind of meaty forehead and bushy brows, and the thick-lipped, down-turned mouth was just as arrogant. Like his son, Stanton had protuberant, low-set ears that stuck out from behind long sideburns, and small, deep-set eyes that flickered from man to man. Despite his husky build, there was the same apelike look.

They all trooped inside, and Stanton jerked his head for them to come up the stairs. "You too, Em!" he shouted, and Wiki could hear the maidservant as she scuttled in their rear. Then, as they arrived at the doorway of a large reception room, he saw the reason she had been summoned. Lined up along one wall, watching the group's arrival with open fascination, were the servants of the house, who looked as if they had been waiting quite some time. After Em scampered to join the line, however, Stanton led the sheriff's party farther along the passage to a well-appointed study.

The room was dominated by a massive desk, which was piled with papers and faced a huge, many-paned window that overlooked the fields. The wall behind the desk was shelved and held rows of black boxes with the names of ships and merchants painted on them in white. Obviously, this was where the business of the plantation was carried out. Wiki wondered if the old man still held the reins or shared the office work with his son.

After stiffly lowering himself onto a seat behind the desk, Stanton busied himself with opening a humidor and selecting a cigar from within it. Though he waved a large liver-spotted hand at the chairs set facing him, the sheriff remained standing, and so did everyone else, too, waiting in silence as Stanton took out a lucifer, struck it, and applied it to the end of the cigar with care. Finally, when the stinging chemical smell of the match had been replaced with the aroma of fine tobacco, he puffed out a cloud and pursed his thick lips, revealing square yellow teeth clamped about the cigar.

He grunted, "So the silly bitch is dead."

Wiki saw George Rochester blink with shock. Stanton saw it too and barked, "It's no secret—the woman was a confounded liability. Hysterical as a bloody jackass—we had thoughts of getting a certificate and confining her someplace for her own safety and the sanity of those around her." He looked again at George Rochester and snarled, "You would prefer me to be hypocritical, sir?"

Rochester opened his mouth, blushing bright red, but before he could say anything the sheriff broke into the exchange, saying, "Mr. Stanton, I would be obliged if you'd tell me what you were doing last night and early this morning."

"For the benefit of these gentlemen?" Stanton demanded. His contemptuous little eyes flicked across Wiki's face. "My son was out for the night. The folks around here are falling all over themselves to amuse and entertain the officers and scientifics afore they sail off to make America proud and famous. It's the height of Virginian fashion—a fad, a fad! It's whist parties here, banquets there, and I've hardly seen hide or hair of my son for the past six weeks, and my daughter-in-law loonier than ever on account of it. So she and I dined alone, as usual—if you can call it alone in a house full of confounded servants. Then I worked at some accounts, after that I retired, and she did God-knows-what. I woke in the night to hear a horse a-galloping down the carriageway, went back to sleep, thought nothing of it, not even when she chose not to turn up for breakfast."

Then he put his great gnarled hands on the desktop, lifted himself partway out of his chair to stare at Wiki, and demanded of the sheriff, "Is this the fellow what found her?"

"Yessir," said the sheriff.

"I see." There was a short, tense pause, while Wiki silently met the penetrating stare of the bright, small eyes. It was impossible to read Stanton's expression. Then, just as abruptly, Stanton slumped back in his chair, saying impatiently to the sheriff, "Well, go and interview the servants, go. They're assembled, just as you requested."

The servants were standing in the same line, except there were more of them, the stable hands having joined the assemblage. The sheriff was silent a long moment, his fists on his belt and his paunch pushing out his vest while he scanned the long row deliberately. Then he gestured in Wiki's direction and said, "Any of you folks seen this fellow before?"

Silence—silence so profound that Wiki became aware of a clock ticking somewhere down the hallway. He could hear George Rochester's breathing and the creak as the sheriff shifted. All eyes were fixed on him, and most of the mouths were gaping open in what looked like utter incomprehension. Then at last an elderly man in a long apron cleared his throat and said, "No, Mr. Sheriff sir." And heads were shaken all along the row.

"You're certain?"

"Not likely to forget an Injun, sir. Wouldn't let 'im in the house in the fust place."

The sheriff pursed his lips, his expression brooding. He said, "Your mistress was taken away in the night. Did none of you see the man who came to get her?"

Again there was silence. Then the same old retainer said reluctantly, "I saw 'im, sir."

"When?"

"In the middle of the night, about eleven or twelve. I heard someone come in, so I got up and looked down the stairwell from the attic floor where the house servants live and saw 'im run up the stairs and go into Mrs. Stanton's room."

"And was it *this* fellow?" demanded the sheriff, jerking a thick thumb at Wiki.

"Of cuss not!" the servant exclaimed, appalled at the very notion. "You think I'd watch a dirty Injun go into the mistress's room without raising hell? Not on your life, sir!"

"So who *was* the man who went into her room?"

Dead silence. Then the old man said reluctantly, "Her 'usband."

"*Tristram Stanton?*" This time the exclamation came from Rochester. Everyone looked at him, and he went bright red and blurted, "Last *night?*"

"It was Mr. Tristram Stanton," the old retainer insisted. "It might've been the middle of the night, but the lanterns in the hall were lit. He looked up when 'e 'eard me and called out, 'Go back to bed, Peter, I don't need you tonight'—it was him, I'd swear it on the Bible."

"How long was he there?" said the sheriff.

"Not long—it was less'n hour later that I 'eard 'im gallop off."

George Rochester tried to interrupt again, but the sheriff raised his palm to silence him, saying to the servants in general, "Did anyone else see Mr. Stanton?"

There was a pause while the assemblage looked at each other and shook their heads, but then the young maid who had let them in bit her lip and said nervously, "Aye, sir, I did—but it was later'n twelve, more like two or three."

Again she looked very frightened. However, she went on gamely, "I 'eard footsteps running up to young Mr. Stanton's study and then run out again, and so I looked and it was Mr. Tristram hisself goin' down. He didn't see me, but I saw 'im. I thought he was off a-hunting rabbits, the way he do sometimes, 'cos he was carryin' a gun."

"A gun!"

"Yessir. A long one."

"Wa'al," said the sheriff, looking brisk and businesslike, "I reckon we should have a look at his study."

Tristram Stanton's study was identical in shape to the one that belonged to his father, but it had a very different atmosphere, being devoted to science rather than accounting. A telescope and various spyglasses were set on a bench beneath the big window. The top of the big desk held astronomy journals instead of the paraphernalia of business; and the wall was hung with weapons, including pistols, knives, cutlasses, and dirks. The centerpiece of the display was supposed to be a pair of fine hunting rifles, but one of them was missing.

The sheriff went over, and carefully lifted down the remaining rifle. "My," he said in professional admiration. "Oh me, oh my." Beautifully crafted, it had two barrels, one above the other, which were designed to rotate. "A revolving rifle—you fire one barrel, turn it, fire the other—get two shots in quick succession," he explained, and reverentially set the weapon down on the desk, away from the piles of journals and alongside a well-brushed top hat that had been left there, brim up, with a pair of fine leather gloves tucked inside.

Then he looked at Wiki and said, "Wa-al, I guess the mate to that there gun was the one that fired the shots into the boat—which puts you and your two little pistols in the clear, Mr. Kernacker-Indian."

Wiki inclined his head, veiling his huge sense of relief. George Rochester, however, wasn't even listening. He blurted, "But it can't have been Tristram Stanton who came here last night!"

The sheriff frowned. "The servants seem certain of what they saw."

"The servants must have been mistaken," Rochester insisted, "because I know for a fact he was somewhere else last night—at the Pierce plantation up Newport News way!"

"You're absolutely certain of this?"

"I certainly am! There was a big crowd, and I doubt if I exchanged five words with him, but I know for a fact he was there. He entertained the whole table with a mighty interesting account of Commodore Thomas ap Catesby Jones's trials and tribulations in getting the expedition underway. You've no idea of the political machinations! Even the procurement of suitable ships was a major endeavor! We drank a toast to poor Commodore Jones *in absentia*. What with the politics and palaver, it's no wonder he declined the command of the expedition, and that they were reduced to giving Charles Wilkes—a mere lieutenant!—the job."

"Table?" said the sheriff, looking baffled. "It was a banquet?"

"A feast!" cried Rochester, greatly animated. "And the table was a famous great one with seating for twenty. Over the first five removes we ate just about everything, animal and vegetable, under the whole blessed sun—a whole squad of menservants heaving along great trenchers of fish, fowl, and meat, sweet potatoes, hominy, and greens—then off came the upper cloth to make way for a complete fleet of desserts, served on the damask linen underneath. And even when the pies and pastries were gone, the banquet was by no means over! Away went the damask, dishes of raisins and almonds were set out on the wood, the port and madeira circulated—and Tristram Stanton was there the whole blessed time."

The door to the passage opened, and Tristram Stanton himself walked in. He stopped short but betrayed no emotion as he took in the fact that his private study was full of men, merely nodding at the sheriff before walking over to the desk. Then he became absorbed with picking up the rifle and studying it carefully, turning it over in his hands.

Wiki frowned, thinking that Stanton's appearance did not quite match his memory of the horseman who had arrived so precipitately at the riverbank this morning. Stanton had changed into clothes suitable for a recently bereaved husband, with black silk stock and black vest, but this did not seem to account completely for the alteration in his appearance. Then Wiki realized that Tristram Stanton's hair was slicked back with some kind of oil, so that it did not flop forward anymore. Feeling curious, he slid closer to the desk.

Stanton murmured, as if to himself, "This is one of a pair—signed by master gunsmith Henry Leman of Lancaster—the prize of my collection. I intended to carry them with me on the expedition." He carried the gun to the wall display, carefully set it back on the pegs, turned and looked at the sheriff, his face quite blank.

The sheriff cleared his throat. "But one of the pair is missing."

"So I see."

They all waited, but Stanton did not go on. The sheriff said, "Could you tell me what you were doing last night?"

Stanton shrugged. "I was out."

"At Newport News," Rochester agreed.

For the first time Tristram Stanton glanced at the midshipman. There was another pause, and then he said, "Correct. I was a guest at a banquet at the Pierce place."

"What time did this banquet begin?"

"The invitation was for four in the afternoon," Rochester replied, when Stanton remained silent. "We chatted and drank grog until the feast, which opened at five."

"And how long did it last?"

Again Stanton left it to Rochester to reply. "We were eating and drinking for six hours, I swear. I had not a notion how elaborate these old Virginians live!"

"And Mr. Stanton was there the whole time?"

"Certainly he was—as I have already told you! I took particular note of it because between the mutton and the ham a man came to the front door asking after him. It was a seaman from the *Vincennes*—I know it because I happened to be in the hall at the time and answered the bell. Now then," mused Rochester, contemplating the ceiling, "what was his name? Certain I know the fellow—an able seaman, reefs, hands, and steers, a useful chap. Potts? Powers? No, that's it!—Powell—that's the name, Powell. Jim Powell, a steady fellow at sea, heavy drinker and gambler on land, alas, served on the old *Peacock* when we was surveying the Georges Banks—"

"Captain," said the sheriff, "if you'd get to the point?"

"Ah!" Rochester started and blushed. "My apologies! Drifted off into memories a moment, but aye, I was the one who opened the door, passing it at the time, and one don't stand on ceremony and wait around for a servant after three or four glasses of good wine, you know. H'm!" he said, as he caught the sheriff's eye. "Asked for Stanton here, so I called out for him."

"And you were there when Mr. Stanton came to the door?"

"No, no—because he didn't, you see." Rochester caught another scowl and hastily elucidated, saying, "No, he scribbled a note and sent it to Powell by a servant. But," he added, as if to make amends for his vagueness, "I certainly saw the seaman stow the note in his hat afore he got underway."

"And you and Mr. Stanton were still there at three this morning?"

"We were drinking madeira at three! It has been a long night, and I can't say I feel the better for it," George candidly confessed, betraying his puritanical New England roots. "We was sailing back to Norfolk as dawn was breaking; and when I got back on board the dear *Swallow*, the watch was swabbing the decks. And hard on the heels of that came the order to trip and stand farther down the river, and so, withal, my bed and I are strangers."

Tristram Stanton stirred, his distinctive voice impatient. "Gentlemen," he said, pointedly opening the door. "I believe that is all, and I trust you are satisfied. As my friend here described, it was a very long night—and I have a funeral and a great deal else to arrange. So if you will excuse me?"

The sheriff hesitated, but then he nodded at the deputies and led the way past Stanton, who was still holding the door. Wiki was the last to leave. As he moved away from the desk he unobtrusively wiped one finger around the inner edge of the top hat that had been left on the desk. There was not the slightest trace of oil.

When he arrived in the entrance hall, Rochester, the sheriff, and the deputies were all ahead of him, yet his nape prickled with an instinct that he was being watched from behind. Wiki glanced back up the stairway—and his gut lurched. Tristram Stanton's father was standing on the balcony of the second floor, his hands braced on the balustrade, and he was leaning forward to stare down the stairwell. Again his gaze was fixed on Wiki, but this time his face was full of expression; it was alive with hatred and fury, thick lips drawn back from tobacco-stained teeth.

Three

When they arrived at the Portsmouth waterfront, a whaleboat from the brig *Swallow* was waiting for them, the six oarsmen at the ready to step the mast, unfurl the sail, and get back to the ship. George Rochester was as impatient as a dog to be off and away, but the sheriff held them back.

He said to Wiki, "Mebbe you've noticed I never questioned you about your reasons for lurking about the riverbank at dawn."

"That's true!" said Rochester, who felt some lively curiosity about this himself.

"Heard you got into an argument last night—with a lieutenant named Forsythe," observed the sheriff, ignoring George.

"Forsythe?" exclaimed Rochester, appalled. Lieutenant Forsythe was an unpleasant customer who had not just a naturally foul temper but a burning grievance as well. Though he out-ranked Rochester, he had been assigned to the *Vincennes* as a junior officer, while Rochester—a mere passed midshipman!—had been given the command of the *Swallow*. That Wiki Coffin was a particular crony of Rochester's would have been like a red rag to a bull.

"He insulted your pretty companion, I hear," said the sheriff, "and spouted some unpleasantries at you as well. Called you something worse than 'Indian,' huh?" The burly southerner shook his head in wondering pity. "Did you really expect him to pay attention when you called him out?"

"Called him out?" Rochester echoed, horrified. "You challenged Forsythe to a *duel?* Oh dear, oh dear, oh dear," he said, and clicked his tongue. Wiki's adaptation to the American way of life was nothing short of miraculous, but occasionally he did make a blunder. However, he had never made a mistake of this magnitude before.

Wiki, who now cast his friend a brooding look, had a temper, as George knew very well. The first time they had met, when they were sixteen, they had collided at the door of a college in the New Hampshire wilderness where they had both been sent as a punishment. George, who had galloped out of the family carriage without looking where he was going, had fallen over Wiki, who had been standing stock-still on the porch, glaring at the forbidding timber portal. Then, when the boys had picked themselves up and sorted themselves out, George had taken in Wiki's brown skin and black hair. The mission of the college had been the redemption of the poor benighted Indian, and so he had blurted, "I should be converting you, not knocking you down, old boy," and had added a loud neigh of laughter. Then he had seen the murderous fury in the other boy's uncannily blue eyes, and the laughter had died.

However, as Rochester also knew, Wiki had a remarkable ability to keep that temper under iron control. Right now the sheriff was being treated to the same icy blue stare, but still Wiki said nothing.

The burly officer said, "Didn't Forsythe inform you that dueling is the province of gentlemen and not for the likes of Indians and kernackers?"

"I simply assumed he was the kind of southern gentleman I would never have believed existed," Wiki said coldly. "A man with neither courage nor honor."

The sheriff, as unmoved as ever, snorted with derisive amusement. "Wa-al, by rights," he said, "I'm supposed to discourage that kind of sport, but you and Lieutenant Forsythe are taking yourselves and your little disagreement off into the wild blue yonder, so I reckon it's safe to return your property." And he handed over Wiki's confiscated pistols, going on to say curiously, "What's a man like you doing on an exploring expedition, anyways?"

"I'm Captain Rochester's linguister," said Wiki, glancing at George.

"You're translating for a windbag?" The sheriff let out a guffaw—the fact that Rochester was bridling with affront and insult completely passing him by—and said, "Wa-al, son, I wish you a whole bundle of luck. What languages do you speak?"

"American English, Maori, Samoan, Tongan, Hawaiian, Rotuman . . ."

"And Greek and Hottentot, too, no doubt," interrupted the sheriff, with unabated amusement. "Wa'al, I congratulate you on your American English—you speak it better than most Yankees of my acquaintance. How do you do it?"

"It's a knack," said Wiki dryly, and at last the sheriff allowed them to get into the waiting boat.

As the boat's crew took up their oars, it occurred to George that the sheriff had neglected to ask something crucial; but before he could frame a question, Wiki handed him the two pistols and then put up his hand, signaling to the oarsmen to hold still while he slipped over the side into the river to clean off sweat and dust. The boat's crew stared, openmouthed at such odd behavior, and then looked at their captain for some kind of explanation.

Meeting their inquiring eyes, George said bracingly, "Don't worry yourselves, lads. He swims better than your average fish."

The men glanced at each other and then studiously away, emanating a definite disapproval of this eccentric behavior, but George was still wearing a reminiscent grin, musing that he could have added that Wiki could hunt like a woodsman, ride like a gaucho, and manage a canoe like an Indian, too. He knew it personally because they had been staunch comrades from the day they had collided in the college portal, and since then they had shared amazing adventures.

George had been packed off to the college in disgrace, with no idea that there he would find a lifetime comrade. After the death of his father, he had been sent to live with his grandparents, who had put him into training for the family legal firm. A few months of this deadly dull pursuit had been enough—George had run away to sea, to be captured on the brink of sailing by his grandfather, who had packed him off to the college instead. The school being a training ground for missionaries, the old man's intention had been to make it possible for the lad to travel to all the exotic places he craved to experience but under a mantle of respectability—a lost cause if there ever was one. George was as determined as ever to head off to sea on the first ship that would take him, but as a dashing jack-tar, never as a stuffy man of the cloth.

Wiki, on the other hand, had been raised in a native village in the far-off southern Pacific, surrounded by his *iwi* and his *whanau*—his tribe and his kin. Apart from his blue eyes, he had been no different from his childhood companions. The life of a warrior had been his natural destiny. Fate, however, had intervened. The way George's family had heard the gossip, Wiki's American father, Captain Coffin, had suddenly taken a notion to track down the son he'd fathered so casually in New Zealand, and had been so captivated by twelve-year-old Wiki's strong personality and sharp intelligence that he'd made up his mind to take him back to Salem. As George's grandmother had remarked, her mouth turned down, the fact that Captain Coffin's childless, middle-aged New England wife might feel rather strongly about it had apparently never crossed the foolish man's mind.

According to Wiki's version of the story, he had realized he was in trouble the instant he'd walked into the neat little Yankee cottage with its wreath of seashells on the front door and clapped eyes on the expression of consternation, outrage, and shame on Mrs. Coffin's face. His only recourse was to adopt Yankee manners and speech as fast as he could—to disappear into the scenery, as it were—and he was lucky enough to have the adaptive talents of a chameleon. As Captain Coffin had exclaimed to George's grandfather, the boy might be a bastard half-caste, but by Jehovah, he learned fast! Proud as punch, he carried Wiki along with him to Boston, Nantucket, and New Bedford when he went there on business, and had taken him along on a couple of coasting voyages to the West Indies, too. However, when he sailed off to the Pacific again he left the boy behind, happily assuming that his wife would be glad of the company. Instead, the instant Captain Coffin's vessel was hull down on the horizon, and the masts and sails fast disappearing from view, she had packed Wiki off to New Hampshire—to be knocked over by George in the college portal.

Their comradeship was founded the instant George learned that Wiki was as determined to get to sea as he was. Then they had got acquainted with the local Indian tribe and had found something else in common. Neither thought much of the college's program for converting the Abnaki, being of the firm opinion that the Indians had been doing perfectly well for the past thousand years and had more to teach the white man than the other way around. Within days they were skipping class to head into the forest and listen to the huntsmen spin yarns about the campfire, and within a year they were participating in the hunting parties themselves. The way George remembered it, the Abnaki thought it a huge joke that two boys who were supposed to convert them to the way of the white man should be converted to the Indian way instead. When the school authorities eventually found out, however, all hell broke loose. So he and Wiki had absconded—like Indians, in a birchbark canoe they had built themselves, paddling three hundred miles down the Connecticut River to the sea.

Now, as George watched tolerantly, Wiki slithered back over the gunwale, the water streaming off his rinsed body and clothes and long black hair. He had his question ready, but then the boat breasted Sewall's Point, on the confluence of the Elizabeth River and Hampton Roads, and his entire attention was taken up by the discovery fleet that loomed ahead, dominated by the *Vincennes* and the *Peacock*, the smaller vessels clustered about the big sloops like chickens about hens, the storeship *Relief* standing off at a distance in the company of the *Porpoise*. They all looked spectacular, but he had eyes for only one vessel—the little brig *Swallow*.

"Ain't she beautiful?" he said. He was scarcely aware that his voice was hushed with a kind of awe and that his face had gone hot and red with bursting pride.

The *Swallow* might have been the smallest craft in the fleet, but she had a dash about her that all the others lacked. Her black varnished hull gleamed like a rapier. "Maybe she's not all that roomy below decks and the accommodations not all that they might be, but she's, oh, such a weatherly little craft," he said. "Wiki, old man, you should've been on board when we come storming down Chesapeake Bay! We overhauled a tubby old merchantman, and you would have laughed fit to bust your breeches to see the poor old slogger frantically putting out extra rags of canvas, convinced we was a pirate!"

"I believe you," said Wiki. Long, low, and black, her two tall masts wickedly raked, it was obvious the brig had been built as a privateer. Now, quite unintimidated by the big *Vincennes* lying just a couple of ship's lengths away, she was tugging at her chain like a greyhound on the leash. "But isn't she rather small for the job?" he inquired. With a rating of just under one hundred tons, the *Swallow* was less than half the size of the trading barks his father owned and commanded and a great deal slimmer than the sturdy, thick-hulled whaleships Wiki knew from his voyaging in the Pacific.

"But what better ship for charting shoals and lagoons?" Rochester demanded. "The brave *Swallow* will venture where the *Vincennes* could never follow!" Then, with an abrupt sense of crisis, he exclaimed, "Hello, what's up?"

There was a bustle on the brig that looked like sudden panic. The hands who had been left on board were rushing about in flustered fashion, looking over their shoulders at the *Vincennes*. Then Wiki's sharp eyes spied a blue-and-gold figure on the poop of the flagship, aiming a spyglass in their direction. "There's some captain or other on board the *Vincennes*," he said; "and he looks like he's studying the state of your ship, set to hold an inspection."

"Oh no," Rochester groaned. "It's Wilkes—his inspections are notorious already. Sheets, there! Haul out to wind'ard!" The whaleboat jinked, taking in a slosh of water, and then braced up as her sail filled, heading for the side of the brig that was out of sight of the *Vincennes*.

Then they were coming about the larboard quarter. "Sail in, there! Unstep mast!" The mast was grappled, and the single sail wrapped about it. A heave and it was lying in the bottom of the boat with its end sticking over the transom. Then the men took up the oars. The stern of the brig was so sheerly curved it seemed to swoop overhead like the wing of some large raven, the black paint dappled with dancing reflections from the water. On the stern board the name *Swallow* flourished in gilt. Above and to each side, the muzzled snouts of two nine-pounder guns poked out, one at each quarter.

The boat came around the starboard quarter and then clinked against the brig's side. Wiki jumped, grabbed the leading edge of a strake, and scrambled up to deck, four of the boat's crew behind him. In the boat, one man and the coxswain heaved on the boat falls while Rochester stood in the middle, and the boat rattled up into the davits. Rochester vaulted from the boat to the deck the instant it was level with the rail, landing with a thump of his half boots.

A flurried-looking older fellow in midshipman's uniform

hurried up to him—Ernest Erskine, Rochester's old-fashioned but highly valued second-in-command. George said hurriedly, "Aye, I know it, Ernest, I know it—clapped eyes on the situation as we came up. Line up!" he entreated the crew. "Toe the line for your lives!"

It seemed to take an unconscionable time; but finally, after a certain amount of swearing, nine seamen, two officers, and the four idlers—the cook, the steward, the boatswain, and the carpenter—stood strung out along the deck as straight as they could, their feet braced on the planks as the sprightly brig danced about on the rippling waves.

The glittering figure on the poop of the *Vincennes* lifted his speaking trumpet and aimed it like a blunderbuss. "You have to learn to move faster than that, you passel of witless virgins!" he hollered. "*Mister* Rochester, I see you at last, sir! Is your vacation finally over? You've consented to come on board because of supper, I doubt not—your galley smokestack has been fouling our air for the past two hours. And that man on your left is a confounded disgrace! Call yourself an officer when you allow your crew to descend to this state? And who the *hell* are you, sir?" The amplified voice rose high in an extremity of outrage. "What mean you by making your appearance on a United States ship in that filthy and uncouth condition?"

It was Wiki Coffin, who had made a fatal decision to stand alongside the brig's sailors. Rochester cast him a reproachful look, but neither said a word. Then, standing rigidly and trying not to listen while the commander of the expedition poured scorn on his friend's wet dungarees and the extravagant length of his unbound hair, George noticed that a five-oared gig was putting out from the *Vincennes* and steering for the brig. A junior midshipman was seated in the sheets with a satchel on his knee.

"Your orders," snapped the speaking trumpet. "The satchel holds a letter with my instructions. I do not require an answer. Simply read them and comply."

And with that the tirade was over. Apprehensive silence reigned as Rochester and his crew watched the boat with the midshipman bob toward them.

Four

The midshipman was the loquacious type, babbling on about the great personal honor of playing a small part in the glorious enterprise that was the United States Exploring Expedition, all the time eyeing Rochester with something like awe. George knew exactly what was in the boy's mind—that not only was Captain Rochester the paragon who had come first in the class in the recent grueling navy examinations, but one who had done the incredible. Though only a passed midshipman (albeit passed with full honors), he, George Rochester, had been given the command of one of the expedition ships and the glorious right to be addressed as captain! Now he was the living, walking, talking proof that even lowly midshipmen could aspire for marvelous things.

Knowing all that did not make George feel any less impatient, however. The satchel sat on the table between them like doom, but he could not open it until the talkative young fellow had gone. When at last he went, George ushered him to the gangway with a briskness that was positively impolite, ran below, tore open the satchel and the envelope within, read the contents with growing consternation and rage, and stamped back up to deck.

"We have to remain behind for the convenience of Mr. Tristram Stanton," he exclaimed to Wiki, who was leaning on the taffrail and looking somewhat more respectable, having changed into dry dungarees and tied his long hair into a ponytail. "We have orders to hang about until his wife is buried, his affairs are settled, and his dunnage is stowed on board. Then we do our best to catch up with the fleet; otherwise, the rendezvous is Madeira. Why *us*, for the sake of Jehovah, why *us?*"

"And why Stanton?" said Wiki slowly, his blue eyes narrow crescents under eyebrows that curled down.

"What do you mean?"

"I'm sure they could have found a replacement—you're always assuring me that any ambitious scientific would kill for the chance to come along on this voyage."

"Oh, Tristram Stanton and Wilkes are great cronies," Rochester assured him. "Wilkes, as an astronomical fellow himself, wanted to do it all on his own—everyone knows that it is the scientifics who are going to reap the glory of the enterprise, not the officers of the expedition. But the department was determined there should be a civilian astronomer on board the flagship, and so Wilkes finally gave in, though he declared he would only accept Stanton because they are as thick as thieves with their lenses and chronometers—and so we hang about here until the soft soap and palaver is over and Stanton's wife is safely interred. And where the devil am I going to put him, I ask you? Not to mention his traps."

There were just three small private rooms on the brig—the captain's cabin, where George lived, along with the five chronometers Wilkes had ordered him to carry; a small stateroom for Ernest Erskine; and another for Wiki who, as a civilian and a scientific, was entitled to a sleeping room of his own.

Wiki shrugged. "I'll shift to the fo'c'sle. After all," he added with a touch of malice, "you wished me to come along on this great venture on account of my seamanship, not because of my talent with words."

This, Rochester was forced to admit, was true. Shipping Wiki as the expedition's linguister had been a last-ditch measure, as his original plan had been that Wiki should come along on the expedition as one of the seamen. This was because Wiki was one of the finest mariners afloat—or so George reckoned. It was a gift his friend owed to the sea apprenticeship he had chosen.

The inevitable horrible confrontation with George's grandparents and Mrs. Coffin at the end of their Connecticut River adventure had led to both sets consenting to allow the boys to follow their ambitions and go to sea. In fact, Mrs. Coffin had been so relieved to get quit of her husband's bastard that she had provided a decently filled sea chest when he'd signed onto the crew of a Nantucket whaler—a deliberate choice because Wiki's aim was to explore the far reaches of the Pacific his mother's people had described in song and story, and spouters were famous for poking their noses into the remotest islands possible.

What Wiki hadn't expected was that he would dislike the whaling business so much and that the slow hunt for the prey would be so unbearably tedious. To make up for this, he had become a confirmed deserter, absconding when his ship arrived at an island he wanted to explore and then shipping on another when he was ready. According to the stories he'd told George, this was easier than it sounded. Spouter masters were used to losing their men on the beach because whalemen jumped ship all the time, and they were just as accustomed to filling the holes in their crew from the stock of destitute seamen on the beach, so his behavior had not been considered particularly eccentric.

There had been other advantages to the spouter trade. While whalemen might have lacked loyalty to their ships and their captains, they were consummate seamen, both on deck and in boats. And while their methods might be harsh, they surely knew how to pass on their remarkable skills. Within a month of shipping, Wiki had learned how to box the compass; heave the lead; haul out an earring; strap a block; and hand, reef, and steer; yet still his education wasn't finished. Six months later, not only could he heave a harpoon and steer a whaleboat, but if the ship was windbound on a lee shore, in a place where it was too deep to anchor and impossible to either tack or wear, he knew exactly how to take in after sails, haul everything hard aback, and boxhaul the vessel safely out of trouble. Two months after that, and he had learned how to jump ship without being caught.

Because of this free and easy attitude, he and George had met up remarkably often over the intervening years, getting together in a dozen ports both American and foreign to pick up the conversation where they had dropped it last and exchange rousing tales about their exploits. Now George recalled anecdotes of many a forecastle experience, and he mused that his friend's offer to give over his stateroom to astronomer Stanton made a lot of sense.

The *Swallow* forecastle held just nine seamen—stalwart fellows, Rochester thought, though he meditated uncomfortably that they were as jaded and dissatisfied as the rest of the expedition's sailors. In contrast to the officers and scientifics, who were burning with enthusiasm for the adventure ahead, the ordinary navy hands were in a pessimistic mood, one and all being cynically certain that it was their superiors who would reap the high honors, never the humble but patriotic tar. Also, they were tired to death of being kept on call at Norfolk while the politicians and the navy department folk quarreled about the disposition of the expedition. Some had been waiting as long as five years.

But Wiki knew how to take care of himself, George decided, so he said, "I'd be obliged if you would move to the fo'c'sle," feeling rather more sunny about life. Then he wandered off to his own cabin to luxuriate in the trappings of being a captain, ignore the pile of paperwork that awaited on his desk, and wind all those chronometer clocks.

Wiki took his sea chest down the forecastle ladder and then stood surveying his new situation with his fists propped on his belt. The forecastle, the abode of the common seamen of the ship, was in the bows, underneath the part of the foredeck where the windlass and the cook's kitchen were set. It was a dark and damp space that smelled of rusty chain and old rope and would be very noisy when the *Swallow* was smashing her nose through rough seas. She had been a sealer at some stage in her checkered past, deduced Wiki, because this sailors' dormitory was fitted out with six double tiers of wooden bunks instead of being supplied with hooks for hammocks, navy-style. They were hulking, clumsy affairs, which cast black shadows that shifted in the flickering light from a single, smoky tallow lamp, and from these shadows five hostile pairs of eyes met his. The only reason there were not nine pairs of eyes was that the starboard watch was on deck, on duty.

From his week of trawling the taverns of Norfolk while waiting for the brig to arrive, Wiki knew he was in trouble. For a start, seamen were traditionally slow to accept strangers. Also, morale was low. The notorious waterfront street of the port—known to sailors the world over as the "River of Styx"—might have been thronged with a cosmopolitan lot of all nations mixed up together, eating, drinking, singing, dancing, gambling, quarreling, and fighting; but whatever their race or culture, they were united in their dislike of this expedition. Contrarily insular despite choosing a life spent at sea, the general opinion of these sailors was that it was a scandal that America should be exploring the Pacific when so much of America itself had not been properly looked at yet. And, as everyone knew, a similar expedition that had set out nine years before had failed ignominiously because so many of the sailors had run away it was impossible to sail the ships.

Since then the seamen who had been waiting for another expedition to be pulled together had watched ship after ship tested in the waters off Norfolk and fail the sea trials. The vessels that were finally assembled were no better than the discards, in the general opinion. Compared to great ships of the line like the *Constitution*, where a lot of them had lived while all this was going on, *Vincennes* and *Peacock* were shamefully small. The *Peacock* might have been painted up to impress lubbers like President Van Buren, but all the varnish in the world could not disguise her wretched condition. Everyone knew that the storeship *Relief* was a dog, while not only were the *Flying Fish* and the *Sea Gull* ridiculously small for a voyage around the world but they had seen rough careers as pilot boats, herding merchantmen from Sandy Hook to New York Harbor. And the *Swallow*—well, she might be very pretty, but in truth she was nothing better than a pirate.

Worst of all, Commodore Thomas ap Catesby Jones, a hot-tempered but thoroughgoing seaman they had all respected, had resigned the command of the expedition. Then a junior lieutenant had been given the job because no senior officer was willing to take it—a junior lieutenant who was notorious as a martinet. The stories of his harsh treatment were legion. They had all heard about the good young fellows who for the most trivial of reasons had been flogged so hard that the fabric of their shirts and trousers had been beaten into the cruel wounds, so that the victims were forced for weeks to pick threads out of the scars. Now the *Swallow* men were all stinging from the long-winded slurs on their appearance and their reputation they had been forced to stand and hark to that very afternoon—and they knew who to blame for it, this upstart Kanaka, that's who. In Portsmouth he had delayed them in an unseemly fashion, first by getting himself arrested for murder and then by bathing himself in the river. Worse still, he was a crony of the captain's and without a doubt the captain's spy.

Wiki, who knew exactly what was going through their heads, quenched a sigh as he looked around for an empty wooden bunk. He would vastly prefer a berth that ran fore-and-aft, so he would not be jerked out of bed every time the brig pitched, and one on the top tier so he could be sure of not having a sea boot planted on his sleeping face as some sailor clambered in or out of the bunk above. There was a spare berth that fitted both specifications, but he knew it was the wrong moment to claim it. Instead, he left his sea chest in a corner, went back on deck, and climbed aloft to reeve off some running gear. The reckoning, he estimated, would come in the dogwatch, the time in the early evening when all the hands were off duty.

He was right. He was leaning on the windlass quietly digesting his supper when he was approached by the other Polynesian in the crew, a huge Samoan whose beautifully tattooed thighs were the size of tree trunks. They introduced themselves in the traditional way, in the Samoan language, traded a few insults, and then settled the disagreement with a bout of wrestling, Polynesian fashion. Wiki came off very much the worst but told himself, as he winced every time he turned over in his berth that night, that he had deliberately let the big Samoan win. After that he stood watches like the rest and took up all the ordinary duties of a seaman, too, knowing without a scrap of doubt that his forecastle companions would make his life very difficult indeed if he was not perceived to be pulling his weight. He kept alert, particularly when working in the rigging, knowing that it would only take a stamp on a footrope to send him crashing down to the deck. However, by the time the boat arrived to deliver Tristram T. Stanton to the ship, he felt relaxed enough to join Captain Rochester on the quarterdeck.

The brig was now floating in solitary splendor. The expedition fleet had been delayed by a gale off Chesapeake Bay but had finally got away on the seventeenth, accompanied by a great deal of signal flying and rolling salutes from both ships and shore that had blanketed the harbor with smoke. Because of the emptiness of the anchorage, the boat was in plain view for much of its approach. Wiki could see Tristram Stanton in the stern sheets, his brown hair flopping in the breeze, boxes and bundles packed all around him. More dunnage, to add to the steady stream of crates and boxes that had been coming on board the brig and filling up his erstwhile stateroom, he wryly perceived. Then, somewhat to his consternation, he recognized the burly figure of the sheriff.

"That reminds me of a question I meant to ask you, old boy," said Rochester thoughtfully, as he lowered his spyglass.

The afternoon light was hard and bright, bouncing off the water. Wiki scowled at Rochester. "What?"

"That duel."

"What about that duel?"

"You must have appointed a second—you have to have a second in a duel. Or maybe you didn't know that?"

"Of course I know that," said Wiki, somewhat snappishly, not enjoying the reminder of his humiliation. The boat was very close now, the headsman reaching out to catch one of the falls that dangled down from the davits. "Jim Powell was in the tavern, too, so I invited him to stand by me."

"Powell? Not the Powell who came to the Pierce place after a message from Stanton?"

"The same man."

"But that's odd! I do think you could've chosen better—he's not the most reliable of men, you know; the whole fleet considers him an infamous liar, as well as a gambler and a drunk. And as your friend," Rochester said reproachfully as the boat clicked against the side of the brig, "I would have expected to have been invited."

"To be my second?" said Wiki, and laughed. It was a contagious giggle, the characteristic laugh of the Pacific. Rochester often thought that Wiki's laugh was the one part of his Polynesian side that would never give way to his American half.

"Don't be ridiculous," he said, having got over his merriment. "You weren't available."

"And neither was Powell," Rochester pointed out.

"That's right." Wiki paused, but there was no time for thought because the boat had been secured, and Stanton and the sheriff were clambering onto the deck. As quick as a cat, Wiki made himself scarce by heading forward.

The sheriff looked exceedingly disgruntled. He turned his head to squint at Wiki, who was keeping a low profile on the foredeck, turned again to glower at Rochester, and said, "I want to speak to that young man."

"To Mr. Coffin?"

Rochester's reticent tone earned him a grunt of sardonic laughter. "Yup, that's the man I mean. He's quite somethin', that kernacker friend of yours," the sheriff went on in candid style. "Looks like jest another black-haired Indian to me, but I had no less than three women come along and knock at my door with an offer to pay bail to get him out of jail—that is, before word got around town that I had let him go. And one of 'em was married!"

"Their motives were merely philanthropic, I am sure," said Rochester loftily.

"You reckon?" queried the sheriff, and snorted.

Wiki came reluctantly when summoned back to the quarterdeck, wondering if the law had changed its mind about taking him off the list of suspects. As he arrived, Rochester was escorting Tristram Stanton below, and the sheriff was glaring after them with the expression of a hound being cheated of a rabbit. It was not until they had disappeared that he turned the frown on Wiki.

Then he said, sounding surprisingly awkward, "You did some pretty smart sleuthing the day you found that corpse. Some Indians have an uncommon knack of working out what goes on in men's heads, I'm told, and mebbe some kernackers have the same talent. So . . . Well, I'd 'preciate your thoughts on this Stanton murder, son."

Wiki hesitated, first getting over his surprise, and then wondering if he should divulge the crazy idea that had occurred to him after he had studied the top hat that had been left on Tristram Stanton's desk. However, he decided against it. They were standing by the skylight that was let into the deck to illuminate the saloon below, and he was uneasily aware that anyone in the after quarters would be able to hear every word.

Instead, he cleared his throat and said tentatively, "I imagine you have a list of all those who benefit from Mrs. Stanton's death."

"Tristram Stanton's the only one, goddammit!" And the sheriff slapped his fist against his leg in frustration. "As her husband, he inherits all her money. Believe me, son, her death was extremely well timed. If she'd gone ahead with a divorce, the plantation would've gone under the hammer. It was her dowry what saved the plantation from the creditors back when she married Stanton, and it was her money that kept it going after that."

"Divorce? I thought it was suicide she threatened?"

"That was the common talk—the story the Stantons liked to put around because it didn't reflect on them as badly as gossip about a divorce."

"I didn't know it was possible for a woman to get a divorce in Virginia."

"Son," the sheriff heavily pronounced, "anything under the sun is possible in Virginia. If she sued for divorce on the grounds of desertion—which she could and would have done once he'd sailed off—she would be declared *feme sole* and regain full control of her own property. The Stantons would have been ruined. Tristram Stanton is the obvious killer—but unless a score of guests and a whole passel of Pierce servants are lying in their teeth, there is no way he could have done it. I went around the confounded fleet, tracking down the men who were at that goddamned banquet, and one and all confirmed that he was there."

Wiki remembered the hatred on the old man's face and said, "Is it at all possible the father did it?"

"It just don't seem logical that the servants would testify that they saw Tristram Stanton—not once, but twice, and the second time packing a gun—just to protect the old man. There's no love for either master in that household. And while he had the power of an ox in his youth, I don't see the old man breaking a struggling woman's neck—he's too lame. And something else that's damn weird—the surgeon says she'd eaten opium."

"Opium?" exclaimed Wiki, startled.

"Yup. The old medic started talking opium poisoning the moment he pulled back her eyelids—and we agreed with him when we found the empty vial tucked away in her bosom. He's positive she would've died jest from that—and yet her neck was busted, too." The sheriff's tone became plaintive. "Why kill her twice, when once was enough?"

"And why break her neck," Wiki said slowly, "when there was a good chance otherwise that people would assume she'd poisoned herself?"

"Son, you've hit the nail on the head," said the sheriff, and sighed gustily. Then his gaze slid sideways to study Wiki's face, while his lips pursed in and out as he deliberated. After a long moment he said, "I'd consider it a favor if you'd keep on thinking about this murder, son—and about Tristram Stanton in particular. If somethin' should come up—"

The southern drawl trailed off. Wiki paused to make sure that the sheriff was not going to finish the sentence; then he said tentatively, "When we went into Tristram Stanton's study, did you notice the top hat that had been left on the desk?"

The sheriff squinted one eye in thought and then nodded.

"When he came in, I thought Stanton looked different from the way he had looked on the riverbank, and then realized he had some kind of pomade on his hair. He had changed into the kind of clothes that are correct for a newly bereaved husband, so the obvious conclusion was that he'd dressed his hair like that for formal occasions—which meant that the top hat should have been greasy inside the brim. But when I looked closer, I found no trace of wax at all, even though the hat was well worn."

"So?"

"Once it seemed evident that the top hat did not belong to Tristram Stanton, I began to speculate about the man who had left it there—which led me to wonder if the murder could have been carried out by an imposter. So long as he was about the right height and build and was wearing the right clothes, he could have gotten away with it. It was dark, remember, and though the manservant was positive he recognized Tristram Stanton, it was probably only a glimpse. And if he had been wearing a hat as he came up the stairs—"

"I see what you mean." The sheriff shifted his boots, making the deck boards creak, while he thought about it. Then he objected, "But an imposter had to know the old servant well enough to call him by name."

"And know his way around the house," Wiki agreed. "There's also the problem of the distinctive Stanton voice, because the servant was insistent that he recognized it. So I wondered about relatives. Is there anyone related to Tristram Stanton who could have posed as him?"

"Wa-al, that's a thought." The sheriff relapsed into a deep silence, frowning down at the warm deck boards between his straddled boots. "There's only one that comes to mind—a cousin, John Burroughs," he said finally. "But I don't see how he could be the murderer, there being no motive whatsoever. He's a scientific like young Stanton, but rich like Croesus—rich the way the Stantons ain't but would like to be. Years ago, the way I heard it, he turned 'em away from the door when they came begging for help to save the plantation, and they've had nothing to do with each other since. Common talk has it that a feud brewed, and now they're deadly enemies."

"Nevertheless, he might be worth looking up."

"Mebbe—but probably not." The sheriff straightened, losing patience with the farfetched and complicated notion, and said, "I'm goin' to look for that missing rifle. In my opinion, if we find the gun, we have the murderer."

"But surely he got rid of it?"

"It's likely he couldn't bear to throw it away. No man who appreciates a fine weapon is going to destroy a rifle like that. He might've stowed it someplace in a hurry after finding there was a witness on the riverbank, but my guess is he'll retrieve it."

"H'm," Wiki said thoughtfully, but before he could ask more, there was a rattle of footsteps on the companionway. He looked around and saw George Rochester rubbing his hands together and looking highly animated. "Sir," he cried over his shoulder to Erskine, who was coming up close behind him, "there's nothing to retard us now—the tide's on the ebb and the wind's in our favor. We'll trip anchor, if you please, and stand down the bay."

"Aye, sir!"

The orders were coming fast, the drawn-out words, "A-l-l visitors ashore!" almost lost in the rattle of, "All hands!" and, "Man the windlass!" Wiki spun on his heel and scooted up the rigging, intent on the big mainsail that was waiting to be loosed. Below him as he sidled out along the yard the gang was working at the windlass to heave the anchor short.

Down went the sheriff's boat, and down the side went the sheriff. The sky and the sea were brilliant, the water dancing and sparkling, tossed up by a brisk, fair breeze. The canvas dropped, snapped, and rippled taut. "Set jibs!" cried Captain Rochester, and with a snatch and a dainty lift of her bow the *Swallow* plucked her anchor.

Wiki's last glimpse of the sheriff was as his boat drew away. The sunlight glittered on the five-pointed badge on his chest. He was not looking at Wiki but at Tristram T. Stanton, who was leaning on the rail directly below Wiki's perch, and his expression was a study in frustration.

Five

*W*ithin days George Rochester was deeply regretting having banished Wiki from the after cabins—not that there had been much choice, he supposed. His stateroom had been the only berth in the after quarters suitable for Astronomer Stanton; and if Wiki had not offered to move forward, George would have been forced to ask him to move into the forecastle—not that he had more than the vaguest idea of what life in the forecastle of a small brig was like. His previous seafaring experience had not included anything that resembled it in the slightest.

After George's grandparents had grudgingly consented to allow him to go to sea, he had approached a sailor he'd spied perched at ease on a New London wharf for advice about joining the navy. George could remember the fellow exactly—an extremely weathered and cynical old salt who had risen as high as captain's coxswain and was now whittling a stick as he sat on a bollard waiting for the captain to return to his boat. Still, a whole five years later, George could bring to mind the way the sailor had spat a great tobacco gob into the sea that rippled about the piles of the pier before calling him a bloody young idiot.

"Dod dog it, don't do it," he'd barked. "Get that crazy notion out of your head! It would be better to hang than turn into a sailor. Study your books, learn a trade, and grow up to be a useful man!" Then, when George had insisted, the coxswain had advised him to go in for the merchant trade and steer clear of the navy. "Look at me," he'd declared, prodding a gnarled, tar-stained finger at his shirtfront. "I've been in the navy all me life, and what good has it done me? They don't teach you nothing better than how to haul ropes, holystone decks, and pull an oar in a boat—they turn you into a confounded dog, to run to a whistle and cringe at a blow. Join the crew of a merchant ship, young man, and learn to be a *proper* seaman!"

Which was exactly what Wiki had done, George mused now. At the time he would have been perfectly happy to take the old coxswain's advice and go along on the whaler with his comrade, but his interfering grandfather had yet again taken a hand. Though finally convinced that George was quite determined to go to sea come hell or high water, he utterly refused to contemplate his grandson going in anything less than a navy ship. He'd made sure that George was set on the right path to becoming an officer by organizing his commission as a midshipman. Both power and wealth were necessary—only the sons of lofty individuals like great navy captains, important merchants, and U.S. senators being eligible—but George's grandfather was both rich and influential.

George, himself, had not been at all grateful, since he'd swiftly found that a junior midshipman's existence was a dog's life indeed. His job was to keep an eye on the men, report on their behavior, and make sure they obeyed orders, so that in effect he was nothing better than a kind of constable's informer, regarded with utter contempt by the men. Still worse were the officers who handed down those orders, most being tyrants who considered their midshipmen nothing better than menials, completely at their bidding no matter how capricious the whim. However, with grit, determination, and unflagging enthusiasm, he had somehow survived his seagoing apprenticeship—all three years, ten months, fourteen days, and sixteen hours of it.

Then he had reported to the Gosport Navy Yard for eight months of instruction in the technical and theoretical aspects of seafaring. George had lived in a boardinghouse in Norfolk and had relished every moment—though, as he remembered it, the dread prospect of the grueling examination to come had cast a bit of a blight on his enjoyment. This had been held in Baltimore before an examining board of senior officers, and he had come through it with flying colors. Not only was he rated as a passed midshipman, but he topped his class—and, because of that, he had been given the command of the dear *Swallow*. He owed that to Captain Wilkes—not that it made him like the fellow any better—because the commander of the expedition had determined that the smaller ships should be given to recent graduates, reckoning that they, unlike the older officers, had not had the time to forget what they had learned.

It was ironic, however, that he should command a small brig when all his experience had been on great men-of-war and particularly so that it should be a brig with a forecastle—or so he freely confessed to himself. On the big fighting ships the seamen slung their hammocks between the great cannon, either on the main deck or the gun deck, which was one tier below, while the junior midshipmen slept on the orlop deck, even farther down in the bowels of the ship. Accordingly, George found it quite a novelty that the *Swallow* seamen should not have just a dormitory of their own but be supplied with permanent berths as well. He wondered if they appreciated the luxury. And having never served on a ship as small as the *Swallow,* he had blithely assumed that the social situation on board this little brig—just ninety-two-feet long and with a complement of just seventeen (including Wiki and Astronomer Stanton)—would be a lot more democratic than on a frigate.

Never had he been so utterly mistaken, George meditated. The only place where the brig's officers mingled with the foremast hands was on deck, and that was just to give them orders. The captain's cabin, with its chart desk and settee and curtained berth in the starboard quarter, was right in the stern, the whole blessed length of the ship away from the forecastle. Forward of this cabin was the saloon, with its big table built aft of the foot of the mainmast, the doors of the pantry and the two officers' staterooms running off to either side. Rochester, as captain, ate his meals in this saloon, with just Astronomer Stanton for company—that is, when Stanton deigned to join him, instead of eating from a tray in his stateroom. Erskine, who was in charge of the deck when the captain was below, ate his meals after George had finished.

Wiki, by contrast, took his mug and plate to the foredeck in fine weather or perched on his sea chest in the forecastle when it rained, and ate in the company of seamen. And Rochester—who on the spur of the moment had decided to join Wiki on the maintop platform, a third of the way up the mainmast, after glimpsing his friend up there while he was parading the quarterdeck in solitary splendor—envied him greatly. Mealtimes in the saloon, he announced to Wiki as he arrived over the futtock shrouds, were an unmitigated bore. Instead of sharing maritime anecdotes and jokes with his old comrade he was forced to try to be polite to Astronomer Stanton, a man he'd decided he disliked intensely.

"He's arrogant beyond belief and confounded tedious in the bargain," he complained, after making himself comfortable on a folded spare trysail. "Most of the time he stays sequestered in his cabin, and when he does condescend to eat at the table he has naught to say but lunars and declinations, just as though a captain don't deal with calculations *ad infinitum* already, in the way of navigating the ship. He's obsessed with astronomics; they're the whole of his blessed conversation, I swear! And the rest of the time he's downright discourteous. Instead of listening when a fellow has something to say, he interrupts or reads a book. I doubt he's looked me in the eye like a decent man even once. I'd never have believed he'd be such poor company."

Wiki said, "Because of that banquet?"

"What banquet? The one at the Pierce place?"

"Aye, I thought you said he kept the whole table enthralled."

"I told you, old boy, he was the very life and soul of the party! Garrulous on the subject of poor Thomas ap Catesby Jones. A story of frustration, I vow!—and one that is highly discreditable to the navy and those who directed its councils. First, there was talk of using the new *Macedonian* as the flagship, but then that fine little craft was taken away from him—it's no blessed wonder he resigned from the command of the discovery fleet in a fury of disgust or that the expedition doesn't kindle the enthusiasm throughout the nation that it deserves!"

"So Stanton seemed angry when he was telling these tales?"

"Not at all! In fact, Stanton seemed uncommon cheerful—altogether different to the person he is now. It was like he had something to celebrate!"

"That's an interesting way of putting it," Wiki said thoughtfully. "*E hoa*—my friend—tell me, did he check his timepiece a lot?"

"Not that I noticed. Why should he do such a thing?"

"He didn't seem as if he was expecting a man to call for a message?"

"I really couldn't tell, old fellow. As I said, I doubt I exchanged five words with the chap. He was right near the top of the table, while I," George said rather broodingly, "was placed near the foot."

Wiki's lips twitched. "The guests were seated in ranking order?"

"No! Virginia gentry are disgustingly democratic! There was a whole fleet of midshipmen from the *Relief* storeship between me and the head of the table, along with a quartet of lobsters—marines, if you please!—from the *Peacock*. I didn't know a single one of 'em, and I have not a notion why I was placed below the salt."

Wiki concentrated on a twist in the splice he was making and then said, "I don't suppose you took note of what he was wearing?"

"What? Who? Stanton?" Rochester cast his friend a startled look and said, "Not particularly. Why should I? Coat, vest, trousers, white shirt, white stock, I guess—no different from the other blessed civilians there, not that there was many of *them*."

"And a top hat?"

"Great heavens, Wiki, I haven't the foggiest idea! He was not in *my* boat—he could have worn a varnished hat with a pretty pink ribbon and I wouldn't have known."

Wiki tucked and tidied loose strands in the splice as he remembered what Stanton had looked like when he had arrived on the riverbank to find his wife's corpse—wearing the outfit George had described, except for riding boots, which George wouldn't have noticed because everyone was seated at the table. Indeed, it was likely Stanton had traveled to and from Newport News by horse. After getting home and hearing the grim tidings of the discovery of his wife's corpse, he must have ridden headlong from the plantation to the riverbank. It was no wonder he looked so disheveled.

George Rochester said curiously, "Why are you asking all this? What does it matter what he wore or what mood he was in?"

Wiki pursed his lips as he used a fid to knock the splice into shape. Finally he said, "The sheriff asked me to keep on thinking about the identity of the man who came to the plantation house."

"Well, I can assure you that it can't have been Tristram Stanton," George said rather testily.

"You and a passel of midshipmen and marines most surely can't be wrong," Wiki dryly agreed. "Yet both servants were so positive it was Stanton they saw."

"It must've been an imposter—just as I heard you say to the sheriff."

So his conversation with the sheriff had definitely filtered down the skylight, Wiki realized, and he wondered if Stanton had overheard it, too. "An imposter had to be sure that Tristram Stanton was not at home," he said. "Though I guess it was commonly known he'd be up at Newport News."

"Strangely enough," said George, his brows lifting as he

took on a meditative expression, "that ain't so. He'd begged off the Pierce banquet on account of wanting to spend the night at his laboratory in Norfolk, tidying up before departure. We was all surprised to see him there."

"*What!*"

"The man has no blessed manners—he simply changed his mind and went along. What his hosts thought, I can't imagine," said Rochester virtuously. "I suppose they simply smiled and laid another place—but don't it go to show that the fellow's a perfect philistine?"

"*E hoa,* what it goes to show is that he has the luck of the devil! If he hadn't changed his mind, he would've been blamed for the murder and hanged for it, too!"

There was dead silence while they looked at each other in speculation. Around them the rigging creaked comfortably and canvas billowed out in a series of great white wings. Sixty feet below their perch, the deck of the brig plunged and rose. The man at the helm was steering full and by, but without paying proper attention to the weather clew of the main topgallant sail, so that every now and then water spatted over the rail and along the deck. However, Captain Rochester was too lost in thought to pay heed.

"Put that way, it looks as if the murderer planned to use Tristram Stanton as a scapegoat," he said at last. "So who hated him enough?"

"The sheriff told me about a cousin, John Burroughs; that they are deadly enemies," said Wiki. "It seems that though Burroughs has pots of money he refused to help out the Stantons when they needed it, and some kind of feud has built up since."

"That doesn't look like a good motive for killing Stanton's wife, not to me," Rochester objected. "If there really is a feud, it seems more likely that Tristram Stanton would kill *him!* And anyway," he went on, "don't the astronomics fellows have to work together in some kind of amicable fashion?"

Wiki frowned, shook his head, and said, "*E hoa,* what are you talking about?"

"John Burroughs—he's with the expedition."

"He's . . . *what?* He can't be!"

"He's assistant astronomer, stationed on the *Porpoise*," said George with dignity. "I'll show you the crew list if you don't believe me."

"Dear God," cried Wiki, struck by a sudden appalling thought. "We have to join the fleet before it's too late!"

Six

*E*ven if he could not comprehend the need for speed, Rochester gallantly responded to the challenge. The elements, however, were not nearly so cooperative. The moderate gale that had been blowing fair and steady hauled to the northeast in the middle watch of the night, which was not only unfavorable but worked up a nasty cross sea as well. For days the waves ran in rows like jackknives, with dark valleys between them, and the brig bounced and banged like a carriage on a rutted road. To Rochester's mind, the only satisfactory aspect of the weather was that Astronomer Stanton was seasick—laid so low, in fact, that George was spared his silent and surly presence.

Then even that contrary wind failed utterly, leaving the brig to lurch about unhappily on a sea that looked like a rippling sheet of glass but still held a sadistic swell, effectively keeping Stanton pinned to his berth. Every now and then a puff would come scudding in cat's-paws across the water, and the sails would billow briefly as they met it, flapping against the masts. Every time, though, they flopped again as the little breeze died, lifeless as wet laundry on a line. Then again the wind would gently gust, but from another quarter, and around the yards would go, while all the time the smell of hot tar rose in the air as the deck boards heated and flexed and tempers on board became short.

By taking advantage of every breath, they gained five miles; but then they lost it all in a squall. Trying to guess the position of the fleet was equally heartbreaking—had Wilkes been delayed by the same fit of doldrums? It was impossible to tell; all they could do was steer for Madeira and hope to find the ships there. When at long last the wind finally swung back to favorable, the brig was sailing in an ocean that was apparently quite empty. Worse still, Astronomer Stanton was back to making his surly presence felt at the table.

" 'Mackerel skies and mares' tales,' " Rochester recited, scanning the cloud-flecked, oyster-colored sky after taking their position at noon; " 'The signs of sweet and pleasant gales'—but whether that signifies we'll raise the fleet is beyond me. I'll wager the ships are scattered. The *Relief* sails like a drover's nag and is bound to be miles behind the rest."

George was on the quarterdeck and Wiki was at the wheel, it being his two-hour trick at the helm. This, Rochester had found, was another opportunity for conversation with his old friend. And now that the trades had returned, the *Swallow* was back to sailing like the thoroughbred she was. All canvas was set, and her sharp bow was fairly slicing through the waves, tossing the crests aside so that foam raced along her polished black hull. Under

Wiki's sure hands the brig heeled steeply as she strongly strode the sea, every sail iron taut with wind. Aloft, the rigging sang and vibrated, while the timbers of the hull creaked in rhythm, and men had to climb uphill to get from the lee side of the deck to the windward rail.

Wiki looked at George and then up at the weather clew of the topgallant and said, "I don't care about the *Relief*. We have to find the *Vincennes* first—then the *Porpoise*."

"If you reckon Burroughs might've posed as Stanton that night, I can understand the *Porpoise*," said Rochester, mightily puzzled, "on account of him being astronomer there—but why the *Vincennes?*"

"We have to ask Powell about that note." Wiki shook his head in self-reproach, saying, "It's been nagging me all along. I meant to ask the sheriff about that letter but ran out of time. We don't know who sent Powell to Newport News to fetch it. We don't even know if it was delivered to Mrs. Stanton. Did the sheriff ask the servants if a note had come for Mrs. Stanton; and if he did, what did they say? Did any of them see her open it?"

"Perhaps once the sheriff knew it was murder, not suicide, it didn't seem important anymore."

"The note was vital! When Stanton arrived at the riverbank he jumped to the conclusion that his wife had committed suicide— because he had sent her a message saying he was determined to sail with the expedition, or so he said. You say the note was sent 'between the mutton and the ham'—what time was that? Did Powell go off in a boat or on a horse? If he delivered the letter early enough, Mrs. Stanton might have taken the opium before the imposter arrived—it might have been suicide, after all."

"But someone stowed that body in the boat!" cried Rochester, completely confounded. "Wiki, it don't make sense!"

"*E hoa*, I agree." Wiki looked aloft, checking the weather clew again, and then back at George's puzzled face. "But if Mrs. Stanton was conscious, surely she would have created a commotion when the intruder came into her bedroom?"

"She might've been asleep—at midnight it's likely she *was* asleep."

"You could well be right—which indicates that she didn't receive the note. If Stanton was telling the truth, the message would have upset her too much."

"So you reckon Powell never got around to delivering it?"

"Or maybe he gave it to a servant, who never got around to mentioning it to the sheriff. The plain fact of the matter is that we won't know *what* happened to that letter until we get to the *Vincennes* and find Powell."

And, as if in response, there was a cry of, "Sail ho!" from the lookout in the masthead.

George Rochester, galvanized, shot up the mainmast hand over fist. Two small clouds lay on the distant horizon ahead, joined by another as the brig kept up her headlong approach. An hour later the clouds had become defined as towers of canvas. Closer still and it became apparent that the *Vincennes*, the *Porpoise*, and the *Flying Fish*, their topsails backed so they made no headway, were clustered about something large and enigmatic in the water. Another hour and George was able to solve the secret with his spyglass.

"It's a famous great tree drifting about in the water, a ship-length long at the slightest reckoning," he reported to Wiki as he passed him in the topgallant crosstrees. "What blessed jungle it comes from, I have not a notion. There are scientifics swarming all over it—taking specimens, I guess."

"Did you see Burroughs among them?"

"Don't know what the fellow looks like," Rochester returned cheerfully. "Never clapped eyes on him in my life." Then he grabbed a backstay and swung down to the deck. When he heard the double thump of George's boots hitting the planks, Wiki followed him.

They met by the wheel, Wiki saying, "Do you reckon we could send a party on board the *Porpoise* to find him?" The sense of urgency that had beset him when he'd heard that Burroughs was with the expedition had diminished over the days but was now beginning to nag again.

"Not without Wilkes's say-so—which, as you know, ain't easy to get," said Rochester moodily. Then he lapsed into deep thought, his head slightly tilted as he scowled at the *Vincennes* in the distance. "How about we show 'em how a real Yankee can do it and sail right around his ship?" he mused. When Wiki opened his mouth to remonstrate, George merely waved a hand, saying with an air of decision, "You'll oblige me, Mr. Coffin, by taking the helm!"

Then he was off, calling for Mr. Erskine and shouting for the boatswain. Within instants, as the word flew around that their captain was going to wreak a little revenge for the tongue-lashing Captain Wilkes had delivered in the Hampton Roads, all hands were on deck.

And all the time the *Swallow* swept down upon the fleet. Signals were fluttering up to the main peak of the distant *Vincennes*. Then, as the moments ticked by, a cluster of brightly uniformed figures could be discerned on the poop deck—staring at the *Swallow* in attitudes of gathering consternation. The brig was dead on course for the flagship, every sail out and bellied taut with wind, the foam dashing along her hull, her sharp bow slicing through the waves and tossing them to either side, apparently utterly set on collision.

George's grin was growing wider with every swish of the sea. He stood with his legs braced, his muscular calves stuck out at the back, one fist gripping the weather shrouds as he calculated speed and distance; Midshipman Erskine as alert as a cockerel alongside him. All hands were poised in their proper stations, seamen standing by lines and sheets, ropes neatly flaked into coils at their feet, Wiki at the wheel with the wind lashing his hair about his shoulders.

On, on the *Swallow* sped in full-bellied splendor, her wake a bubbling light green, her bowsprit aimed unerringly at the poop of the *Vincennes*. Now the group of officers standing there could be more clearly spied, staring spellbound at the brig as she tore down upon them. Moments rushed by in the creaking of rigging and the swish of water, and then—just as impact seemed inevitable—"Ready about!" George bellowed, and, "Ready about!" Midshipman Erskine yelled.

Wiki heaved down on the wheel as the seamen hauled, and around the *Swallow* came, her spanker boom slamming and her foresheets slapping taut. Another bawled order and she had straightened up and was sailing along the flagship's starboard side, heading for her bow. Looking up as they sped by, Wiki could glimpse stunned faces lined along the other ship's rail.

Then another series of hollered orders, a heave on the wheel, and the brig did a circuit of the flagship's bow, perilously close to the long bowsprit. A haul at the braces and back along the larboard side of the *Vincennes* the *Swallow* ran, losing speed but still sending foam seething along the hull of the sloop of war. Then, with more singing out, the arcing wake of the *Swallow* darkened and then disappeared, as the brig braced around, very slowly, and sheered past the flagship's stern.

It had been the most flamboyant display of seamanship imaginable, a spectacular maneuver that had been carried out with flawless precision. Bemusedly, Wiki heard the sound of cheering, and then realized that every man jack on board the brig had thrown his hat in the air with a roar of delight. The *Swallow* sailors were going to describe this with pride in a thousand seaport taverns; in the space of just a few moments the dubious shipboard morale had shot up to euphoric.

However, looking up again as they glided past the poop of the *Vincennes*, he could discern Captain Wilkes's expression—and the commander of the expedition was not at all amused, Wiki discerned. Nor was Wilkes impressed. This, Wiki deduced, was not going to be lightly dismissed as a display of youthful high spirits.

"At last I see you, *Mister* Rochester!" the speaking trumpet blared. "But I also see that you have not achieved maturity in the interval! It would be better that you attend to your duties instead of indulging in fancy spectacle—and that you should rendezvous in good season, as instructed, instead of dawdling!" And on Wilkes ranted, while Rochester stood ramrod straight and wooden faced and Wiki, equally expressionless, studied the sky. "You will oblige me by getting a boat over here," the tirade finally ended. "I wish to receive Mr. Stanton on board—and you too, *Mister* Rochester, with a good explanation for your tardy arrival. Let's see if you can lower a boat with the same flourish that you sail your ship!"

Unfortunately, however, obeying the order took an hour or more because of the large amount of astronomical gear that had come with Stanton, and which had to be hastily loaded. By the time the boat finally pulled away the sun was dropping, and the shadows were growing long. The boats clustered about the floating forest giant were gathering up the scientifics and their specimens and ferrying them back to the respective ships. Wiki waited on deck, watching. Then it was dark, and Rochester had still not returned.

Seven

*I*t was night. Wiki looked around, deliberating. The gun brig *Porpoise* was now the closest ship to the *Swallow,* lying about a half mile away; he could see her lamps spring into life one by one, flickering as they swung from their fastenings in the shrouds.

Making up his mind, he stripped to the skin, clambered over the gangway, and dived. The water was crisp with salt, but not particularly cold, streaked with phosphorescent trails left by the fish that swarmed about the drifting tree. Wiki breasted the distance methodically, lifting his head to check his destination every now and then, shaking his long hair back over his shoulders. He finally arrived at the bow of the *Porpoise,* clambered up until he could reach the martingale chains, and then scrambled over the bowsprit.

There was a seaman between the knightheads, leaning over curiously to see what the noises were about, and for a moment Wiki expected him to shout a warning to an officer. However, the man kept silent. As the lantern in the fore rigging flared up a little, Wiki saw that he was a Pacific Islander, a compact fellow who was bare chested, so that the fringes of dense tattoos about his waist showed above his belt, and realized with some surprise that there was another Kanaka in the fleet. Even though this man was only about half the size of the huge Samoan on the *Swallow*, Wiki hoped he was not in for another bout of wrestling.

However, the first words revealed that this was a Rotuman, one of the most peaceable and considerate people of the Pacific. With superb good manners he ignored Wiki's nakedness. The ritual introduction took a long time, the ceremonious exchange of genealogies being succeeded by the new politeness of Oceania—an exchange of stories of how they had come to be on board American ships. Softly chanted Wiki:

> *I am te kakano whakauru, a man of two tribes*
> *My name is Maori, but I am also William Coffin Junior.*
> *I have been educated with white men*
> *I have sailed the sea in their ships*
> *And I have lived in their houses on shore.*

The Rotuman, predictably, had left his island on a whaler, reciting:

> *I have traveled faroff lands and distant seas,*
> *I have seen the island of America*
> *And the snows of the northwest coast.*

And Wiki, with equal courtesy, replied:

Ma noa la se maoen 'ae 'e fue—
Be careful not to drift away
The southern snows are colder still
And your relatives await on Rotuma.

By the time good manners had been satisfied, the moon had risen and Wiki had dried off. It was only then that the Rotuman felt free to ask the question that must have been burning inside him—why in the name of all the spirits had Wiki arrived on board in such an eccentric manner. He listened with great interest and then remarked that a shark *'aitu* must have protected Wiki during his long swim from the *Swallow*, the shark being the totem god of his village at home. Quelling a grimace, Wiki commenced questioning him about Astronomer Burroughs but with frustratingly little result.

Wiki's grasp of Rotuman, a difficult language that was a blend of Polynesian and something much more alien, was serviceable; and because of his experience on American ships, the Rotuman's English was fair. However, the name "Burroughs" meant nothing to him. Wiki did his best to explain, but got no more than a repeated shake of the head. Astronomer Burroughs was on another ship, Wiki deduced at last—or maybe not with the expedition at all, which raised new speculations about the murder of Stanton's wife. Before he could question him further, however, a seaman strode toward them from the waist, hailing them in English.

To Wiki's amazement, it was Jim Powell. The American sailor started violently when he recognized Wiki, demanding, "What the hell are *you* doing here?"

Unlike the polite Rotuman, Powell stared blatantly at Wiki's naked physique. Feeling at a humiliating disadvantage, remembering this man's betrayal, his patience tried to the limit, Wiki did something very rare for him—he lost his temper, and snarled, "Where the hell did you get to that night in Norfolk?"

He hardly noticed the Rotuman quickly making himself scarce. Staring aggressively at the American, he braced his shoulders and flexed muscled arms, expecting to see a lifted fist. Instead, however, Powell stepped back a pace and mumbled, "I couldn't help it."

"It was a matter of honor! You had agreed to stand by me!"

"Not my fault. Lieutenant Forsythe gave me a job to do—and anyways, that duel was never going to happen."

Forsythe? It was Forsythe who had sent Powell to collect a message from Tristram Stanton? It was news to Wiki that there was any kind of connection between the two southerners. Was Forsythe Stanton's lackey? It was beginning to sound likely.

He said contemptuously, "So he got you out of the way by ordering you to take a boat to Newport News."

"How do you know where I went?"

"Never mind. What I want to know is what happened to that note."

"What goddamned note?"

"The note that Astronomer Stanton wrote for you to carry to his wife."

"There wasn't one," Powell said sullenly.

Wiki said with disdain, "You're lying. You were seen stowing it in your hat."

"Oh, that." Powell shrugged, his eyes moving about evasively. "I lost it."

"I don't believe you."

"My hat fell off when I got back into the boat, and the letter landed in the mud. So I threw it away." He looked at Wiki resentfully and said, "That happened to me once when I was sailing with Wilkes a couple of years back—he sent me off with a letter what got dropped in the mud, just an accident, mind you, and I delivered it in good faith. But when he heard about the state it was in, he had me bent over a cannon and flogged across the bum. Cruel, it was—I couldn't sit down for weeks."

Wiki paused, on the verge of calling him a liar yet again, but then changed his mind. Jim Powell was so obviously reliving a grudge, the story was likely to be true.

So he gave up and said instead, "Whereabouts on the *Porpoise* is Astronomer Burroughs living?"

"Burroughs? He ain't—he's on the *Vin*."

Wiki's brows flew up as he wondered what the encounter had been like when Tristram Stanton arrived on the *Vincennes,* expecting to take up the station of astronomer on the flagship, and found his hated cousin in his place, he mused that Wilkes might be quite taxed to settle matters between them. Without doubt, George would have quite a yarn to tell him when he got back on board the *Swallow*.

Then he observed to Powell, "I thought *you* were on the *Vincennes*."

"Well, I'm not," the other said moodily. "Men are being reassigned from ship to ship at his majesty's whim, but he'd better not shift me to the *Vin*, 'cause I'll murder him first chance, I swear it." Then he looked around as a shout rang out from the shadows aft and hissed, "Do me a favor and get off this goddamned ship."

Wiki hesitated, but then turned, clambered out onto the bowsprit, and dived into the sea. Then he surfaced and looked about, lifting his head above the choppy little waves. The *Swallow*, being less than half the size of the bigger gun brig, looked miles farther away than the *Porpoise* had on the outward leg; and the swim seemed much longer, too. When Wiki finally arrived alongside the *Swallow*, it was only thoughts of the Rotuman's shark *'aitu* that gave him the strength to clamber up the side of the brig, and even then he might not have made it if a helping hand had not been stretched down.

It was George Rochester, his long face unnaturally white in the reflection of the lantern. "Burroughs was on the *Vincennes*." he said urgently, as Wiki arrived dripping on the deck. "But I got there too late!"

Wiki, cold, wet, and panting for breath, shook his head in numb confusion.

"We had to break into his stateroom," Rochester jerkily went on. "The door was locked, and no one had a key. Then all we found was his dangling corpse—still warm, but too late! We cut him down and the surgeon did his best, but his neck had been broken—by the fall we supposed. There was a chair on the floor where he'd kicked it over."

"Burroughs is *dead?*"

"Aye," said George solemnly. "Burroughs hanged himself."

Next morning the expedition ships were still laying aback around the great half-submerged log, and the boats with the scientifics were busily rowing back and forth. The day was beautiful, the sea smooth, and the wind light; and Captain Wilkes, it was very apparent, felt in no rush at all to get to the south. Accordingly, he was in a mood to be tolerant of the scientifics' hankering after specimens. Wiki, in the maintop, could see men putting out lines and seines and hauling in a great mess of fish. Somewhat to his relief, they were not bringing up any sharks.

"They'd be better getting their ships underway," remarked Rochester, joining him on the platform aloft that was still their informal meeting place, Wiki having been too weary the night before to even think of shifting out of the forecastle. "The *Relief* sails like a drover's nag, just the way I told you, and detained the progress of the fleet more than somewhat before Wilkes got tired of the constant hindrance and sent her on to Rio."

"And yet he was critical of the time we took to rendezvous?"

"He was, he was indeed," said Rochester, and sighed very deeply. He gazed about the sparkling scene from under the speckled shade of his battered straw hat, his long face gloomy.

Wiki paused and then said reluctantly, "I would like to see the room where Burroughs hanged himself."

Rochester glanced at him and said, "Well, you can't."

"I thought you might want to pay another visit to the *Vincennes?*"

"Not bloody likely. But even if you went there with me, it would be no good. Tristram Stanton has taken up residence in that room."

In the same place where Burroughs's spirit had so recently been sundered from his body? The sparse black hairs on Wiki's brown forearms stood on end as gooseflesh crept over his skin. It would have been difficult enough for him to study the room, even. Though his American side understood that shipboard space should not be wasted; the idea of sleeping where the lost *kehua* still prowled was utterly abhorrent.

After a moment he managed to comment, "The door was broken down."

"I don't think Stanton cares about that. He was all anxiety to get established on the ship. He scarcely waited for the corpse to be removed before shifting in."

"Did anyone find the key?"

"The surgeon and I looked in Burroughs's pockets after we'd given up all hope of reviving him but couldn't find it. Someone—Stanton, I think—remarked that he'd probably tossed it out the sidelight before putting his head in the noose."

"So you had no chance to talk to Burroughs at all?"

"I told you, I was too late! Captain Wilkes," said George moodily, "detained me for an hour or more. He went through the brig's logbook with a fine-tooth comb, nitpicking his way through the entries. Every blessed decision I made, he would've made a different one. Then, when I finally got out and along to Burroughs's stateroom, it was to find quite a crowd there. Tristram Stanton had set to a-hollering that the door was locked and he could get no answer; that he was certain Burroughs was there inside and something was very wrong. We hammered on the door and yelled awhile, and finally Stanton put his shoulder to it."

Remembering the astronomer's hefty build, Wiki had no doubt that the lock had given way in short order. He observed, "You said the body was still warm."

"Aye. That's why we sent for the surgeon. He said that Burroughs had been dead for twenty minutes at the most."

"So there was a chance that he was still alive when Stanton started yelling?"

"Well, he sure didn't bother to reply," said George morbidly. "I guess he had his mind on what he was doing. Mind you, he could've been confused because the surgeon said he'd given himself a nasty knock on the head some time before putting that noose about his neck. On a low beam, I suppose." George went on with distaste, "Tristram Stanton's a cold-blooded swab if I ever met one. I know they were enemies, but they was family, too. You'd think he'd observe the decencies afore rushing to claim Burroughs's cabin and his assistant."

Wiki frowned. "The expedition supplied Burroughs with an assistant?"

"Nope, Burroughs carried along the man who's been assisting him for years. Aye, I know it—a scandal, no less. The quarters reduced, a big deckhouse added to the *Vin*, a fo'c'sle built on the deck of the *Porpoise*, officers bunking together instead of enjoying staterooms of their own—and all to make room for the blessed scientifics. Yet Astronomer Burroughs insisted on having his own personal servant and paid a hefty sum for him to come, it seems. Invaluable chap, must be. Not only worked in the scientific assisting way, but was a kind of valet as well. Name of Grimes," Rochester added.

"And Tristram Stanton has taken him over, this man Grimes?"

"Aye—typical family arrogance, don't you think?"

Wiki agreed with him but didn't bother to say so. Instead, he said slowly, "I think it's probably a good idea for me to present myself to Captain Wilkes. After all, I am the expedition's linguister."

"Well, you'd better dress up a little, old man," said George moodily. "And then maybe he won't realize that you was at the helm when we made that infamous circuit of his ship. I'll lend you a shirt and vest."

Eight

$\mathcal{U}$nexpectedly, Captain Wilkes made the first move. While Wiki was debating how to go about introducing himself to the commander of the expedition, a message arrived from the *Vincennes* requesting the attendance of Mr. William Coffin, linguister, at the earliest opportunity. Wiki, arrayed in his best bib and tucker, arrived at the gangway of the flagship in short order, to be met by a chubby-cheeked junior midshipman, who kept on glancing at him with awe as he escorted him aft.

Wiki, for his part, was looking about at the hectic scene on the main deck. The *Vincennes* was only a second-class sloop of war; but at 780 tons, she was more than twice the size of any ship he had ever sailed in. Looking down the nearest hatchway, he could see a long line of ladders zigzagging through tiers of decks, with darkness at the bottom. Overhead, the towering masts seemed lost in the sky, connected by a maze of rigging. Her huge topsails hung loose, braced at different angles to keep the ship still, but the lower sails were all brailed up so that he had a clear view. Two launches the size of small schooners were set in struts amidships; the boats in which the scientifics were rowing about would be stowed inside these when the *Vincennes* was on passage.

About three dozen men were sitting and standing about the foredeck passing away off-duty hours in reading, sleeping, sewing, or spinning yarns. Other sailors were running hither and about, more or less arranged into a gang for each mast, kept at work by boatswains and their mates, their pipes shrilling, while the officer of the deck watched them, speaking trumpet in hand. To Wiki's discomfort, it was Lieutenant Forsythe, the bulky, foul-mouthed southerner he'd made the blunder of challenging to a duel. They exchanged brooding looks but said nothing. Wiki kept on striding along, following the midshipman, who was pressing obliviously onward to the house that had been built at the stern to accommodate Captain Wilkes, the scientifics, and their gear.

It was a large affair, nearly forty feet long and over fifteen feet wide, not ornate, but nicely painted. At the forward end, a door at the break of the deck led to a paneled corridor lit by a skylight let into the poop deck above. Varnished wooden doors punctuated one wall of this passage, all shut, but evidently belonging to staterooms, though a notice on one door indicated it was a pantry. A long dining saloon was separated from the corridor by a credenza topped with a decorative partition of turned wooden spindles, through which Wiki could glimpse a polished mahogany table that was big enough to seat twenty. Revolving armchairs were screwed to the floor all about it, and in the sky-light hung castors filled with crystal glasses and decanters that tinkled slightly as the ship rolled a little and threw glittering re-flections interspersed with rainbows.

The rest of the house was taken up with a big room that ran across the stern. At the doorway to this, the young mid left Wiki with an awkward little bow as he went. Wiki stood in the open-ing, unnoticed for a moment, looking around. Because the *Vin-cennes* was a very plain ship, there were no quarter galleries but the skylight let in plenty of illumination—which was lucky, he thought, because the room was full of drafting tables and chart desks. Chronometers ticked in serried rows, and rolled charts filled big pigeonholes in the bulkheads. This, obviously, was the center of operations.

There were four men in the room. One was Tristram Stan-ton, seated at one of the desks making calculations on a sheet and referring to an ephemeris. Wiki, who had seen him seldom on the *Swallow,* was surprised once again by his hefty size—more fitted to a drover, he thought, than a high-bred southern planter. However, the brown hair that flopped over his meaty forehead, the ears that protruded from behind his thick sideburns, and the small, alert, simian eyes were all familiar. A tall, thin man hov-ered near the astronomer, his back bent, a large timepiece in one hand. When this fellow looked up Wiki was shocked by the drawn pallor of his face. His eyes were reddened and pouched, as if he had not slept. Then the other two men, who were standing deep in conversation, finished what they were saying and looked around. The taller of the pair came forward, and Wiki forgot the astronomers.

So this, he realized, was Captain Wilkes. Though Wiki had heard a great deal about him, he had never seen him before. To his surprise and hidden amusement there was a distinct resemblance to his friend, George Rochester. Like George, Wilkes was long nosed and long faced; and while the commander of the Expedition was dark haired and did not follow the fashion for sideburns, he had the same benign expression, partly because his full-lipped mouth was tipped into a constant small smile. Knowing Wilkes's reputation as a tartar, Wiki was certain the fixed smile was deceptive, but nonetheless an impression of benevolence was there.

The man with him was a tubby, barrel-chested fellow, so short he only came up to Captain Wilkes's shoulder. He was red haired, with the florid complexion that so often went with that coloring, but his sideburns were flecked with gray. His voice had been loud as Wiki had come into the drafting room, his tone very jocular.

Before Captain Wilkes could say anything, this fellow exclaimed, "Young William Coffin! Don't say you don't know me, dear boy!"

"Sir?" said Wiki, vainly trying to chase down any sense of familiarity.

"Smith's the name—Lieutenant Lawrence J. Smith."

Wiki bowed his head, smiling neutrally. The name meant nothing.

"I shipped with your father as a lad of fifteen."

"Ah," said Wiki, feeling no wiser. Lieutenant Smith was over forty years of age, he estimated. When this man had shipped with his father, he, Wiki, had not even been born.

"I had applied for a midshipman's warrant in the U.S. Navy but was advised to get experience in the merchant service first. Captain Wilkes here got the same recommendation—don't you remember it well, Charles? You didn't find as good a berth as I did, I'll wager!"

"*Hibernia* to France as a ship's boy—and no, it was *not* pleasant," said Captain Wilkes in his well-educated New York accent. "However, every sailor must learn to take the rough with the smooth, and so it can be considered a salutary experience. I," he added precisely, "benefited to the extent that I emerged from the experience with the rank of second mate." Then his permanent smile shut tight again.

The tubby lieutenant rattled on, "It must have been 1826 when I became reacquainted with your father—I'd removed to Salem, Massachusetts, and so of course took great interest in the affairs of the East India Marine Society, great interest! You were twelve—had been in the Land of the Free for just a few weeks at the time. But a marvel you were, a wonder to behold! Born a cannibal New Zealander and yet able to speak English as freely as if you had spent all your days in Salem. Your father assured me that you were conversant with sailor talk before you even arrived in Boston, having picked it up most wonderfully on the voyage home, but since then had flown—yes, flown!—ahead in your adaptation to American ways. Charles," he said to Captain Wilkes, "just listen to him talk, I beg you!—and see if you're as amazed as I was."

At that, Captain Wilkes took over the conversation, asking many questions about Wiki's background and the languages he spoke, while Wiki answered with the bland politeness he had cultivated over the years for this kind of cross-examination. It was indeed a revelation, Captain Wilkes concluded, that a barbarian could take on the trappings of civilization so completely. He then went on to express a hope that Wiki fully understood the enormous privilege of being allowed to take part in this world-shaking enterprise, the great United States Exploring Expedition. His scientific passengers were enchanted with the voyage so far, he said.

"In fact," Captain Wilkes added, sounding surprisingly ingenuous, "the novelty of our situation has been quite enough to interest the *entire* company!"

"Indeed, sir," said Wiki, not at all sure how to respond.

"Even the ignorant sailors are quite fascinated! It has been amusing for me to watch them huddle around to see fish being dissected and then to hear Jack and his shipmate bandying scientific names—'hard words,' they call 'em!—back and forth."

Wiki nodded and smiled, and Wilkes prattled on about the geological, astronomical, botanical, zoological, and anthropological aims of the expedition, with occasional interlocutions from Smith. Wiki had often heard George repeat that Wilkes had a reputation for being conceited, ambitious, and arrogant, and that it was little wonder the navy had invited three other captains to take over the command after Thomas ap Catesby Jones's angry resignation, before being reduced to appointing this man. Listening to Captain Wilkes's enthusiastic outpouring and watching the fire in his large, intelligent eyes, however, Wiki meditated that his unfortunate manner might stem from a single-minded devotion to science rather than egotistical pride.

Then all at once the commander ran to a stop, cleared his throat, and said, "You probably know that the expedition was struck with *tragedy* last night."

Wiki fought down the impulse to look at Stanton, who appeared to be absorbed in his calculations, but was undoubtedly listening raptly. He said carefully, "Astronomer Burroughs?"

"Yes." Wilkes seemed to become aware of the audience, too, looking up and saying, "Gentlemen, would you mind—?"

Lieutenant Smith harrumphed and apologized, coming to an abrupt realization that his company was no longer wanted, and took a brisk leave. Stanton, however, moved much more reluctantly. Wilkes and Tristram Stanton were cronies, Wiki remembered—it was only because of their friendship that Charles Wilkes had agreed to have an astronomer on board the *Vincennes*. However, the chilly silence in which Stanton rose from his desk and gathered up his papers was not friendly in the slightest, and his back, as he strode out of the room, was stiff with annoyance. He had to duck his head as he went through the doorway. The thin man scuttled after him; then the door was shut.

Wiki listened to their steps go off down the hallway until they faded with distance. Then Captain Wilkes, sounding businesslike, said, "The Portsmouth sheriff gave me a letter to hand over to you if circumstances demanded it; and though he did not make his thoughts at all clear, this suicide *does* seem to be the kind of thing he had in mind because we can't get *around* the fact that Burroughs was Stanton's cousin."

Then he groped around in a pocket, came up with a folded wad of paper, and handed it to Wiki, who was feeling extremely puzzled. It was not some strange mistake, he saw, because the name "William Coffin Jr." was clearly inscribed on the front. When he looked up, Captain Wilkes said, "It's a letter of authority, along with instructions concerning how to send reports of your progress with the Stanton murder case. I was also requested to assist you to such extent as I see fit. Oh, for heaven's sake," he said irritably, when Wiki stared. "Read it and see for yourself."

It was a grand parchment affair, highly embellished with a seal, a red ribbon, the coat of arms of the port, and a number of impressive-looking signatures. The text authorized the bearer, William Coffin Jr., to act on behalf of the sheriff's department of Portsmouth, Virginia, and demanded full cooperation and assistance as the said William Coffin Jr. might request. *Dear God*, Wiki thought, and only barely stopped himself from shaking his head. It did not surprise him that the sheriff, who had struck him as an obstinate character, was pursuing the investigation from afar; but he would never have guessed that he'd be the one chosen as his proxy—though, now that he thought about it, the sheriff had been heavily hinting at something like this when he'd come on board the *Swallow* with the boat that had delivered Astronomer Stanton.

He looked back at Captain Wilkes with a frown, his mind racing. "So you believe, sir, that Astronomer Burroughs's suicide is connected in some way with Mrs. Stanton's murder?"

"I don't believe anything," Wilkes said testily. "Burroughs was a very private person about whom I know very little. I accepted him for the expedition *only* because of Stanton's strong recommendation, and even then he was assigned to the *Porpoise*. If Stanton hadn't been delayed by the obsequies for his wife, Burroughs wouldn't have been on the *Vincennes* at all. But the requirement of the navy was that an astronomer should be on board the flagship, and so I was forced to bring him over."

"Stanton *recommended* him?" Wiki exclaimed, disregarding the rest.

"He gave him a most glowing recommendation."

"But they're supposed to be enemies!"

"Evidently you were misinformed," Captain Wilkes said coldly. When his lips were no longer curved in that fixed smile, the contrast was quite intimidating. "Which makes me wonder why the sheriff of Portsmouth should have chosen *you* to be his deputy," he went on with a snap.

"The sheriff didn't tell you?"

"He did not."

"I see," said Wiki. He paused, thinking hard, and then said, "On the night Mrs. Stanton was killed, someone came to the Stanton house. Two of the servants testified that it was Mr. Tristram Stanton himself. But more than a dozen officers from the fleet gave evidence that he was at a banquet in Newport News at the time."

"I already know that," Captain Wilkes said, his tone impatient.

"Which left the identity of the man who came to the house a mystery—a mystery that the sheriff would very much like to solve," Wiki doggedly went on. "The imposter was quite an actor—he convinced one of the servants that he was the master, which couldn't have been easy. He had to have the distinctive Stanton voice, and he had to know the house quite well—not only did he address this fellow by name, but he went unerringly into Mrs. Stanton's room."

"So?"

"One man who might have managed to bring it off was Mr. Stanton's cousin, Astronomer Burroughs."

Captain Wilkes frowned. "You really believe that Burroughs—a *most* respectable man in his profession—would try a trick like that? Why in God's name would he do such a thing?"

"I agree that it sounds very strange, sir."

"But the sheriff wants you to chase up this strange notion?"

"Well, of course he doesn't know that Burroughs hanged himself," Wiki said. "And I haven't read his instructions yet either. But I expect you're right. I should say it's possible he would regard the suicide as an admission of guilt."

"But how can you possibly prove it? Your suspect has put an end to himself and left you with nothing but guesses!"

"If I could talk to Burroughs's assistant—a fellow by the name of Grimes—maybe it would help."

"Then do it," said Captain Wilkes, and turned away decisively to ring a small bell for the steward.

Nine

*G*rimes turned out to be the man who had been assisting Stanton, which did not surprise Wiki at all. On Captain Wilkes's instructions, they were closeted together in one of the staterooms that ran off the passage—a cramped room so full of equipment and supplies that it was obvious no one slept there. Strong hooks were driven into the massive ceiling beams—for hammocks or mosquito netting, Wiki assumed—and large net bags of onions hung from these, filling the air with a dusty, pungent smell. Looking around, he spied a box and sat on a corner of it to study his companion.

Enough light seeped in a sidelight window for Wiki to be struck yet again by the misery on the thin man's face. Added to it was a kind of muted horror at being trapped in this small space with a South Seas savage, so Wiki kept his voice gentle as he said, "Captain Wilkes has asked me to investigate the sad death of your employer."

A flicker of stunned incredulity briefly altered the tragic expression. "*You?*"

"The sheriff of Portsmouth has deputized me as his agent on board the expedition."

And Wiki handed over the letter of authority. As he watched the astronomer squint at the flourishing words, he mused wryly that Grimes looked just about as thunderstruck as he himself had felt when he'd first read it. However, the astronomer made no comment as he handed it back, so Wiki began the cross-examination.

"You were greatly attached to Mr. Burroughs?"

Grimes's expression immediately softened. "Mr. Burroughs was a fine gentleman, completely wedded to his craft."

"You'd worked with him for a long time?"

"Five years—nearly six—but it was more than that, you understand. All his life was astronomy—we worked together just about twenty-four hours of every day and night. He was a great man, sir—if he had survived, the expedition would have made him truly famous. The world would have appreciated his gift for science."

"Coming on this expedition was very important to him?"

"Certainly. Everyone knows," said Grimes, with a hint of reproof in his tone, "that the scientifics who are lucky enough to be part of this discovery fleet are bound for honor and glory."

"But was he nervous or apprehensive when he boarded?"

"He was in the highest of spirits—and even more so when we were shifted from the *Porpoise* to the *Vincennes*. He was most conscious of the honor of being on board the flagship, particularly as Captain Wilkes is well known in the astronomical way."

"So you had no expectations whatsoever that Mr. Burroughs was likely to—"

"To commit suicide?" Grimes burst out. "I was shocked, never so shocked in my life! I—I couldn't believe it—I—I still can't take it in!"

There were tears running down his face. Wiki tactfully waited, looking down at his hands instead of watching the other man's misery. Then he said, "When did you find out that you were joining the expedition?"

"Not until the start of August. Mr. Burroughs had applied for a place with the discovery ships many times, pressing his case with the Department of the Navy. For a while he had high hopes of Commodore Thomas ap Catesby Jones, but then Commodore Jones resigned and Mr. Burroughs had to start all over again. And it was not until the beginning of August that he at long last got a satisfactory answer. It was a triumph—a triumph of persistence."

"Was it a surprise to you?"

"It was only what he deserved, a great man like him! He was a better astronomer than other men I could name!"

There was sharp anger mixed with the deep sorrow on the other man's face. Wiki tried another tack, saying patiently, "Did he have much to do with his cousin Stanton?"

Silence. Grimes pursed his lips and for a moment seemed on the verge of coming out with something, but in the end he merely muttered, "He got the position on the strength of Mr. Stanton's recommendation."

"So Captain Wilkes told me. Did you expect Mr. Stanton to do him such a big favor?"

Another long pause, while Grimes perceptibly made up his mind about how much to confide. Then he mumbled, "I—I think a sizeable sum of money might've changed hands. Mr. Stanton was very much in need of the ready, and Mr. Burroughs was willing to pay anything—a small fortune, if necessary—to come along on the expedition."

So bribery was a distinct possibility. Wiki, thinking that the chances that Burroughs had been the murderer of Mrs. Stanton were rapidly increasing, said, "Do you remember what day you and Mr. Burroughs came on board the *Vincennes?*"

"It was just a couple of days before the fleet sailed. Afore that, we was on board the *Porpoise*—a whole two weeks we was there. As soon as he got the news that he'd been accepted, Mr. Burroughs started moving his equipment on board."

Wiki said in a flat voice, "Oh." He couldn't help it—his theories had been building up so neatly, and yet they were so easily exploded. Burroughs could not possibly have been the imposter if he was on board the *Porpoise* at the time. Realizing this, he felt dashed.

He said, "You were living on the *Porpoise* right up to the day you were removed to the *Vincennes?* A whole two weeks?"

"Well," said Grimes judiciously, "I wouldn't call it *living*. We still slept on shore."

"Ah." This was a different matter altogether. "And did Mr. Burroughs go out in the evening at all? I know the scientifics were in great demand as guests," Wiki prompted.

"Only one night, he did."

"Do you remember when?"

Wiki held his breath as Grimes calculated, muttering under his breath, but the date was the right one—it was the same night the man who had passed himself off as the master of the house had called at the plantation and Mrs. Stanton was murdered.

Wiki said tentatively, "I don't suppose you'd have any idea where he went?"

"I would not have presumed to ask," said Grimes, on a note of reproof.

"Did you notice his mood?" When Grimes hesitated, Wiki prompted, "I should have imagined that he was reluctant to go out when there was so much packing and planning to do."

"Oh, he was very cheerful. So splendid he looked, all rigged out in his best formal fig—claw-hammer coat, stiff white shirt; vest, fit for a royal presentation he was. I know it because he brought the clothes to me to brush and sponge. I'd never before seen him look so grand."

"And . . . a top hat?"

"Of course! He never went out without one."

"Did you see him when he got back?"

"When I saw him again I was on the *Porpoise*. It was well past noon next day."

"And what was his mood like then?"

"Excited—excited. Just had the news, you see, that we was being shifted onto the *Vincennes*."

"Did he know why he was being moved?"

"They said Mr. Stanton wouldn't be able to join the expedition on account of his wife committing suicide," Grimes added, and looked away as he said the last word, blinking hard.

"The news of the suicide affected Mr. Burroughs?"

"Not so anyone would notice," Grimes said, adding rather defensively, "The shift to the *Vincennes* preoccupied our minds so—we was busier than ever."

"And when it became officially known that she had not committed suicide at all—that it was a case of murder—?"

"He said nothing about it to me, though I noticed he went a bit quiet—abstracted, as if he had something on his mind. He would stop in the middle of something and stare into space, if you know what I mean. But then he'd get busy again—we had so much to do, and he was so looking forward to the voyage."

"Did the sheriff talk to Mr. Burroughs—or to you?"

"No, sir, neither of us. We passed his boat once when we was pulling over to the *Vin* with a load of equipment, and he looked around with an inquisitive expression on his face, but he didn't call out or anything. He was heading for shore, and I guess he was on some kind of errand."

"I see," said Wiki slowly. Everything had fallen into place— but still something nagged. Then he was roused from his deep reverie by Grimes giving a little cough and saying, "Is that all, sir?"

Wiki gave up trying to pin down the stray thought and stood up, narrowly missing a clout on the head from a bag of onions. "I thank you," he said. "You've been most helpful."

As he emerged from the house onto the bustling deck, he hesitated, blinded by the sudden bright sun. There was a burly figure standing by the weather mizzenmast shrouds. For a moment he thought the silhouette was Tristram Stanton, but when his sight adjusted he recognized Lieutenant Forsythe.

Neither said a word. Wiki turned on his heel and headed for the gangway, where the boat from the *Swallow* waited.

Ten

At six that evening a gun was fired on the *Vincennes*, and the flags were lowered to half-mast. All hands were lined up in good order on the decks of their ships to witness the burial of the remains of Astronomer Burroughs. Though the service was taking place on the flagship, Wiki thought that most sailors would have been able to follow the words from memory—*We therefore commit his body to the deep*—as the distant canvas bundle slid down the plank from under the flag that had been draped over it.

No doubt, mused Wiki ironically, the chaplain was inspired to add at least some words of the prayer that put the whole raison d'être of the exploring expedition in a nutshell—*Preserve us from the dangers of the sea, that we may be a safeguard unto the United States of America, and a security for such as pass on the seas upon their lawful occasions*—a prayer that was heartily echoed by the ever-growing host of American whalers, sealers, and merchantmen who risked the reefs, shoals, and savages of the great Pacific. They were men like his father, who, through organizations like the East India Marine Society of Salem, had lobbied the U.S. government for many years to send out an expedition to chart those reefs and shoals and at the same time subdue those savages who might threaten the safety of American mariners—a responsibility Captain Wilkes was acutely aware of and, as he had said publicly and often, was determined to carry out to the letter.

Three ragged musket volleys cracked as the corpse hit the water with an unheard splash to be lost forever in the deep blue sea—and Wiki still did not know what Stanton's cousin had looked like. *Confound it,* he thought, he should have asked Wilkes to let him see the body—it was just primitive superstition that had held him back.

During the second dogwatch he tapped on the door of the captain's cabin, and when he heard a grunt from within he turned the handle and went inside. George was busy with papers at his desk, so Wiki lowered himself to the edge of the settee that ran under the stern windows. While he waited, he slumped into his favorite thinking position, forearms along his thighs, his hands lightly clasped between his knees. The five chronometer clocks ticked heavily in the creaking silence, not quite in rhythm with each other.

He was thinking deeply about Jim Powell's claim that it had been Lieutenant Forsythe who had sent him to Newport News to collect the note from Tristram Stanton. Powell was a notorious liar—but was he lying now? The memory of the scene in the Norfolk tavern was as vivid in Wiki's mind as the pattern of the carpet under his feet, but none of it carried any kind of hint that

Jim was going to head off on a mission for Forsythe instead of staying behind, as he had promised to do.

As a memory, it was markedly unpleasant. When Forsythe had stormed in the door of the ordinary, Wiki had been in close conversation with Janey, his pretty fair-haired companion of the evening, expecting no kind of trouble whatsoever. They had been sitting in a nook with Janey's friend—a red-haired, Irish-looking girl—and her beau, Jim Powell, who had joined them without being asked. Wiki had been secretly wishing that Powell would take the redhead away and leave them alone when the door had crashed open and Forsythe had burst in on his way toward the tap. Then, when he clapped eyes on Wiki and Janey, he'd stopped dead.

Wiki remembered the southerner's glowering look. For some unknown reason he had been spoiling for a fight, and the sight of Rochester's half-caste friend in intimate conversation with a fair-haired southern girl had given him the excuse that he wanted. Wiki remembered every single insult, and how Forsythe's derisive laughter at the very idea of dueling with a half-caste Kanaka had hurt worse than all the insults put together—but he did not remember anything to indicate that shortly afterward the foul-mouthed lieutenant would send Jim off to Newport News to fetch a note from Tristram Stanton.

And what about Burroughs—had he indeed been the man who impersonated Stanton that night at the house? And was there a link between Burroughs and Forsythe? All three men were Virginians, Wiki mused. When George at last put down his pen and turned in his chair, Wiki said at once, "*E hoa*, what did Burroughs look like?"

George grimaced. "Ghastly. His end wasn't pleasant. When we cut him down his head flopped to one side and his mouth fell open—and there was some gore running from where he'd banged his head, as well as the horrid burn of the rope on his neck. And his face was swollen and purple—almost black. But it was mostly his expression that sent chills up my spine—a look of startled horror."

Wiki winced because so much of the description matched his memory of the dead body of Stanton's wife. That both had ultimately died of a broken neck seemed very ironic.

He said, "I meant his physical description. Could you tell he was related to the Stantons?"

Rochester considered the idea. "Burroughs's body was about the same kind of build as Tristram Stanton's—barrel-chested, I guess. I didn't see him standing up—not exactly, but my impression was that Burroughs was a bit shorter."

"Being shorter wouldn't be noticeable from a stairway."

"That's true," Rochester agreed with his eyebrows hoisting high, but then added, "You have to remember that it would have been a simple matter for a thinner man to pad himself out to pass as Stanton, too. Just about any man could have gotten away with it, just as long as his hair and clothes fitted the general appearance."

"So what color was Burroughs's hair?"

"Hard to remember because my attention was taken up by that awful face. It was dark and coarse like Tristram Stanton's, I think, and his ears stuck out the same way."

"He had sideburns?"

"I do remember sideburns." Rochester fingered his own fluffy side-whiskers, studying Wiki thoughtfully. "You seem quite determined that Burroughs was the man who went to the Stanton house that night. You've learned something, old fellow."

"Burroughs was invited to join the expedition only because

of Stanton's strong recommendation—I heard that from Captain Wilkes himself. And Burroughs's servant, Grimes, told me outright that he thought Burroughs had bribed Stanton to put in a good word for him."

Rochester's brows had reached his hair. "I remember you saying that Stanton was short of the ready. You reckon a big sum of money was involved?"

"The way I reckon things happened, no money at all was involved. I think Burroughs was asked to do Stanton a favor."

"What kind of favor?"

"To go to the plantation house the night his wife was murdered."

"My God, Wiki! Are you trying to tell me that Tristram Stanton *bribed* Burroughs to put his wife out of the way—and Burroughs agreed to do it?"

"I think the sheriff would jump to that conclusion if he were here."

"H'm," said Rochester, and pulled at his long nose, thinking deeply. Then he looked at Wiki and said shrewdly, "So you've made up your mind to delve a bit further to prove him right or wrong or whatever. But how can you hope to do that?"

"He left a letter of authority with Captain Wilkes, deputizing me to carry on with the investigation."

George's mild blue eyes opened wide. "Is this some kind of joke?"

Wiki produced the document and once again watched incredulity chase disbelief on the reader's face. "But why *you?*" George exclaimed when he was finished.

"Captain Wilkes was equally amazed," Wiki dryly replied.

"So that's why he came on board to talk with you when the boat delivered Stanton," said Rochester, light dawning. "I wondered about that. He'd already left that letter with Captain Wilkes?"

"So it seems," Wiki said, having worked this out himself. "And, having left it, he had to get me up to date—share his thoughts and findings, just in case something happened that justified this letter being handed over."

"And Captain Wilkes considered Burroughs's suicide a justification for telling you that you're now sheriff's deputy? Because he was Stanton's cousin?"

"So he said."

"And your guess is that the sheriff would reckon Burroughs's suicide was a virtual admission of guilt?"

Wiki hesitated, thinking that the sheriff had seemed to believe that the murderer was still on the loose in Virginia, because he had talked about hunting down the missing rifle. However, he shrugged and said, "That's what I told Captain Wilkes at any rate."

"Well," said Rochester, frowning, and stopped. He shifted uneasily in his chair and then said, "I didn't know the fellow at all—but I find it hard to believe that Burroughs was the kind of man who'd go along with murder. It just ain't logical that he'd do it, not even to get a position with the expedition. If anyone ever found out—"

Wiki meditated that Burroughs's assistant would never believe it, either. Then George went on, "Maybe he was bribed to get the body out of the house and into that derelict boat and then shove her along on her way to the sea. You've said already that she could've been dead of opium poisoning before anyone arrived."

"You've forgotten the little matter of her broken neck," Wiki said dryly.

"Maybe he dropped her after she was dead, and her neck snapped."

Wiki grimaced. "I don't think that's possible," he said, though he didn't feel all that certain. "If the body was still warm, it would have been completely limp; and if rigor mortis had set in, which takes a couple of hours, she would have been as stiff as a board."

"Well, it's an answer to why she didn't raise hell when the imposter walked into her room. Yup," said George decisively, "I reckon she was as dead as the dodo when Burroughs—if that is who it was—arrived."

"But I don't see how Stanton could possibly predict she'd kill herself before Burroughs came to dispose of the body," Wiki objected.

"You said Stanton confessed that he'd sent her a note that would have upset her considerable."

"I can't think of any message cruel enough to make sure of that—and anyway, it was never delivered."

Rochester's eyes opened wide again. "How the devil do you know that?"

"Jim Powell told me."

"*Powell?*"

"Aye. He said it fell out of his hat into the mud, and so he threw it away, because Wilkes had once beaten him for delivering a muddy letter."

George shook his head, looking baffled, and then hazarded, "You saw Powell on the *Vin?*"

"I saw him on the *Porpoise* last night."

"But I thought he was on the flagship."

"Well, he's not." Wiki wondered briefly what Captain

Wilkes would say if he knew that there was at least one man in the fleet with murder against him in his heart.

"Anyway," Rochester said, "Powell is an infamous liar. Steady seaman, but unsteady man—drinks, gambles, and so forth, you know."

"I do know," said Wiki somberly. Then he sighed, returning his mind to the note. "If the plot—if there *was* a plot—had gone as planned, and Stanton's wife had died of that overdose of opium, the note Stanton described would have made a verdict of suicide almost certain. So why did Stanton leave it so late to send it to her? Why write it in the middle of the banquet and not earlier, when he could be sure of it being delivered in time?"

Rochester shrugged. "Don't ask me, dear chap—as I said, I was right at the other end of the table and scarcely spoke to the man, only to call out to him that there was a fellow—Jim Powell, as it turned out—at the door."

"Maybe Stanton arranged it simply to draw attention to himself and make sure people remembered he was there."

"I think people were paying him plenty of attention already," said George.

"So you said," said Wiki. He was frowning, lost in thought. "You also said he was in great spirits," he observed at last.

"Definitely."

"As if he had something to celebrate."

George opened his mouth but then shut it again as he tipped his head slightly to contemplate Wiki, one eyebrow higher than the other, an attitude that was supposed to indicate alert understanding. "And you reckon he was in high spirits because he'd successfully set up the murder of his wife," he stated.

"If so, the note might have had something to do with it."

"I don't see how," George objected, after giving this some

serious thought. "I can see him plotting murder, yes—because Tristram Stanton is a cold-blooded swab if there ever was one—but if a note was involved it would only make sense if Powell was *delivering* some kind of message to let him know that everything was going according to plan. But Stanton was in high spirits before Powell ever arrived, and, what's more, he didn't even get up from the table—there was no way Powell could've slipped him a message. And it don't signify anyway," George concluded with decision, "because you say that Powell told you that the note was never delivered."

"You're right," agreed Wiki, and fell silent, studying his loosely linked hands between his knees and the carpet that covered the deck between his feet.

After a moment he lifted his head to contemplate George again, saying, "What do you know about Lieutenant Smith?"

"Lawrence Smith?"

"That's the one. He was conversing cozily with Wilkes when I walked into the cabin this afternoon."

"Oh, they've been shipmates for years—both joined the *Independence* in Boston at the start of 1818 and have often been on the same ships, I believe. In fact, I heard that they were together on the *Porpoise* last year, doing that survey of George's Banks. Smith's a kind of scientific, too—has an amateur interest, just like Wilkes does, only it ain't astronomy. What is it, now?" George asked himself, studying the deck beams. "A kind of superior linguister—what do they call it? Philology? He takes great notes of chants and poems and odes and suchlike, so maybe that ain't the right blessed term at all. Anyway, it's something to do with words and language—though not just straight translating, like the job you've been shipped to do, old boy."

"Ah!" Wiki exclaimed. At long last the hint of familiarity

that he had been hunting down throughout the awkward conversation on the *Vincennes* was there. Now he remembered an acquaintance of his father's who had been fascinated by the Maori passion for proverbs and riddles and had questioned him at great length, carefully spelling out the phrases as he wrote them down. This, he realized, must have been Lawrence J. Smith—only he had seemed terribly old at the time.

Then he said slowly, "So the chances are that he—like Tristram Stanton—joined the expedition because Captain Wilkes asked for him especially?"

George shrugged. "I suppose it's possible," he allowed. "However, I can't think of any favors Captain Wilkes might have done him—you have to bear in mind that he's simply a subordinate on the *Vincennes*."

This, Wiki remembered, was part of Wilkes's policy of giving the command of the smaller vessels to men at the bottom of the navy list—men who, like George, had passed their examinations so recently they had not had a chance to forget what they had learned.

"But doesn't it seem likely that Lawrence Smith and Tristram Stanton are cronies, too?"

They stared at each other in speculation, but then George spread his hands. "I can't help you with that one, old chap," he said, and let out an unexpected guffaw. "Can you picture that bantam trying to impersonate Stanton?"

"Not easily," Wiki admitted.

"And while he might talk a person to death, I can't see him doing anything more physical."

"But there might be some other connection."

"Well, old fellow, you're the sleuth—that there paper tells me so. Let me know when you've worked it out," said Rochester, and with another unseemly hoot of amusement returned to his paperwork, saying over his shoulder, "Captain Wilkes sent orders with the boat. We make sail at dawn and abandon this floating tree—and high time, too. It's October already! Springtime in the south! I reckon he's only just remembered that if he wants to explore the Antarctic, he needs to get into high southern latitudes before the end of the year."

Eleven

The next day dawned sweetly, with a smooth sea and a fine topgallant breeze. Stray noises drifted over from the other vessels—the shrilling of boatswains' piped calls and the regular cries of the lookouts. Bells ringing the half hours marked the time for swabbing down decks, for change of watch, for breakfast.

For a while it looked as if nothing much was happening, but then, suddenly, without warning, the lower sails of the *Vincennes* loosed and dropped. Wiki could hear slapping sounds echo over the water as canvas flapped against masts and distant squealing as the yards were hauled around and braced. Far-off shouting and the sails lost their wrinkles as they tautened. And all at once the flagship was moving. Gradually, then faster, the *Vincennes* was gathering way. A gun was fired as a signal to follow.

"All hands on deck!" Captain Rochester hollered, and Erskine cried, "Stand by to make sail!" An orderly confusion commenced, half the men dashing aloft to pluck at buntlines and cast off gaskets, while the rest grouped on deck to haul on sheets, lines, braces, buntlines, and halliards. "Stand by!" cried Erskine. "Let fall!"—and canvas unfurled with a deafening rattle. "Sheet home and hoist away!" Around came the yards; out fluttered the jibs. "Haul taut! Jib halliards, there! Hoist away!"

And the brig came to life. Wiki, at the helm, felt the sudden lift as the sails snapped taut and the *Swallow* picked up her skirts of foam, eagerly launching herself across the sparkling sea. "My God, ain't it a magnificent spectacle?" rhapsodized Rochester, a dozen hours later. Wiki, who was in the main topgallant crosstrees overhauling some reeving, moved over for George to join him. They stood there companionably, lightly holding onto lanyards a hundred feet above the sea. Again it was the dogwatch, a leisured time on board. Around and below their perch the sails of the *Swallow* spread and descended like huge white wings, while on their lee the other ships sailed in line, the *Vincennes*, *Porpoise*, and *Peacock* tall pyramids of luminous canvas that reflected the red and orange of the lowering sun, the schooners clusters of golden triangles, all of them racing closehauled toward the first stars of the night. "Ah, Wiki," George said on a long breath of contentment, "this is the life for me."

The pace, however, was not maintained. If Captain Wilkes had indeed felt some kind of urgency, it quickly dissipated. The ships were constantly hauled aback to accumulate scientific data. Boats were lowered so that the biologists could poke and peer at the depths. Multitudes of glass containers became filled with live animalculae frisking in saltwater and dead fish floating in alcohol. The fleet sailed back and forth over a small stretch of ocean to establish beyond all doubt that there were no shoal waters there, despite the reports of past navigators. Hydrographical and meteorological observations were regularly made and faithfully noted.

A particularly irritating job was assigned to the *Swallow,* that of charting currents. Two kegs, one full of saltwater and the other half full, were connected by a five-fathom line and then thrown overboard. The theory was that the full keg, sinking, would pull the half-full keg just below the surface, and that with a log line attached to the connecting line, it was possible to get a reading that was uninfluenced by wind and wave. In practice, it was not at all easy. If the top keg leaked, both rapidly sank to the bottom; and when the log line was hauled to bring them up again, it invariably broke, and then a report had to be written, while all the time the fleet dawdled south.

There were other annoyances. Because the victualing officers back at the navy yard had disliked Wilkes so much, the provisions were second-rate, so Wilkes decreed that the fitness of his sailors should be maintained with healthful habits. Cleanliness inspections were a regular feature, often held by Captain Wilkes himself from his station on the poop of the *Vincennes,* so that his fault-finding speaking-trumpet sessions became more hated than ever. In the still evenings, spare sails were lowered into the water to make shark-safe pools so that all hands could have a swim. On the flagship the small squad of marines marched and countermarched away the day.

Spiritual well-being was not neglected, either. On Sundays the fleet chaplain held divine service on the deck of the *Vincennes,* and all the captains were expected to demand that the crews muster in their best square-collared white frocks tied with black silk neckerchiefs, clean blue jackets and trousers, and shiny black hats and shoes, to listen to yet another repetition of the expedition prayer, along with a relevant passage from the Bible—a rule that was universally loathed. Then Wilkes had an additional idea—that gun crews should be trained and gun captains appointed. The first flat calm, he said, would be an opportunity for exercising the cannon.

"I thought it was a mission of peace and the cannon was just for show," Rochester complained to Wiki. "And to tell the truth," he admitted, "cannonry ain't my strong point—I know how to signal a gun crew to let them know how close to the target they got, but that's about the limit of my skills."

They were standing on the quarterdeck studying the two stern chasers that were all the cannonry the brig boasted. They were long-snouted beasts, painted a somber black and speckled with rust, each set solidly on a four-wheeled carriage and securely tied down so that they would not break loose if the brig pitched violently, and kill the men by running over them, and sink the ship by smashing holes in her stern. Before, they had seemed simply part of the deck furniture, but now they had suddenly taken on a new significance.

"Perhaps we need an armorer," said Wiki. "Do they have armorers on navy ships?" His only experience of such gentlemen was on a London whaleship he had once joined briefly in the Sea of Japan, where the blacksmith had been called "the armourer" and had been in charge of the ship's weapons.

"Excellent idea!" said Rochester, with great animation. "Except that I think we call the chap the 'gunner.' Whom shall we appoint?"

He and Wiki and Erskine devoted a great deal of thought to it, discussing the various men on board in detail. In fact, the choice was obvious—a lanky foremast hand by the name of

Dave, who had come on board with a musket as long as he was, along with a fund of bloodcurdling yarns about hunting bears and worse in the mountains of home.

"He must know his firearms," Rochester decided. "Folk tell me they make their rifles themselves! The mountain men reckon the regular manufactured ones aren't accurate enough, or so they say. In fact, I have heard that they learn to use 'em straight from the blessed cradle—and to run at top speed while they do it! Imagine it, young boys being trained to load and fire rifles at the same time as they run. Amazing, don't you reckon? Picture a little lad managing a long, heavy rifle, a large powder horn, a bullet bag, a priming-powder horn, and dashing along meanwhile with all that equipment rattling and banging—firing to kill, and then heading for the horizon and reloading all at once and at the same blessed time! Remarkable, truly. Let's have him."

"I'm not sure that mountain men have much to do with cannon, sir," Erskine objected, but was easily overridden.

Forthwith, mountain man Dave was summoned. He was not at all modest about his ability, declaring he could handle any weapon coming, this not being his first berth in a man-of-war by any means, and was even more delighted at his elevation in rank than George Rochester was at getting the job delegated. Wiki watched him as he set about counting and cataloguing the brig's armory—twelve 1819-vintage Hall breech-loading rifles and an assortment of swords, pistols, knives, dirks, and cutlasses, plus a dozen vicious contraptions that were a combination of two weapons, being a broad, sharp blade attached to the underside of the barrel of a pistol.

These, the mountain man handled with reverence. "Elgin cutlass-pistols," he said to Wiki, who—like every Maori warrior he knew—was fascinated by weapons, firearms in particular, and so was paying close attention. "Designed and made expressly for the expedition," Dave added, in a tone of awe. He immediately held classes in cutlass work, saying swords were just for show, being so easily broken, and so the crew enthusiastically practiced the skills of chopping and slashing with the big heavy cutlasses, hammering murderously at each other in pairs. Then he introduced them to the Elgin cutlass-pistols, teaching them to fire first and then lunge in with the blade. Another frontiersmen favorite was the foot-long Bowie knife, a single-edged affair with a handle made of horn and a brass strip along the back. Dave taught the men how to chop down fast, to break the other man's blade, and then push forward to gut him, cutting edge upward, all in one homicidal action.

The two nine-pounder Long Toms, however, were his special pride and joy. As Rochester confided to Wiki, on his previous ships his impression had been that the main job of the gunner was to keep up an incessant dissatisfied growl about his guns. Dave, by contrast, treasured his charges; he groomed the old stern chasers as if they were prized stallions, rubbing them bright with brick and canvas, and then coating them with a mixture of lampblack, beeswax, and turpentine until they shone like mirrors. The various rammers, sponges, priming wires, caps, and fuses were spruced up likewise—and then he turned his attention to training both captain and crew in the management of these pampered contrivances.

George Rochester's role was to stand on the quarterdeck with a speaking trumpet, while the Samoan, a large, intimidating figure in a loincloth that showed off his great tattooed thighs to advantage, drummed out a call to quarters on a length of log. "Silence fore and aft!" George cried, as the men hurriedly assembled, to be echoed by Midshipman Erskine:

"Wet and sand the decks!"

"Take off your muzzle bags and withdraw your tompions!"

"Cast loose your guns!"

This led to a bustle of activity, as the bags and barrel plugs that protected the muzzles of the cannon from saltwater were taken out and put aside, and the tight lashings that held the guns in place were cast away. Men hooked on rope tackles, one to each side of the carriage to heave the gun up to the gunport in the rail, and a train-tackle behind to run it back for loading. After that, they seized the breeching—a stout rope secured to the brig's hull by two ring-bolts, one to each side of the carriage—and looped it to a knob at the back end of the gun. This was long enough to allow the cannon to recoil after every shot, but prevented it from running amuck all over the deck.

All this, Captain Rochester watched benignly, his part in the drama being finished. It was now the turn of gunner Dave, who snapped out orders in quick succession: "Chock your luff—stop, vent, and sponge your guns—cartridge, wad, and ram home—load your shot, wad, ram home—man side-tackle falls, run out!"

The cartridge was a flannel bag with three pounds of powder in it, and it was rammed down the muzzle of the gun until the man assigned as gun captain, poking about in the innards with a priming iron thrust through the touch-hole, could feel it was in place, at which he hollered, "Home!" Then the nine-pound shot went down, followed by a wad, both rammed hard. That done, the men clapped onto the side-tackles and shoved the loaded cannon up to the gunport, pushing its muzzle out as far as it would go.

Aiming the brute was the next job. "Crows and ha-a-a-nd-spikes!" Dave roared, and crowbars and handspikes were thrust into place and levered, heaving the gun right or left according to the mountain man's whim, with a great deal of grunting and swearing.

"Elevate your guns for a long shot!" This was a job for the two gun captains, who used wedges shoved underneath the breeches to raise the snouts high enough to rip cannonballs through the sides of enemy frigates—the task for which stern chasers were specially designed.

"Cock your locks, blow your match, watch the weather roll, stand by . . . FIRE!"

The captain had punctured the cartridge with his priming iron, used a goose quill to fill the touch-hole and the powder pan above it with priming powder from his horn, the hammer of the flintlock had been pulled back; and just in case it didn't work, the slow match—a kind of fuse—was smoldering. The gun, theoretically, was set to blast.

Instead, they practiced hour after hour, all heaving and dumb show, with no satisfying smoke and thunder at the end, just a lot of dissatisfied swearing from mountain man Dave. While exciting at first, it rapidly became tiresome. The only man on board who was happy with the constant gun-drill was the Samoan, whose drumming was becoming more stirring by the minute.

Even if Dave had been pleased with the performance, Captain Rochester could not have allowed a live firing. "If I let 'em fire willy-nilly and without his say-so, Wilkes would have my intestines for a bandanna," he candidly confessed to Wiki.

They were standing at the taffrail, the spanker boom swinging a little above their heads because they were yet again hauled aback. George had just returned from the *Vincennes*, where he had delivered his journal for Captain Wilkes's weekly inspection, journal keeping being another requirement of the expedition. "They're all finding this dumb exercising a bore," he said, meaning the captains and officers of the other ships, with whom he associated quite freely. Wilkes encouraged his captains and officers to lower boats and exchange visits, particularly on Saturdays, to carouse in a temperate and seemly fashion, and drink a toast to wives and sweethearts. The officers of the expedition, he declared, were the cream of the U.S. Navy, and he wanted them to become a tight-knit team of loyal comrades, like Admiral Nelson's legendary Band of Brothers.

"But of course we simply have a good growl and drink rather a lot of wine," said George. Then he handed a card to Wiki and said, "Your company is craved by the mids of the *Vin*."

"My what?" Wiki blinked.

"Next Saturday. The junior midshipmen of the *Vincennes* have invited you to a feast. I had to deliver many soothing reassurances that you would not try to eat any of *them*," he added with a grin. "And then they asked if you ate your meat cooked."

Twelve

*D*o you think us awful outrageous, Mr. Coffin, sir?" inquired a red-cheeked lad.

Wiki withdrew his stare from a fascinated survey of his surroundings and gazed at his questioner. Obviously, the young man expected an answer, but Wiki found it very hard to think of one.

He did not think his hosts outrageous at all, just extremely high-spirited. There were six of them, their enthusiastic chubby faces belying the primness of their uniform—dark blue clawhammer coats with a single line of gold buttons running down from gold-embroidered stand-up collars. Their trousers were white—two of them were grand enough to have white satin breeches to haul out for special occasions such as this. It was beyond Wiki to guess why they had invited him here, but it was certainly an interesting experience.

The midshipman who had spoken was named Dicken, Wiki thought—his friends called him Jack. Like the rest, he was fit to bust with the honor and glory of sailing with what they all insisted on calling the first, great, national exploring expedition. "Just imagine, sir!" one of them had cried—"a country that but a short time ago was a mere discovery itself, taking its place among the most elevated nations of the world!" Captain Wilkes, they were all quite certain, was a genius of the stature of Captain Cook, and they hero-worshiped him unquestioningly. "Long life to him!" had been the first of their spirited toasts.

Wiki smiled and said, "Why should I think you outrageous?"

"Because we are not refined, Mr. Coffin!"

They were also rather drunk. Wiki said very solemnly, "Does a midshipman need to be refined?"

"Assuredly, sir! It is by no means enough that an officer of the U.S. Navy should be a capable mariner!" the young fellow declaimed, and to Wiki's surprise the other five joined in the chorus: "He should be a gentleman of liberal education, refined manners, punctilious courtesy, and the nicest sense of personal honor!"

Wiki hazarded, "You're quoting someone."

"Aye, sir!"

"The great John Paul Jones, sir!"

"It's drummed into us all by our superiors, sir!"

Then the mids competed vigorously to relate the story of the epic battle that took place on September 23, 1779, between the English *Serapis* and the American rebel ship *Bon Homme Richard,* commanded by the immortal John Paul Jones. It had been a bloody conflict, Wiki was assured, the two ships tightly locked together in combat. The first raking broadside had cruelly blasted the *Richard;* but though the English commander had called out to Jones to surrender, he and his crew had tenaciously fought on, their ship sinking fast beneath them. So withering had been the fire from the tops of the rebel ship that the English captain had torn down his colors—and the *Bon Homme Richard*, foundering fast, was the victor.

"I have not yet *begun* to fight!" a midshipman by the name of Keith roared, and all the other midshipmen roared it out, too, raising their glasses of wine in salute. This, Wiki gathered, had been the immortal reply made by John Paul Jones when the English had invited him to surrender. The party was getting very merry, he meditated further, and he wondered if Captain Wilkes would hear about it and send a lieutenant to calm them down.

Meantime, he returned to a fascinated study of his surroundings. This might be the mess room of the mids, and the place where two of them slept, but it reminded him of nothing so much as the reception room of some low house of entertainment. The bulkheads were entirely draped with white-and-crimson curtains. There was a large mirror on one wall and silver candlesticks perched all about. A huge vase was filled with artificial flowers made out of painted feathers—a souvenir, he supposed, of Madeira. A bureau stood in one corner, and a fancy washstand, its china bowl and pitcher decorated with sprigs of green and gilt, was set in another. Brussels carpet and Chinese rugs covered the floor, and two long couches were built along the fore-and-aft walls. Though upholstered in blue damask they were evidently used as berths at night.

The wall opposite the looking glass was hung with dirks, daggers, a couple of the famous Elgin cutlass-pistols, fancy swords, and two massive cutlasses. Wiki studied them with mixed feelings of avarice and discomfort. In most of the Pacific communities he knew, weapons as valuable as these were kept wrapped in mats or tapa cloth so that their *mana* and *kaha* could not be stolen by malicious spirits. A hand weapon not only assumed the strength and valor of the owner, but acquired the power of the lives it had taken as well. After all these years he still found it amazing that Americans should take the substantial risk of so boldly putting their arms on display.

Then, again, his attention was claimed. A voice piped up from the head of the table almost as if he discerned Wiki's thoughts. "Mr. Coffin, could you tell us something of your history? The traditions of your ancestors? Stories of your youthful days?" he cried.

It was Keith, one of the two midshipmen who lived in this room. He looked sincere and serious, but was possibly rather drunk. Wiki smiled, leaning back easily in his chair, and said, "You want me to recite my *whakapapa?* I warn you, it takes a long time."

Whakapapa? The strange word excited them. Two of them asked him how to spell it and carefully wrote it down. "Your . . . ancestry?"

"Aye—my mountain and my river, my ancestral canoe, and my genealogy, too. Anyone who cannot recite his *whakapapa* is *tutua,* 'a nobody.' "

"Oh dear, then we are all *tutua,*" one said, and they all laughed.

"No one expects a *pakeha* to recite his or her genealogy— except perhaps for Queen Victoria."

"Is that what you call us—*pakeha?*" And again the scribes wrote the new word down. "Sir, can you tell us how your people felt when Captain Cook arrived?"

Wiki paused for thought, studying them with hidden amusement, and decided to tell them a story. "My grandmother told me that when the first European ship came into their bay, *her* grandfather declared to the people that the men who sailed on such outlandish craft must be wandering ghosts—*tere tu paenga roa*—because they had come from the far side of the horizon where the spirit realm lies. Then the ship came to anchor, and the boats pulled to shore.

"And when the people saw the men facing backward as they worked at their oars, they knew that *koro* was right—that they were goblins, whose eyes were in the backs of their heads. The children and women ran into the trees, my grandmother with them, but the warriors stayed on the beach, ready to fight. Instead of attacking the warriors, however, the goblins began to collect shellfish and eat them with enjoyment, so the women calmed down, thinking they must be quite a lot like ordinary men. They took *kumara*—our sweet potato—and fish to the goblins, and showed them how to roast it in an oven in the ground. And when they saw them taking pleasure in the well-cooked food, my grandmother said that the women thought perhaps they were not goblins after all.

"Next day the boats pulled ashore again, and this time the men brought a gift of some of the kind of food they ate on the ships. My grandmother said that some of it was very hard." Wiki held up a ship's biscuit. "She thought it was pumice stone that had been enchanted because it tasted sweet. She said the people liked it very much. The sailors' meat, however, was fat and salty, and the people disliked it greatly. She told me that this was what convinced her grandfather that these were ordinary hungry mortals and definitely not supernatural beings. These men had heard about the good food of Aotearoa, and they had come because they wanted to find out what good food was like."

This part of the yarn was a joke, because the cold winters,

thick forests, and poor soil of New Zealand made growing food notoriously difficult; and Wiki's people sighed often, in proverb and folklore, for the fertility of their lost ancestral land, Hawaiki. However, he did not bother to explain, feeling quite sure that his audience would not understand the wry humor—and, anyway, his little story had enchanted them enough, he saw. They were childlike themselves, and so the simple tale appealed.

Then a shout of delight went up as the door opened and their mess steward arrived with a great sea-pie made of meat and onions and potatoes—"Hash with an awning," they called it, because of its pastry top. "Rouse up some more of that capital claret, dear fellow," said Keith to the steward, and more bottles were fetched. A toast was drunk to wives and sweethearts— "May they never meet!" quipped one, and they all rolled about with laughter as if they'd never heard the joke before. "A blessing, a blessing," someone cried, and they chorused irreverently:

Five, six, rigging to fix
Seven, eight, don't be late
One, two, join the crew
Three, four, take up your oars!

And knives and forks were wielded with a will.

"Do you enjoy sea-pie, sir?" Wiki's neighbor politely asked.

"Of course," said Wiki. "But it must be well-baked," he added gravely.

"We collected together a thousand dollars to spend on extras for our mess, and Keith spent six hundred of his own in the bargain. After all, three years is a long time to be away from the amenities of home, don't you think, sir?"

Wiki's eyebrows were higher than ever. A three-year voyage

about the world was certainly quite a proposition, but nonetheless he was very impressed by the amount of money these lads had at their disposal. He knew from George Rochester that the custom in the navy was for officers to make their own eating arrangements, only staples like flour being provided by the ship, but for the first time he realized that the families of these young gentlemen were rich.

"And Keith furnished this cabin, sir. Don't you admire it?"

"I do indeed," said Wiki solemnly.

"What age are you, sir?" another boy asked him. "Do you know it? Do your people keep count of the years?"

"I'm twenty-four," said Wiki. Up until this afternoon he had felt quite young, but these boys made him feel old.

"Sir, I couldn't help but notice that you're not tattooed," said another. "Don't New Zealanders tattoo themselves like other savages?"

"Warriors have a *moko*, a tattooed face," said Wiki, and then added by way of explanation, "I was taken to America when I was twelve years old."

"Do you ever think you will get one?"

Wiki had often thought of it. He said, "It's not really my choice."

"Why, who chooses?"

"The father, the grandfathers—it's *taumaha*, a serious matter that demands a lot of deep discussion."

It wryly amused him to imagine what his father would say if approached with such a proposition. Captain Coffin was still sailing the Pacific, trundling from one lagoon to another after sea slugs—*bêche-de-mer*—and pearl shell, to trade for tea in Canton. They met up occasionally, usually in some foreign place, and Wiki invariably enjoyed his father's company. Not only did they have a lot in common, both being seafarers, but Captain Coffin was so unstintingly and flatteringly proud of his only son.

"If you got your face tattooed, sir, do you think they would put you on display in America?"

"Perhaps," said Wiki. It was one of the reasons for not getting a *moko*.

"What was your mother's name?"

What strange questions they asked. "Te Rau o te Rangi," Wiki said. His people often changed their names at a whim, but that was the name he had known her by. She had been a celebrated beauty—Captain Coffin had certainly been bowled over by her looks, and there were songs likening her to the planet Venus. "She was a famous swimmer," said Wiki. "Many men challenged her, *pakeha* sailors among them, but she beat them all."

"And your father, sir?"

Wiki smiled, understanding now that the question about his mother had been asked to tactfully lead the way to this one, and said mildly, "Captain Coffin of Salem, Massachusetts." Then he watched their faces. Most of them knew that part of his history already, he saw; he did not feel surprised about it, knowing that scuttlebutt—shipboard gossip—was both fast and accurate. However, a couple of his hosts lifted their brows as if suddenly realizing why their guest had been carted off to America at the tender age of twelve.

"What were your feelings when you left your home?" one asked.

"Excited. Sad." Wiki shrugged. Several men of his tribe had gone off on American ships before; and while some had not come back, others had returned to amaze the *iwi* with their exciting yarns and become people of importance, and so following in their wake had not taken a great deal of courage.

"It was an adventure," he said.

"What were your first impressions when you landed in America?"

Wiki meditated. When he was a child his grandmother had repeated to him the famous prediction of the prophet Te Toiroa of Nukutaurua—that in times ahead their land would be chattering with *te reo kihikihi,* the cicada language, which was how his people came to describe the incomprehensible twittering talk of the *pakeha.* And while twelve-year-old Wiki had thought he understood English well enough by the time he arrived in Boston, his first overwhelming impression had been of being deafened by the meaningless clamor of cicadas—that these busy Americans rushed about battering each other with a constant rush of words. And they interrupted each other all the time! In his home village interrupting a speaker had been the height of discourtesy, but in America, or so it had seemed to him, it was meant to be a sign of great interest in what was being said.

From past experience, however, Wiki knew that it was not a good idea to let on that his first impression had been that Americans were rather less refined than the people at home. "I was greatly impressed by the immense buildings and the wonderful bustle of business," he answered solemnly instead.

"And you're a true-blue American now, sir—ain't that marvelous? They tell me you're a sheriff's deputy in Virginia, Mr. Coffin—is that true?"

Wiki asked sharply, "How did you hear that?"

Keith waved a casual arm. "Scuttlebutt, sir," he said.

"Everyone knows it. Are you investigating that astronomer what killed himself?"

Wiki narrowed his eyes. "Why, is there something to investigate?"

"We all wonder why he did it, sir."

"You were surprised when you learned about it?"

"Astounded, sir! He spent all his time fussing about with his instruments and seemed perfectly happy with life. He just didn't seem to have any reason to put an end to himself."

"Did any of you work with him?"

The boys all glanced at each other. "Not really," one said. "We have orders to assist the astronomers with their observations—it's meant to be good practice for us, but Mr. Burroughs's assistant didn't like us to hang around and watch even, let alone try to help."

"He was jealous, perhaps?" Wiki suggested, remembering Grimes's obvious devotion to Burroughs.

"They were as close as cats, sir," Dicken agreed. "Didn't have much to do with the rest of the ship at all. Privately closeted together day and night with their instruments and observations. I feel sorry for the assistant, now—he must heartily wish he had been present to put a stop to the desperate act. Does he have no idea why Mr. Burroughs should do such a thing, sir?"

They were all looking at Wiki expectantly. He was frowning, thinking that that was the question he'd forgotten to ask Grimes—what had he been doing and where had he been at the time Burroughs hanged himself.

He evaded the question, saying wisely, "My people have a saying, *Ko nga take whawhai, he whenua, he wahine*—for the source of trouble, look for land and women."

"You wonder if Astronomer Burroughs put an end to himself on account of a petticoat?" someone demanded, and all six laughed heartily. "You'd be better to look to Lieutenant Forsythe for quarrels over the nancy girls, Mr. Coffin!" another exclaimed, and they all giggled again.

For a nasty moment Wiki thought they were referring to his failed attempt to call Forsythe out after the foul-mouthed southerner had made his gross advances to Janey. Then, however, it became evident that Lieutenant Forsythe was unpopular with these boys—"Commander Wilkes gave old Forsythe a proper dressing down for bullyragging me unmercifully," piped up one midshipman. "Three cheers for our gentleman commander!" chorused the others, with some sloshing of wine.

"Forsythe's a famous sharpshooter, though," said Keith, when the hubbub had died down. "He brought his own rifle on board—his granpappy gave it to him when he was ten years old, he says, which must mean that it is awful ancient, but I've never yet seen him miss his mark."

Keith's voice was wistful, betraying a youthful passion for firearms and marksmanship. Wiki mused that being a crack shot was a new side to Lieutenant Forsythe's character, but not particularly unexpected.

"It hangs from a famous large rack of antlers in his cabin," the chubby-cheeked Dicken volunteered. "Would you like to see it, sir?" he said brightly. "I'm convinced Lieutenant Forsythe would be happy for you to view it, it's such an awful fine trophy."

Wiki shook his head, smiling faintly, certain that Lieutenant Forsythe would not be happy in the slightest, and to his relief they returned to the ghoulish topic of astronomer Burroughs's demise.

"When you talk of land being a bone of contention with your people, sir, do you mean property—like money?" another mid asked. "I heard that Burroughs was a warm man, but he didn't appear very rich. The steward said he brought nothing much at all in the way of extra provisions, and that his clothes were just about rags."

"Perhaps he was bankrupt," said one. However another, in a perceptible Virginia accent, assured him that it was universally known that Burroughs hadn't been short of the ready.

Wiki said quietly, "There's also a third cause of conflict—*kanga.*"

They all looked at him. "Curses," he said. "Slurs on a man's reputation—his *mana*. Something to destroy his honor and his name."

There was a long silence, and then Keith said hesitantly, "I can understand that."

"You can?"

"Aye, sir. If there was something in my past that I hoped was forgotten—"

"Or hoped would never be revealed?" said Wiki, after waiting to make sure the sentence was not going to be finished.

"Aye, sir."

"Particularly when a man was on the verge of achieving his life's ambition?"

"Aye, sir," said Keith again. He seemed suddenly sobered, saying quietly, "If there was something in my past that would ruin such a glorious prospect, then I would perhaps rather die than face the consequences."

"The surgeon said Burroughs banged his head," said Dicken, and they all looked up at the massive beams that held up the deck above. "Would a bang on the head cause anyone to sling up a noose and put his head inside it, Mr. Coffin?"

Wiki shrugged and spread his hands.

"He was so excited to be part of the expedition," said another midshipman.

"So I heard," said Wiki, assuming he meant Burroughs.

"It would be a dreadful shame if he was sent home, don't you think? Do you know if he'll continue to assist Mr. Stanton, sir?"

Wiki blinked, realizing that the boy was talking about Grimes. Then he frowned, struck by a sudden thought. Had Grimes been as excited as Burroughs was at the chance to join the expedition? He had said something that suggested that, he remembered.

Then Dicken said brightly, "Would you like to see the room where Astronomer Burroughs hanged himself, Mr. Coffin?"

The budding idea dissolved. Wiki looked sharply at the smiling boy and said, "Is that possible? I thought that Astronomer Stanton had taken over the room."

"Oh, he has, sir—but Mr. Stanton has gone to the *Porpoise* with Grimes to fetch some equipment that was left behind when Mr. Burroughs shifted from the *Porpoise* to the *Vin.*"

"But surely the room is locked?"

"Oh, the door is still broken, sir," said Dicken, waving a careless hand. "They take forever to fix things on this ship."

Wiki's fist clenched hard on his thigh with abrupt irritation with himself. He had assumed that the stateroom where Burroughs had committed suicide was one of those opening off the passageway in the deckhouse—*but none of those doors had been damaged.*

He said as calmly as he could, "Aye, I do think I would like to see it."

Thirteen

They clambered up a ladder to the gun deck, one tier above the orlop deck where the junior midshipmen berthed. Then Dicken led the way with his supple adolescent knees bent outward, so that the top hat with a cockade he'd popped on his head would not be knocked off by the beams. Wiki's back was bent uncomfortably as he followed, his eyes flickering all around. Shadows led off fore and aft. Apart from themselves, the deck seemed empty of men.

Tautly lashed-down carronades squatted along the side of the ship, shiny black paint glimmering in the stray rays of sun that leaked through the red-painted rims of shut gunports. Between them Wiki could see hammock hooks and the faint glint of tin numbers that were nailed onto the bulkheads. He briefly wondered what the figures were for, but then decided that each gun must have its own number, which seemed logical. More light fell down dimly in dusty squares from scuttles in the main deck above, randomly delineating neatly stowed sponges and rammers, and racks symmetrically piled with shot. It seemed evident, though, that the Department of the Navy had taken a bet that the *Vincennes* wouldn't need to fire a broadside on this expedition because cabins and storage rooms interrupted the measured lines of cannon. However, Wiki saw that their walls had been constructed of canvas stretched tautly on light wooden frames, mounted parallel to the sides of the ship. If the *Vincennes* did have to prepare herself for a major battle, he deduced, these could be swiftly and easily removed.

Dicken kept on going all the way to the stern, where cathedral-like shafts of dusty light wafted down from scuttles to streak the walls of more substantial and permanent cabins. These, Wiki deduced, were originally paint and sail lockers, now converted into staterooms and workshops. Then the midshipman came to an abrupt stop, waving an arm at a door that was cracked and splintered but had been wedged shut from the outside.

"Would you like me to open it, sir?" he said.

Wiki paused. On the main deck above a drum was rolling for the six p.m. distribution of grog to the men. They were standing directly below the deckhouse where Captain Wilkes and most of the scientifics lived and worked, he thought. He looked up at the beams and solid oak planks, meditating that their thickness must be the reason no one had heard the commotion when Stanton had been hammering at this door and shouting out— while all the time Burroughs, inside this room, had been swinging from the noose about his neck.

Which made it odd, he thought later, that a sudden

crescendo of unearthly shrieks of horror filtered down from the main deck so clearly.

Wiki whirled and sprinted for the ladder, the six boys close at his heels. When he burst out into the light, the first man he saw was Lieutenant Forsythe, who was evidently in charge of the deck again, because a speaking trumpet dangled from one hand. The southerner was staring rigidly up at the main topgallant sail but saying and doing nothing—all the noise was coming from the boatswain, who was screaming incoherently. Then Wiki saw the human pendulum that was swinging with the roll of the ship a hundred feet above the deck, writhing and fighting the noose about his neck.

A hand pushed Wiki out of the way. It was George Rochester, snapping at the screeching boatswain, "Calm down, sir! What the hell has happened here?"

The petty officer's eyes were round and staring with horror. "There was somethin' amiss with the main topgallants'l, sir—it was snagged. The lieutenant—Lieutenant Forsythe—he called out to slack the main topgallant buntline, at the same time ordering Powell on the topgallant yard to overhaul it. The sail bellied out full and the rope whipped out, snapped back, caught Powell around the neck, whipped out again with him snarled up in it, and snatched him off the yard. One awful cry came from his lips—and there he dangles now. I saw it happen, sir—"

Powell? It couldn't be, thought Wiki confusedly. It was odd enough that George Rochester had materialized—though it was Saturday, the day the journals had to be handed in to Wilkes, and Rochester was wearing dress uniform. But Powell was on the *Porpoise,* surely. He remembered him swearing to murder Captain Wilkes if he was ever shifted to the *Vincennes*. The squirming body was horribly distinct, swinging against the clear sky with every roll of the ship.

Lieutenant Forsythe seemed to gather his wits. Wiki saw him take a breath and lift the trumpet. "Let go that rope!" he blared to the gang of men at the foot of the mast who were numbly hanging onto the buntline. Rochester spun round, exclaiming, "Lieutenant, if they let that rope run he'll be dashed to the deck, you'll kill him—" but Forsythe did not seem to hear, instead screaming into the speaking trumpet, "Let that bloody rope run, I say, let go at once!"

And Rochester shouted at the top of his lungs, "Belay that! Don't do it!"

Forsythe dropped the trumpet. His face went red and then white. His eyes, like the boatswain's, were staring. He spluttered, "*What?*"

George merely cast him a harried glance. "Slack the rope gently—handsomely now! Gently! Gently!" he shouted, and the men at the foot of the mast numbly started to obey. Then he looked at Wiki and jerked his chin upward. The unspoken order was clear. Wiki kicked off his shoes, leapt for the rigging, and tore upward, hand over fist.

It was as if the whole ship was emerging from a paralysis, brought to life by Rochester's vigor and force. All about Wiki ropes sang and vibrated as a host of sailors followed him up the rigging. He was the first to reach the main yard. Then he rapidly sidled outward, reached up, grabbed Powell around the waist— and it was indeed Jim Powell, though almost unrecognizably black in the face.

He was still struggling, though feebly, and making horrible strangling noises. The ship rolled, and Powell kicked as he swung. Wiki slipped, lost his grip, snatched at a rope, missed, snatched again, and snagged it with the tips of his nails. Somehow he saved himself. Then two, three, men were alongside him. On deck, sailors were easing the rope gently, hand over hand, and gradually the buntline slackened. The body was dangling over the maintop. They were able to bring him in.

Jim Powell was laid down on the lofty platform. Rigging thrummed, and Wiki saw the ship's surgeon mounting the shrouds, as sedate as if the ratlines were the rungs of a ladder at home, his medical bag hanging from one shoulder. With a detached part of his mind Wiki meditated that someone should advise the doctor to hold on to the shrouds, not the ratlines, because ratlines were notorious for coming away. His main thought, however, was that the surgeon may as well have saved his breath—Powell was certainly dead. The rope had wound about his neck several times, like the coils of a boa constrictor.

However, the old medic, after inspecting the victim, was merely astonished. "My God!" he exclaimed, his countenance red with amazement. "What stuff do they use to make these hardy tars? He's alive!"

They put Powell in the stateroom nearest to the door of the deckhouse to recover his wits and his equilibrium before attendants arrived to take him down to the regular sick bay in the bowels of the orlop deck. Small as this stateroom was, it was packed with men, and the babble was deafening. The air stung with the fumes of the spirits of hartshorn the surgeon was wafting back and forth under Powell's nose. Then everyone shouted out excitedly as Powell's bloodshot eyes blinked twice and stretched wide. They all waited for his first words.

"I heard the drumroll for grog," he croaked, and lifted himself on an elbow. "My ration—where is it? I want it."

"There's none for you," the surgeon advised sharply.

"What's that you say? No grog for me? Why so?" Powell demanded in that awful rasping voice. His face was turning from black to purple, and his eyeballs were flushing even redder.

"You should be thanking the good lord above for your miraculous delivery from the jaws of death," said the doctor primly, "and not lusting after liquor."

"No grog? When I came as close as *that* to breaking my bloody neck? That's damned hard, damn my eyes it is!"

Judging by the expressions on the faces of the seamen who had helped lay Powell on the berth, they heartily agreed. However, they kept their counsel. They also headed out of the cabin, having been reminded that they would forfeit their own grog if they didn't hurry along. Wiki reluctantly began to move, realizing he was beginning to look conspicuous, but all at once the door was blocked by the ship's purser, who, it seemed, had heard about the exciting near-tragedy and had come to check on the victim.

"His first words were to ask after his grog," the surgeon said, not bothering to lower his voice. His tone was scandalized.

"Seamen!" expostulated the purser, and looked down at Powell in magisterial fashion, his hands clasped behind his back. He made an impressive figure in white breeches and a blue clawhammer coat with two rows of buttons swerving down from a stand-up collar, white silk stockings, and shiny black pumps with little bows on the toes. He smelled of cigars and sherry.

"Do you expect he will live?" he asked the doctor.

"A mustard plaster, cupping, and blistering will set him up as right as rain," the surgeon declared. "I'll fetch a couple of loblolly boys to get him down to the sick bay and will attend to them there. There ain't no emergency that I can see, the good lord be praised. But I flatly refuse to prescribe paregoric, and as for grog—" He snorted. Then he headed out of the cabin, no doubt back to his own wineglass, Wiki mused, sipping and supping being standard throughout the fleet on these convivial Saturday afternoons.

"Jim Powell, you should prepare yourself to thank God for your providential escape," said the purser, evidently ready to offer a prayer.

"Hard lines, I call it," Jim muttered instead. "Might as well be dead, for all the use of what being saved has done me."

"You must put your faith in our noble surgeon. Hold hard to hope, my boy!" Then—after reminding Powell that according to the terms of his contract with the ship, the expedition, and the navy, the cost of medications would be subtracted from his pay, along with the sick bay bill—the purser departed in the surgeon's wake, and abruptly Wiki and the man he and Rochester had saved were alone.

Jim was mumbling constantly, his head rolling from side to side in a manner Wiki thought must be very painful, considering the condition of his neck. Feeling increasingly alarmed, he wasn't sure that Powell could see him, let alone know who he was—the red eyes were terribly unfocused. "Damned hard," the seaman kept on hoarsely mumbling. His arm lifted, and his fingers groped blindly at the air in Wiki's direction. Wiki's first reaction was to take a step back toward the door, ready to yell for the doctor, but then Powell said his name.

"No grog, think on that," he muttered, so low that Wiki could scarcely hear him. "And that bloody purser only called to make sure I was alive on account of I'm in debt to the ship for fifty dollars, damned hypocrite. Him and his sick bay bill, when he don't give a damn otherwise if I'm alive or dead, cheating bastard. I almost break my bloody neck, and they won't spare me my rightful grog. Hard lines, I call it—hard lines indeed. It's my fair ration, and I goddamn need it."

Without a word Wiki turned and left the cabin. He looked about the deck, spied the butt where the master's mate was rationing out rum mixed with lemon juice and water, asked for a tot, and carried the brimming pint carefully back to the stateroom. Powell was still alone and still cursing in a black mutter, which stopped abruptly as one eye opened wide and he spied what Wiki held.

"Gawd bless yer, my friend," he croaked, and sat up with amazing alacrity, all at once looking quite alive, instead of hovering on the doorstep of death. Wiki, who—like everyone else in his *iwi*—greatly disliked the taste of alcoholic spirits, watched, unwillingly impressed, as the pint went down like a creek down a hole.

Then Jim had finished and was feeling about with his tongue for droplets in the stubble on his chin. Wiki said, "How long have you been on the *Vin?*"

"Could've felled me with a feather when I was bloody summoned to appear on board the flagship," mumbled Jim instead of answering. "That bloody tartar Wilkes shouldn't be restin' easy, knowin' the black murder what lives in my heart." Then, after peering into the mug to make certain sure it was empty, he held it out to Wiki with a coaxing grin that looked truly awful in the congested wreckage of his face. "Get a tot for yoursel'," he wheedled. "You get a ration, just like everyone else in this goddamn' fleet—and then if you ain't all that thirsty, perhaps you could spare a few drops—"

Wiki merely looked at him, folding his arms to emphasize the silence.

"Not that I ain't grateful for what I got already," Jim hastily assured him, and then added with an elaborately penitent air, "I've been thinkin' about that note——"

"What note?"

"You're a good friend, fer a Kanaka, and I 'ave to tell you it's bin on me conscience that I told you a lie."

"Which lie?" Wiki asked sardonically.

"I do regret telling it, I swear! I told you I tossed that note Lieutenant Forsythe sent me to Newport News to fetch, but I didn't. I delivered it. And I read it on the way," Powell husked triumphantly. "I c'n read, you know. I ain't as ignorant as some might think. And I reckon I might remember what I read, given a little something to lubricate me wounded voice and me poor shocked brain."

Wiki studied him meditatively, wondering whether to believe him. "You delivered it to Mrs. Stanton?" he queried.

"No, I did not." The seaman was grinning craftily. "I could tell about how it went to a cove what you nivver would believe—that the man who was waitin' for it was——"

The harsh rasp stopped dead. A shadow had fallen over them. When Wiki turned he saw George Rochester standing in the doorway, with two wooden-faced, red-coated marines at his shoulder. Wiki had scarcely taken in the shocked expression on his friend's paper-white face when still more men arrived—the surgeon, still looking as if something directly under his nose smelled bad; two sick bay attendants—loblolly boys—in disgustingly spattered aprons; and, behind them all, the bulky shadow of Forsythe—no, not Forsythe. Instead, it was the astronomer, Tristram Stanton, easily confused with the lieutenant because they were so much the same build. The doorway was packed with men—the scene had all the confusion of a dream. Wiki was frowning. Why was Stanton here, when it was Forsythe who should be checking up on the man he could have killed with his poor judgment?

Then he heard Jim Powell husk, finishing the interrupted sentence, "... *Forsythe!*"

Wiki said blankly, "What?" When he turned and stared at Jim, the suffused face was still writhing in a wheedling smirk, but in his eyes there was a flicker of awful fear—or so Wiki thought, but then the seaman began to sing. Had Jim Powell gone mad? He was drunk—of course he was drunk. Wiki turned back to the door, and his attention was seized again by the shocked, fraught look on George Rochester's face.

Rochester seemed unaware of the surgeon pushing past him to get into the room and grip Jim's shoulder to stop the drunken crooning. His long face was so bleached of color that his cheekbones stood out, and he said in a queer, flat voice, "Wiki, you have to come with me now—the boat is leaving; we have to go straightaway to the brig."

Wiki said blankly, "To the *Swallow?*" He didn't want to go to the brig at all; he wanted to question Jim Powell further, but the loblolly boys were heaving the seaman up from the bunk, so he reluctantly backed out of the way. Rochester seemed unaware of what was happening, not even turning his head as he stepped aside to let them out, all the time keeping his desperate eyes on Wiki's face.

"Captain Wilkes has removed me from the command of the *Swallow.*"

"*What?*"

"He's given the brig to Forsythe."

Fourteen

or God's sake, *why?*" said Wiki, but knew the answer before he heard it. Rochester had publicly countermanded the order of a superior officer—and worse still, an officer who had been in charge of the deck of another ship. It made no difference that by calling out he had saved a man's life. It was a crime—a court-martial offence. He could count himself lucky he'd been let off with just the loss of his command. Without a doubt, Captain Wilkes's tirade had been awful.

They were back on the *Swallow*—for the last time, Wiki thought unhappily. The two marines were waiting on deck, standing sentry at the gangway, to make sure that Rochester handed over the command in due and proper fashion, he supposed, though maybe Wilkes was crazy enough to believe that

George might turn pirate and try to run away with the brig before Lieutenant Forsythe arrived. George Rochester sat slumped at the chart desk in the captain's cabin, staring into space with an awful, blank, shocked look. Wiki was busying himself packing George's clothes in his sea chest. It was the least he could do.

"What's going to happen to you?"

Rochester said numbly, "Wilkes reassigned me to the *Vincennes.*"

"What about Erskine?"

"He's going onto the *Porpoise.* Forsythe is bringing Passed Midshipman Zachary Kingman with him."

Wiki knew Kingman vaguely—a tall, gaunt man with a face like a skull. Older than most men of his rank, he had wasted so much time at the gambling tables that it had taken more years than usual for him to pass his examinations. Wiki mused with sad irony that the after quarters of the brig were going to be a lot less refined.

"So we're shifting onto the *Vin,*" he said, thinking that it would give him a chance to question Jim Powell again—alone in the sick bay, once the surgeon had taken himself off and the attendants were busy about other work. And now that questions about Astronomer Burroughs's death had been raised, a priority would be to talk to Grimes as well.

Rochester's hand shot out and gripped his arm. "Not you!" he said fiercely. "You have to stay with the brig."

"*What!*" Wiki exclaimed, horrified. "I'm not staying *here!*"

"You must!" Rochester spoke through stiff lips, so that his voice was flat and queer. "I can't—I don't—trust Forsythe. He's a tyrant and a bad seaman besides."

And maybe a murderer as well, Wiki grimly mused. "But what the devil can *I* do?"

"Look after the brig for me—please."

"But *how*, for God's sake?"

"You're the most resourceful man I know—I know you can do it." Rochester said again, his voice shaking just a little, "Please."

Wiki took a deep breath. Then he said steadily, "When you get on board the *Vincennes*, you must see Jim Powell again—go to the sick bay, get him alone, and make him talk."

"Powell? Why?"

"Didn't you hear what he said?" Wiki paused, looked at George's face again, and decided that his friend had been too shocked to take in a single word. Carefully, he said, "When I saw him on the *Porpoise* he said he'd dropped the letter in the mud, and then thrown it away. I thought he was lying, but he told me a convincing story about once being cruelly beaten because he'd delivered a muddy letter and how he'd made a vow that he'd never let it happen again. Today he confessed that it was indeed a lie. He told me that he'd read it, and delivered it, too—but not to Mrs. Stanton. He said he gave it to Forsythe!"

Rochester blinked. Then he said slowly, "D'you reckon he really read it?"

"I don't believe he can read much of anything. It's probably yet another lie—but you have to try to get him to tell the truth."

"How will I know it's the truth when I hear it?"

"Keep up the questioning—try to trip him up. What's important is what he read—or what he says he read. As soon as you find out, you have to let me know."

"Don't you think he was simply drunk and blathering?"

Wiki grimaced. As the loblolly boys had carried him away, Jim Powell had been back to his silly singing, crooning and mumbling a little verse that seemed mostly composed of the two

144

words, *"All's well."* The tune was "Nancy Dawson," traditionally piped to inform the crew that the grog was ready to be given out. *Damned rum,* Wiki thought. Without the grog, Jim would not have revealed as much as he did—but he certainly hadn't expected him to sink the mug so fast. After the joltingly close brush with death, Wiki supposed it was little wonder it had gone straight to Jim's head.

There was an echoing click as a boat arrived at the side of the *Swallow,* a hail from the deck, and a sharp thump of boots as the marines stamped to attention. Rochester compressed his lips, visibly braced himself, and looked about for his cocked hat. "This is it, I guess," he said tightly. Instead of shaking hands, each gripped the other's right forearm, the way they had often done, but more forcefully than ever before. Then, just as George reached the bottom of the companionway, he turned, his expression concerned. "I've been meaning to ask you something," he said.

"Yes?"

"When I told you that Burroughs was with the expedition, you were suddenly anxious to catch up with the fleet. I've never understood the urgency."

Wiki managed a careless flip of his hand. "It was when I realized that it was possible that Burroughs was involved in the murder—though to what extent I couldn't possibly guess. And murderers seldom stop at one killing, I believe."

Rochester's frown lifted. "But Burroughs put an end to himself—and so the danger is over."

Wiki thought about what the midshipmen had told him. He remembered how he'd had to keep his head ducked down to miss low beams as he'd followed Dicken to the stateroom where Burroughs's dangling body had been discovered. And because of

Powell's revelation, it seemed that the man who was taking over the brig could have been involved in the murder of Tristram Stanton's wife. Wiki remembered Forsythe's frozen expression while Powell dangled by the neck from the buntline; he thought about Forsythe's order to let go the line, which would have killed Powell if Rochester had not swiftly contradicted it; and he remembered, too, the impression of mortal fear that Powell had emanated as the crowd arrived in the stateroom doorway, and the way the seaman had hissed Forsythe's name.

However, he kept his tone casual. "I'm sure you're right," he agreed.

Shouting echoed down from the deck as some ruckus developed about the unloading of the boat. Rochester stood indecisively, and then with a sudden movement gripped Wiki's shoulder briefly before turning for the companionway stairs. He ran up them two treads at a time. Wiki watched his comrade go and then slowly opened the door of his stateroom.

Though he had moved back into the cabin when Stanton left for the *Vincennes*, up until now, Wiki had spent very little time in here. The room was small enough to start with, and its space had been reduced still farther by a locker that had been built into the break of the quarterdeck, the back of which intruded on the wooden berth so that it was six inches too short. When he lay on his side he had to keep his knees bent, and when he lay on his back he had to prop his feet up on the locker back, and lie with his abdomen hollowed. There was not even a chair. Because he had spent his waking hours on deck, or in Rochester's room, or at the mess table in the saloon, he had not needed one. His sea chest was poked underneath the berth, alongside some astronomical equipment that had been left behind by Stanton. A few books were stacked under the small sidelight, but otherwise there was very little sign of his occupation.

After a long moment Wiki roused himself, changed his good broadcloth for dungarees, and put the formal clothes away in his chest, scattering camphor into the folds to keep away the moth. Then, after pushing his sea chest back out of sight, he sat down on the edge of the berth and slumped forward, his forearms propped along his thighs, his fingers lightly entwined, contemplating the dusty planks between his feet. It was reminiscent of the hours when he had been imprisoned in the old sugar house at Portsmouth because, just as then, he was trying to recall every element of the scene on the bank of the Elizabeth River. This time, though, he was concentrating on Forsythe.

When he'd spied the derelict boat drifting down the stream and stepped out from under the tree, Wiki had assumed without hesitation that the shot that rang out had been aimed at him—by Forsythe. Now he wondered why he'd jumped so swiftly to that conclusion. Was it because he had been waiting for Forsythe, along with Jim Powell and whomever Forsythe had chosen to be his second? Or was it because, in that blur of motion when he'd caught a glimpse of the rifleman, he'd instinctively, without consciously realizing it, recognized the man?

It was a struggle to recollect small details exactly. Wiki remembered the dark figure outlined against the brush and the sky, but it had been just a blurred glimpse as he had rolled over, tossed the heavy pistols away, and dived in a flat arc into the river. Had the man been wearing black—or was it a trick of contrast with the paling sky? Wiki's impression was that he had been tall and big—but it could just as easily have been a goblin on a horse, he now thought ironically.

But if Powell had indeed named Forsythe as the man who had received the message from Stanton, the southerner's involvement in the murder was a distinct possibility—and Forsythe was a large man, large enough to pass as Tristram Stanton, if the light was poor and he was dressed in the right kind of clothes. Wiki had twice been fooled by a trick of the light into thinking Forsythe was Tristram Stanton. He was also a crack shot, according to the midshipmen, and the aim of the man who had been shooting at the sinking boat had been unerring.

So was it at all feasible that Lieutenant Forsythe had been the man who had posed as Tristram Stanton, gone to the Stanton house, murdered his wife, and placed the body in the derelict boat? It was indeed possible, Wiki decided—but was it likely? There had to be a motive, and to all appearances Forsythe didn't have one. Where Burroughs could well have been bribed with the promise of a place with the expedition, Forsythe didn't need a word put in on his behalf because he was with the expedition already. Being a gambler like his crony, Kingman, Forsythe could have been bribed with money, perhaps—but Tristram Stanton did not have that kind of money available, not until his wife was dead and he'd inherited her estate.

Wiki remembered leaving the tavern with his fair-haired girl after issuing that crazy challenge. When he'd invited Jim Powell to be his second, Jim had agreed, though with a condescending grin. Janey had been shaking with shock after Forsythe's vicious verbal attack and weeping stormily. Most of his attention had been on her; but he did remember Forsythe and Powell standing together as they watched him go. At the time he had assumed that they had been discussing the duel, but instead it seemed that Forsythe had been giving orders to Powell to take a boat to Newport News and collect a message from Tristram Stanton. *If*, for once, Powell was telling the truth.

The timing was right. The banquet had started at five, Wiki remembered—the party had met at four, and drunk grog and talked until five, when the feast had begun. The meats had probably been served about eight, Wiki calculated, and George Rochester had said that Powell had come "between the mutton and the ham." Then Powell had left with the note and had taken it to Forsythe—but where had they met? If it had been Portsmouth, not Norfolk, it would have been possible for Forsythe to ride to the plantation house after learning whatever the message had to tell him and get there between eleven and twelve, when the old manservant had been roused by someone coming up the stairs. That was another of the questions he should ask Powell—where had he gone to deliver the note?

Wiki felt restless and impatient. He needed to see Jim Powell again—and quickly, too—because he did not believe that George knew enough to ask the right questions. He particularly wanted to ask Powell if he thought it at all possible that Lieutenant Forsythe had had murder in mind when he called out to the men to let go the rope. While no one could have predicted that the buntline would loop about Jim Powell's neck and snatch him off the yard, Forsythe could have seen it as a first-rate opportunity to get rid of an inconvenient witness.

Then, just as he was wondering how to get back on board the *Vincennes*, he heard a tap on his stateroom door. To Wiki's surprise, it was dusk. Rochester had been gone about a couple of hours. The sounds of the boat leaving, and Forsythe and Kingman taking over the cabins, had been nothing more than a background to his thoughts.

The knock, he belatedly realized, was a reminder from the steward that supper was ready. Wiki stood up, flicked his long hair away from his face, opened the door, and stepped into the saloon. It was time to ask Forsythe some probing questions—even though it could easily prove to be an interview with a murderer.

Fifteen

The brig's messroom was square, its scant space mostly taken up with a table built aft of the mainmast. When Wiki walked in, closing his stateroom door behind him with a small but loud click, the two men who were already at the table turned their heads to stare challengingly. Lieutenant Forsythe sat in the chair at the sternward end of the table where Wiki had been accustomed to seeing George Rochester presiding, and Passed Midshipman Zachary Kingman sat on one of the benches that were screwed to the floor on either side.

They said nothing. Wiki had the impression that they had been talking and had abruptly fallen silent when he opened his door. Then he wondered who had been left in charge of the deck—the boatswain? The cooper? Perhaps Forsythe had brought another midshipman on board with him; Captain Wilkes's predilection for shifting men about the fleet certainly made that possible.

There was a small bench built between the bulk of the mainmast and the foot of the table. Wiki swung a leg over this and sat down. The lamplight from above fell fully on Forsythe, while Wiki himself was in shadow. Forsythe's face was flushed and sweaty, Wiki thought—but that could have been the effect of the lantern. His mouth, however, was definitely loose and damp. There was a half-full bottle between the two men; evidently they had been celebrating. Again, Wiki wondered about the officer on watch. Despite Rochester's instructions to him to look after the brig, it was obvious that if he checked he would be begging for trouble, and so he kept his mouth shut.

Both Forsythe and Kingman had got out of uniform and were wearing loose shirts with the sleeves rolled up. Kingman was so cadaverous that Wiki could see the double bones that made up his forearms, barely covered with thin, weathered skin, so that the limbs looked ancient and mummified. Forsythe's forearms, by contrast, were meaty and muscular. They were heavily tattooed, too, each with a coiled snake writhing from wrist to elbow. On the table, between Forsythe's hands, a flat, dark-colored object rested. Wiki looked at it and heard his own intake of breath. It was hard for him to look away.

Forsythe had been watching him intently. Now he picked the object up so that the light caught on it and said, in his southern drawl, "D'you know what this is?"

"Of course. It's a *mere*." The leaf-shaped war club was very old, and had been carried in battle many times. It was stained dark at the edges, and the simple spiral carving at the handle end was rubbed and blurred.

"A stone ax, I'd call it. What's it made of?"

"*Pounamu*—greenstone."

"Is greenstone valuable?"

"Very." A greenstone *mere* was the supreme hand weapon, the mark of a chief, a potent signifier of his *mana* and his rank.

"You want to know how I got it?"

Not particularly, Wiki thought. He said nothing but simply waited.

"A New Zealand chief gave it to me, on account of he didn't have no use for it no more."

Still Wiki did not speak, so Kingman, in an exaggerated voice, said, "He *gave* it to you?"

"Wa-al, he didn't say nothin'. He just lay there and watched me as I took it."

Kingman rolled his eyes. "That sounds mighty careless of him."

"Wa-al, there was this bullet hole in his forehead." Forsythe mimed raising a rifle to his eyes, aiming it and firing. "Pinged him first shot, from 190 yards," he said. "Asked for his head as a trophy," he added.

Wiki didn't ask if he'd been given the head. Look down at us, lord, he mused ironically, and see what a contrast we make— the civilized tattooed *pakeha* and the uncivilized untattooed savage. Tribal warfare, marked by an endless cycle of insult and revenge, was part of his heritage; if he had been honest when the midshipmen asked about his impressions of America, Wiki would have confessed that he was still constantly amazed by the value Americans placed on human life. In the past, however, his mother's people had fought with wooden spears and clubs like the *mere* Forsythe held. Since then had come the white man's musket, which killed from a distance and destroyed many more men than had fallen in traditional battles. Now, not just in New Zealand, but throughout the Pacific, white sailors were drafted by the leaders of warring tribes for their war skills and their murderously efficient guns. Wiki supposed that most of these mercenaries went off with some kind of loot after they had won the battle for their patrons. He leaned back as the steward put a sea-pie on the table—his second sea-pie of the day—thinking that it would be as palatable as the first.

Three mugs of tea were served, and then the steward disappeared into the pantry. Forsythe put down the war club to help himself. For a while there was nothing but chomping and slurping noises, and then the lieutenant looked at Wiki and observed, "So you got yourself arrested by the sheriff back at Portsmouth, huh?"

Wiki lifted his brows, intrigued by the change of topic. "As you can see," he said, "he changed his mind."

"And I wonder why you was lurkin' on that riverbank when that boat bobbed along." Forsythe snickered and said, "Been waitin' a tidy long time, hadn't you?"

Wiki said sharply, "How do you know that?"

Forsythe's eyes narrowed. Then he tapped the side of his head and said, "Brainwork. We had a little appointment there, remember."

"An appointment you didn't keep," Wiki observed.

"And you confounded know why—and you're bloody lucky I didn't, or you'd be six feet under right now."

"Yet when I left the tavern you were in deep consultation with Powell."

"Deep consultation, garbage. I was just givin' him the message what I'd come into the tavern to pass on—that he was wanted down at the waterfront."

Wiki frowned. "A message from whom?"

Forsythe shrugged. "Don't know."

"What do you mean, you don't know?"

"Exactly what I say, damn it!" Forsythe's fist landed on the table so the dishes all jumped and clattered. The pantry door opened and the steward's inquiring face poked through then retreated in a hurry. As the pantry door clicked shut again, Kingman was looking from Forsythe to Wiki and back, his mouth hanging open in a grin.

Then Forsythe said, his tone more controlled, "A junior mid marched up when I arrived on the wharf and said that Powell needed summoning, and when I told him to damn well deliver the message himself he was gone without even listening."

Wiki snapped, "I don't believe you."

"Believe what you bloody well like, but that's the way it happened."

"What I believe," said Wiki deliberately, "is that you sent Powell to Newport News with orders to come back to the riverbank with a note from Tristram Stanton."

"*What?* What note? Why the hell would I want a note from Tristram Stanton?"

"That's the story as I heard it—from Jim Powell himself."

"Then he's lying, the double-dealing little swab. And I was never on the riverbank!"

"So how do you know I kept the appointment?"

Again Forsythe tapped the side of his head and said smugly, "Brainwork. You was arrested there, wasn't you? And then the sheriff carted you off to the old prison on the waterfront in Portsmouth."

"I think you were lying in wait," Wiki reiterated doggedly. "And I think you saw the boat with Mrs. Stanton's body come floating down the river."

Forsythe went red. "You bloody well couldn't be wronger if you tried, so you can put that little idea out to pasture."

"So where were you?"

"None of your goddamned business."

Wiki paused, staring at him. Then he said, in a casual tone, "How long have you and Tristram Stanton been cronies?"

Forsythe's eyes popped and his face went bright red. Then he let out a series of raucous guffaws. His meaty shoulders shook, crumbs spluttered from his open mouth, and tears of mirth ran from his eyes. Kingman giggled too, though uncomprehendingly, and Wiki watched, blank faced.

Finally, Forsythe sobered enough to blow his nose with a loud honking sound. Then he said derisively, "And you reckon you know such a lot, clever Mr. Coffin. Tristram Stanton thinks I'm lower than pig shit—on account of his wife was my cousin, and he was scared pissless I'd take her money."

Wiki said, stunned, "Tristram Stanton's wife was your *cousin?*"

"Second cousin," Forsythe amended. "Related through our mothers." Then he warned, "Don't you get it into your head that there's anythin' to deduce from that—she was from the rich side of the family, I from the poor side, and I was never welcome in the Stantons' house. Not that I didn't call—when I could be sure that Tristram Stanton was not around so I could talk her into lendin' me some cash without him buttin' in. It was our family money, earned by my forefathers, not his! But I sure didn't hang around for the funeral."

Instead Forsythe—like Burroughs—had been on the *Vin-*

cennes, at sea, when the obsequies were held. Thinking deeply, Wiki said slowly, "Tristram Stanton wasn't at home the day his wife died."

Forsythe bared his teeth and said, "So I heard."

"And you were sailing soon—and lieutenants need a tidy sum to contribute to the mess, or so today I learned."

"Cleverer than ever," said Forsythe, and helped himself to another huge portion of pie. "Yup," he said indistinctly, "soon as I heard he was away, I went around to beg Ophelia for some ready—because, by God, I needed it."

Wiki said blankly, "Did you say *Ophelia?*"

"Yup, O-phe-lee-ah." Forsythe drew the word out scornfully. "Somethin' else you did not know, huh?"

Wiki silently shook his head. The name was like a strange revelation. He remembered that in Shakespeare's *Hamlet* the spurned Ophelia had drifted off to suicide by drowning, singing a soft, demented song to herself as she floated through the reeds. For the first time the staging of the dead body in the drifting boat made some kind of sense.

"If you ever have pickaninnies—and God forbid you do— my strong advice is not to name them after anythin' in Shakespeare. Ophelia was a pathetic whining bitch, not altogether in control of her wits—like her namesake, folk told me. Didn't surprise me in the slightest to hear she'd ridden off in the dead of night, climbed inside that derelict boat, punted herself off, and taken poison."

Wiki said, "She didn't die of poisoning." Then, remembering his conversations with Rochester, he immediately wondered if he was wrong.

However, Forsythe was not disposed to argue. "I heard that, too," he admitted. "But hell, suicide was on the cards. She'd threatened to do herself in more times than a camel can fart on a bucket of hay."

"Nevertheless, she was murdered."

"And Tristram Stanton was the man what snapped her neck."

Wiki's eyebrows shot up in surprise at the other's flat tone. "As much as I would like to agree," he observed, "the evidence doesn't point that way. Twenty men from various ships in the fleet have testified that Tristram Stanton was in Newport News at the time."

"Wa-al, whatever the evidence, the fact remains that he had every good reason to put her out of her misery—which I did not! She didn't give me money then, damn her wizened heart, and I sure don't benefit from her death. So don't look to me for a motive, Mr. Deputy Coffin," Forsythe said aggressively, and took a slurp from his glass. "At least while she was alive I had prospects. Now I have none."

Deputy? So Forsythe knew about the sheriff's letter of authorization, Wiki realized—like everyone else in the fleet, it seemed. But had Ophelia Stanton really refused to give him the money? After all, he *was* her cousin—and he *was* off about the world for at least three years. Forsythe must have settled his mess bill somehow, and the money must have come from somewhere.

However, that conclusion did not feel quite right. Wiki remembered the southerner's glowering look as he had stormed into that Norfolk tavern—he had been looking for trouble, he realized now, simply to vent his frustration, which indicated that he just might be telling the truth.

He asked, "What time did you give up and leave the house?"

"What do you mean?" Forsythe demanded suspiciously.

"I'm sure you didn't concede defeat easily—I think you needed that money badly."

The lieutenant scowled in silence a moment, ruminatively picking his teeth with a long fingernail. Then he admitted with a defiant air, "I was prepared to argue my case till kingdom come, but that craw-faced old bastard threw me out."

"Stanton's father?" Wiki looked at the lieutenant's thick, muscular, tattooed arms, remembering the stiff, painful way Tristram Stanton's father had moved. "You're exaggerating, surely," he said, with unconcealed disbelief.

"He got the servants to throw me out," Forsythe amended. With an irritated movement he shoved back his chair, stood up, grabbed the bottle, jerked his chin at Kingman, and headed for the captain's cabin. "And it took a dozen of 'em to do it!" he yelled over his shoulder as he opened the door. Kingman followed, and the door slammed shut behind them.

Sixteen

It was a relief, at first, to emerge into the cool darkness of the deck. The brig had orders to keep pace with the *Vincennes* and was accordingly under easy sail—as the whole fleet knew, Captain Wilkes was not in any particular hurry yet. All should have been serene, but as Wiki looked around he was gradually beset by uneasiness. The moon-lit sea was calm, but the brig rolled unhappily, and the hull and rigging creaked more loudly than they should, with a particu-larly loud wrenching groan from the spanker boom over the helmsman's head.

And the ocean was emptier than Wiki had expected. He looked about at the black shimmer of the water and then clam-bered up the main rigging to the crosstrees. From there he could glimpse the masthead lights of the *Vincennes*—but the flagship was about three miles away, much farther than he had expected. He could see another dot of light from the distant *Peacock*, but the gun brig *Porpoise* and the schooners *Flying Fish* and *Sea Gull* were nowhere to be seen.

The last thing Wiki wanted was for the *Swallow* to be separated from the rest of the ships—but instinct told him there was something else the matter as well. He studied the familiar scatter of bright stars and sniffed the air. There was the usual smell of salt from the sea and pitch from the rigging, but there was an oiliness about the atmosphere he did not like.

Slowly, he slid down to deck hand over hand along a backstay, his ankles crossed over the tarry rope. When his feet touched the planks he looked about for the officer on watch, but the quarterdeck was deserted. There was just the man at the helm, who was watching him curiously.

He was Michael, a boy from New Bedford who had gone one voyage on a whaler before joining the navy. They hadn't sailed together before, but they knew people in common, and Michael was accustomed to seeing Wiki doing seaman's duties on the *Swallow*. Wiki arrived alongside him, keeping his manner casual, and looked at the binnacle compass. Their course was more east than he had anticipated, while the bad weather he sensed was coming from the north.

He looked up at the complaining spanker boom and observed lightly, "That spar needs a bucket of water. I'll take the helm for a spell, if you like, so you can give it a drink."

Michael looked surprised but readily gave over the wheel. Wiki guessed the lad could do with a drink himself. He saw the boy walk forward through the darkness to the scuttlebutt by the fore hatch, swig down a beaker of water, and after that, relieve himself over the bows. Then he watched Michael drop a bucket into the sea for water to throw over the jaws of the spanker boom.

Meantime, Wiki worked and tested the wheel, finding, as he had suspected, that the brig was crabbing badly. The feel of her was even stiffer than he had expected; in fact, every jerk and quiver that emanated up from the rudder made him feel still more uneasy. Then Michael arrived back on the quarterdeck. Wiki watched him as he clambered onto the rail, stood there poised, braced himself, and tossed the water upward. Miraculously, the boom's groaning stopped.

Michael jumped down. Wiki gave back the helm, saying, "There's a big under swell setting her to leeward, rather more east than she should be." He had already brought the wheel up a couple of points and hoped the lad would follow suit.

Then he walked forward toward the outline of the man on lookout in the bow, who stood poised between the knightheads. The smooth, muscular, bare-chested silhouette had led him to believe it was Sua, the huge Samoan, but as he drew near Wiki realized to his surprise that it was a Polynesian he had never seen before. Another casualty of Captain Wilkes's trick of reassigning men all over the fleet, he mused.

This Pacific Islander was not as large as Sua but stoutly built just the same. When Wiki arrived alongside him, he was gazing across the glassy black sea to the north horizon, swaying easily on his broad bare feet, but seeming very alert. He was wearing trousers, so Wiki could not see what tattooing he might have on his legs; but when the man turned his head, he greeted Wiki in Samoan.

They introduced themselves quietly and briefly, omitting most of the ritual. Sua's sailor name was Jack Polo, while this fellow had been dubbed Jack Savvy. Only Wilkes, mused Wiki wryly, understanding the implications of the names—that one came from the island of Upolu and the other from the island of Savai'i—would so blindly put men of the same race, but of differing tribes, in the same forecastle. However, most of his attention was on the lightning that was playing low down on the northern horizon.

Dark shadows were streaming across the stars. Jack Savvy was looking at the veiled sky as well. "Not good," he said, and hunkered down, placed the flat of his hand on the deck, and seemed to listen to what the hull was saying. After a long moment he straightened. "Not good," he said again.

Wiki nodded. He wondered what the barometer read but couldn't check, as it was in the captain's cabin. Was Forsythe keeping an eye on it? He felt doubtful. The brig abruptly gave a heavier roll, and Wiki felt a fine rain dash across his face. He paused for thought, acutely conscious that he had no right to give orders, but then said in Samoan, "I'll take a turn around the deck and make sure everything's snug and secure."

"I'll come with thee," the man from Savai'i said.

"Better not—you're on lookout duty. It's not a good idea to leave your post for long. I'll stand in your place a moment while you rouse up someone from below."

Wiki saw the Samoan nod. When he came back from the forecastle, Sua, predictably, was the one with him. At home they might be in opposing tribes, but on a Yankee ship they were shipmates with much in common. Together, Wiki and the bigger Samoan went around waking up the men who were supposed to be on watch but had been peacefully asleep in corners instead. Then they set about securing loose gear, including taking down an awning and furling it tight.

The *Swallow* was rolling still more heavily by the time they had finished. The puffs of wind were coming at shorter intervals, and with each gust the spats of rain were getting thicker. What in the name of all the spirits, Wiki wondered, was Forsythe thinking? Surely, particularly considering that his promotion to the command was so new, he should have displayed more concern for his ship. But there had been no movement from the captain's quarters. Either Forsythe and Kingman were roistering still, albeit very quietly, or else—more likely—each had retired to his berth.

He said to the big Samoan, "Who is the officer on watch?"

Sua shrugged, looked around, and said, "The bo'sun?"

Wiki said, "Better rouse him up."

The boatswain, a good man and a crony of Midshipman Erskine's, was a stickler for the rules. When he came up rubbing bleary eyes, Wiki expected to be roundly reprimanded. However, he seemed to be just as unhappy that Erskine was no longer on the brig as Wiki was at Rochester's demotion, and just as alarmed that there should be no officer in charge of the watch. He looked about, studied the sails and the sea, and nodded. Then he went and stood by the helm, his left fist clutching the weather shrouds, so much in command of the quarterdeck that it would have been tactless of Wiki to remain.

The saloon at the bottom of the companionway was still empty. The plates and mugs had been taken away, but otherwise it looked just the same as he had left it. Wiki went into his stateroom and went to bed—without removing his clothes. Listening to the gusts of wind whining about the rigging, it seemed prudent to him to turn in all standing.

He didn't expect to sleep much, but instead dropped at once into a heavy slumber, to be abruptly woken by shouting in

Samoan, accompanied by loud banging on the deck above his head.

Both Samoans were yelling, their shouts panic-stricken. After a confused moment he understood what they were so urgently trying to tell him. Wiki tumbled out of bed and through the door into the saloon, crashing against Forsythe. It was very dark. The single lamp dashed back and forth on its hook, throwing enormous shadows. A clattering came from the pantry, where every dish and spoon was on the move.

The lieutenant seemed abruptly sobered. He snapped, "What the hell is happening? What the devil are those savages bellowing?"

Wiki said briefly, "Man overboard—the bo'sun." Without waiting for an answer he dashed up the companionway.

When the door slammed open he stopped short involuntarily, pinned in the doorway by a vicious gust of wind. Above, the rigging was thrumming and whistling. The decks were awash, and while he stood there a torrent sloshed past his legs and down the stairs. In the wild blackness of the deck he could glimpse men struggling with wet snapping ropes forward, and other men gathered at the amidships rail.

Wiki felt Forsythe shove on his back at the same time as the gust let go and stumbled headlong out into the storm-wracked night. The brig was flying under just a couple of rags of canvas on the topsail yards, pursued by huge waves that came rolling in from the north. The full moon flickered in and out as clouds scurried across its face, and Wiki could glimpse the frightened expressions of the two men at the helm who were together struggling to hold the brig on her course. Why the hell hadn't the boatswain sent someone to fetch Captain—*Captain*, for God's sake!—Forsythe up to deck before the brig had sailed into such danger? Then Wiki understood that the storm he and the Samoans had sensed lying just over the horizon had come all at once, squalling down upon them.

Thunder grumbled, looming closer, closer. Then there was a louder clap, so deafening Wiki's eardrums popped. Lightning fizzed sharply, destroying his night vision for a moment, and the wind gusted. Then rain came out of the blackness, hissing down with malignant force, tossed back and forth like a solid, living curtain with the gusts. Waves materialized, lifted, crashed over the stern, and rushed in cascades along the deck. The brig was fleeing before the storm, but the storm was winning the race.

Wiki worked his way to the group at the rail in short rushes, timing his movements to keep his footing on the tossing deck. Both Samoans were there, still yelling in their native tongue, pointing at a figure that was floating just a dozen yards away. The brig had unexpectedly dipped her starboard rail under the water with a particularly hard gust—every man on deck had been thrown sprawling. All the rest had finished up in the scuppers; but when they had struggled to their feet again, it was to find that the boatswain had been washed into the hungry sea.

Intermittent moonlight flickered over the small, distant figure, now being drawn past the stern of the vessel. Men, both Samoan and English, were yelling at the tops of their voices and struggling aft to reach out over the taffrail. But there was nothing that could be done—rescue was impossible. Bringing the *Swallow* about would simply spell a swift end to the brig, and there was no way a boat could live in that sea.

Then, to Wiki's amazement, one of the enormous waves picked up the boatswain and swirled the struggling figure closer. For an endless moment the boatswain was poised on the foaming crest while the wave lifted, lifted, towering above the stern of the brig—and then, like a man spitting out a cherry stone, the wave threw the boatswain over the quarter bulwarks, rushing on to foam along the starboard side.

The body crashed up against a gun and finally stopped, wedged by the carriage. Somehow Wiki struggled up to where the old boatswain lay stunned and gasping, to find he was indubitably alive. As he gripped the boatswain's shoulders and heaved, Wiki thought that was the second miraculous escape he had witnessed—but there was still the question of whether the *Swallow* would survive the night.

Forsythe said curtly in his ear, "Get that man below and give him a glass of grog." Then the lieutenant took charge of the deck, barking out a stream of curt orders that flew forward in the shrieking wind. Took charge just as if the *Swallow* had not got into these dire straits because of the captain's lack of responsibility. George Rochester had called Forsythe a bad seaman, Wiki remembered. His poor judgment on the *Vincennes* would certainly have killed Jim Powell if Rochester hadn't interfered, and the brig would most surely have been lost if the Samoans had not roused their inattentive captain by hammering on the skylight and yelling out to Wiki.

However, half drunk though he might be, Lieutenant Forsythe rose to the challenge. All night the *Swallow* rolled and tumbled, the gale whistling about her, the hours punctuated with the howling of the wind, urgent shouting, and the thump of feet and the dragging of canvas and ropes as the men struggled to follow his orders. Everyone slipped and fell constantly, but Forsythe hung on, an indomitable fist gripping the vibrating shrouds.

When at last dawn crept over the horizon the sky had a wild

and terrifying appearance. Great waves were still pursuing the brig as she scudded before the gale, but the *Swallow* lived. The deck was a grim sight, littered with torn rigging and damaged spars, but the brig sailed on as bravely as before. As the day went by the wind gradually diminished, and by sunset the *Swallow* was under full sail. At last, after eighteen hours of incessant labor, the order, "That will do, the watch," was given, and half the crew could go below and seek some rest—but still Lieutenant Forsythe clung to his station on the quarterdeck. It was not until the second watch was sent below that he went down to seek his own berth.

The following morning, however, Wiki found that Rochester's second assessment—that Forsythe was a tyrant—was right on the mark. Four bells had just struck, and Wiki was lying on his berth with his feet propped up on the locker that intruded so on his bed space, reading a book, when he heard the peremptory shout for all hands on deck. He frowned, thinking that it might be time for the morning ration of grog, but that the tone of the order did not seem quite right. Swinging down his legs, he stood up, straightened, ducked under a beam, and padded up the stairs.

When he opened the door at the top of the companionway all the men were assembled in the waist, and the atmosphere of stifled rage and disgust was almost palpable. He could see hands curled into fists. The men stood, brace legged, in hostile attitudes, and no one spoke or moved.

Then Wiki took in the scene on the quarterdeck, and his breath hissed out with shock. The two Samoans were triced up in the rigging. Their shirts were pulled down off their backs and hanging down over their spread legs, and their outstretched arms were tied high in the shrouds so that their bare toes just touched the planks. When the brig rolled they grunted as they struggled to keep the wrenching weight off their wrists. Jack Savvy let out a faint whine of pain.

Lieutenant Forsythe, in full dress uniform, the gold epaulette on his right shoulder glinting, stood facing the crew, his eyes narrowed, his right hand resting on the hilt of his sword. Passed Midshipman Kingman, also in full dress rig, stood beside him, a multiple lash held loosely in his bone-thin, big-knuckled hands. Nine thin plaits of rope trailed from the handle, each knotted at the working end. This, Wiki realized with horror and disgust, was the navy's notorious cat-o'-nine-tails.

He pushed his way through the assembled men and went straight up to Forsythe. He said, "What the devil is going on here?"

"Punishment," said Forsythe, his eyebrows high. "And pray get the hell off my deck."

Wiki ignored that, staying exactly where he was. He said tightly, "Punishment for what?"

"For speaking their native lingo. Speaking their own language is against regulations."

"It's against regulations for a Samoan to speak Samoan?" Wiki demanded incredulously.

"Of course. It can't be allowed. They could be plotting mutiny."

"That's bloody ridiculous!" Wiki could see the powerful muscles of the Samoans' naked backs and shoulders flex and writhe as they fought to keep their weight from dislocating their wrists. "They were speaking Samoan in the panic of the moment—as you know perfectly well! And they worked as hard or harder than anyone else to save the ship—she could have gone down if they hadn't roused us up. For God's sake," he demanded furiously, his voice shaking with outrage, "what do you expect of them?"

169

"I expect rules to be damn-well obeyed. If you wasn't a civilian, you'd be triced up there alongside 'em, you goddamn uppity savage." Forsythe lifted his voice. "Twelve lashes each. Summon the bo'sun to carry out the punishment."

Wiki snapped, "Wait." Then he went up to the Samoans and, one at a time, he laid his cheek against the other man's so that their tears mingled with his; and in their own language, his voice low, he explained what was happening.

"I am a warrior," Sua softly intoned:

There is a craving within me for a gun to hold,
A war club to grasp, a spear to aim—
Look and see my wretched state
Look and see a disemboweled fish
A stranded shark, a lost albatross—
Yet a warrior I remain.

Wiki stepped back, watching them both brace themselves for the ordeal. He cast a glance at Forsythe, feeling distantly surprised that the lieutenant had not interfered when he had spoken to the men, but Forsythe was merely smirking. "Put a barbaric curse on me, did you?" he idly queried, and without bothering to wait for a reply, called again for the boatswain to carry out the sentence.

Now, however, there was a hitch. When the boatswain arrived on deck he looked much the same as usual; but when he was informed of the crime, he stared at Forsythe, turned his head to spit over the rail, and then declared himself too sick and frail after his near-drowning to comply. Then, without waiting for an answer, he stumped back to his bed.

Forsythe did not appear to care about this, either. He nodded at Kingman and, poker-faced, the midshipman wielded the multiple lash.

There was strength in the skinny arms—by the time he had finished, blood was trailing down the smooth brown backs, staining the waists of duck trousers and marking the upper swirls and curves of the blue tattooing that indicated the proud heritage of these warriors. At long last the two men were cut down. Wiki sent a vial of salve to the forecastle and then clambered aloft to scan the empty sea.

The weather could not have been in greater contrast to the storm—while the brig still rolled heavily with the undersea swell, the surface of the water was like a sheet of glass, and there was a haze across the horizon. The wind had dropped completely. The sails hung straight up and down, slatting noisily against the masts with each pitch. After a while Forsythe sent up orders for the mainsail and foresail to be brailed up, to stop the irritating noise. Apart from that there was nothing to do but watch the horizon for a sign of the *Vincennes*.

The next day they located her—because of the distant sound of cannon.

Seventeen

*G*eorge Rochester was in a fix. He hadn't thought much about it when he'd been assigned a gun crew; but now that the *Vincennes* was beset by a flat calm, and the storm was reduced to a nasty memory, Captain Wilkes had decreed that the cannon should be exercised. And because mountain man Dave had been so efficient during exercises on the *Swallow*, George had totally forgotten the orders that were as much a set part of the routine as the cadences of a catechism.

He'd had troubles enough with being reduced to someone so lowly as a mere passed midshipman on the sloop of war. The supreme head of the *Vincennes* was, of course, Charles Wilkes, who—probably because he was technically only a lieutenant himself, without even the right to fly the commodore's pennant, let alone wear the double epaulettes and gold lace of a captain—

was a real stickler for rank. Below him was the first lieutenant, and below the first lieutenant were all the other lieutenants, all in subrankings of their own; then the sailing master; then the purser, surgeon, and chaplain, along with all *their* subordinates; and so on down to the humblest of the officers, the midshipmen, whose job was to summon bad-tempered, sleepy seamen out of their hammocks when the night watches were changed, muster the gun crews when the ship was at quarters, and report every blessed move to the lieutenants. It brought back horrible memories of the dog's life of a junior midshipman. After the glory of the quarterdeck of the *Swallow*, it was a daily humiliation.

Faced with a great ugly cannon and an expectant gun crew, George realized that here was a problem he should have anticipated long before. Over the few months at the Gosport Navy Yard, he'd been taught mathematics, chemistry, English, natural philosophy, and French—plus, for God's sake, the intricacies of steam machinery!—but it had been blithely assumed by his instructors that he had learned all he needed to know about cannonry during his years at sea. And that, unfortunately, had not been the case. Over his time on various ships of war, George, like his fellow junior mids, had been left to educate himself as best he could in the midst of a thousand interruptions.

He had taken part in many live exercises and had even played his part when the cannon were fired in earnest during campaigns against pirates and slavers, but his only role had been to peer out through the gunport, gauge how close the shot had come to the mark, and indicate bearings with much flapping of his hands and arms. He'd turned often to look at the men who serviced the gun—men who had looked like imps out of hell, dripping sweat rags tied above their grim, smoke-blackened faces—but it had been through a stinging fog of gunpowder fumes, and it had been far too noisy for anyone to hear what anybody else shouted, unless they were right up next to one's ear. In the roar and confusion each man had to know without telling what job he was to do because it was impossible to work the guns otherwise. Dumb exercises, though, were a different matter, because it would be mortifyingly obvious if a fellow called out the wrong command; and, if he did make a mistake, Captain Wilkes's scorn would be awful. Again George wished most heartily that he had paid a lot more attention during the exercises on the dear *Swallow*, instead of leaving it all to Dave.

His responsibility on the *Vincennes* was one of the two nine-pounder chasers, along with its crew of ten—a captain, a loader, a rammer, and a sponger, two side-tackle men, three train-tackle men, and a powder boy—all of whom were watching him in happy anticipation. Normally, a crew serviced two cannon, one on each side of the deck. When the first was fired, they raced across and got the second one ready, and so they went back and forth for the duration of the battle—but at least, because the armament of the *Vincennes* had been greatly reduced to make room for the scientifics and their equipment George was spared that. The flagship could boast just eight ugly, stumpy carronades, plus the two long, nine-pounder guns on the poop deck, so George had been assigned just one of the latter while another passed midshipman had charge of the other. That, however, was scarcely a relief.

After the Samoan's stirring drumming to quarters on the *Swallow*, the tinny rattle beaten out by the ship's drummer boy sounded oddly dissatisfying. "Wet and sand the decks, knock out ports, take off your muzzle bags, withdraw your tompions, and cast loose your guns!" cried Captain Wilkes—orders that were familiar enough, being the same ones Rochester had hollered out on the *Swallow*. His gun crew cast loose the lashings that housed the gun tight against the bulwarks and whipped out the tompion bung swiftly enough, but George noted with some pride that their actions were not nearly as smooth as the exercise had been on the brig. But then his five tackle men clapped onto the tackle ropes, ran the gun carriage inboard, and stared at him expectantly. His complacency abruptly faded.

George had prepared himself as best he could. After consultation with a junior midshipman named Keith—who should have been a mountain man in George's private opinion, being quite obsessed with arms in general and cannon in particular—he had compiled a list of orders, which were jotted down on the palm of his left hand. "Chock your luff!" he began, reading it out with assumed confidence—but the men did absolutely nothing, just stood there holding tackle ropes, or with their bits of equipment at the ready, their heads turned as they continued to watch him, while overhead little fluffy clouds passed serenely over the limpid blue sky.

There was an awful pause while George's mind went blank. Then, with a start, he realized that the instruction simply ordered the men at the tackles to maintain tension to counter the roll of the ship, something that they were doing already, to prevent the great carriage from running amuck all over the poop deck and smashing their toes. He'd been on the verge of repeating the order in a peremptory fashion but stopped himself just in time. Well, he meditated, it was a relief that he'd saved himself from that particular embarrassment, but it didn't do much for his confidence. He had to clear his throat before shouting, "Stop vent and sponge your gun!"

At that, thank God, two of the men moved. The fellow who had been appointed captain of the gun leaned over the breech and solemnly placed a piece of leather over the touch hole, while the sponger leapt forward, dipped a sponge on the end of a long pole into a bucket of water, and pushed it up and down the barrel of the gun. The idea was to douse any sparks from the last discharge, George deduced—though it seemed rather odd, considering that the gun had not been fired yet. However, he was not prepared to ask any questions, being fervently grateful that the men seemed to know what to do.

"Cartridge, wad, and ram home!"

This led to quite a little flurry of activity, as the powder boy fished a cylindrical bag of gunpowder out of his leathern bucket and heaved it across to the loader, who shoved it up the barrel. Then the rammer stepped up, inserted a wad, and pushed it up as far as it would go. The captain of the gun bent over again to poke his priming iron through the breech and wiggle it.

Looking up at George, he said solemnly, "Home!"

This, George felt paramount to certain, meant it was safe to charge the gun. However, the next order on his list was confusing because it read, in tiny smeared letters, "Round shot, canister, or stand of grape"—which offered a choice of projectile. He stared down at his palm with his eyebrows high and then looked about vainly for inspiration, while the expectant silence went on and on. *Single round shot* was designed to smash holes in the sides of enemy ships, while *grape*—a canvas bag packed with shot—was used to clear enemy decks of men, and *canister*—a tin can filled with musket balls—was calculated to destroy enemy rigging. And who could possibly guess what kind of target lived in Captain Wilkes's imagination?

Then, to George's intense relief, he heard the captain of the gun hiss, "I think I'd choose round shot, if I was you, sir."

"Round shot, dear fellow? Capital!" said George, and

watched the loader heave up a great nine-pound cannon ball and roll it down the barrel. "Ram home!" he cried, and the rammer leaped forward with his wad and rammer again and worked manfully to pack another wad down to make certain the ball didn't roll back again and thud ignominiously to the deck.

"Man side-tackle falls, run out!" The two side-tackle men hauled mightily at the ropes, running the gun up to the rail and forcing the barrel out as far as it would go. At last, to George Rochester's huge relief, he was back on familiar ground. Squinting out over the sparkling sea as he had done many times in the past, he fixed his eye on an imaginary enemy ship and hollered, "Crows and handspikes, elevate your gun!"

This was followed by a lot of satisfying grunting and heaving, along with grinding noises as the cannon and its carriage were tackled with handspikes and crowbars and wrenched back and forth until George had it pointed at the great man-of-war he had conjured up in his mind.

"Cock your lock, blow your match, watch the weather roll, stand by . . . FIRE!"

But just as on the *Swallow*, the charge was not detonated. Instead, the dumb show was repeated *ad nauseum*. At about the dozenth repeat, Rochester noticed that some of his men were mimicking that confusing order to load, muttering in a chant:

A couple of round shot, canister, stand of grape,
Two midshipmen and a master's mate,
Wad and ram home your charge!

George found it difficult not to laugh, which was duly noticed by his men, who were looking more saucy by the minute and threatening to become undisciplined. Suddenly, however, there was a difference. As everyone watched raptly, a boat was rowed out, and a barrel was rolled over the transom and into the water, so that it bobbed a couple of hundred yards off. In the distance, the *Porpoise* and the *Flying Fish*, their sails as limp as those of the *Vincennes*, were watching, too.

The barrel was half-full of seawater, George speculated, because it floated well down, reminding him of that tedious business with the kegs and the log line when he'd had the job of measuring currents. Because it was weighted, this barrel stayed more or less in the same spot, instead of lightly dancing off on the breast of the rippling sea. Then the boat rowed away, leaving every man on board the *Vincennes* to stare in speculation at the slowly bobbing object.

Captain Wilkes was at the ready with his speaking trumpet again, hollering for silence. As they listened, George's gun crew looked at each other with broad grins, understanding that the cannon were going to be exercised in reality, with the barrel as a target—and that it would take the form of a competition, to see which gang would smash it first. The powder boy was bright red with excitement. Even George felt energized, for the first time distracted from dragging worry about the dear *Swallow*, which had been lost to sight for seven long days and had cost him a great deal of sleep.

"Sir," said the gun captain, looking extremely animated.

"Yes?"

"I'd choose grape, this time, sir."

"Grape?"

"Aye, sir! Let's blast that barrel to smithereens, sir!"

"Make it so," said Rochester, catching the spirit, and swiftly the gun was sponged, charged, loaded, rammed, and run up to the rail. His crew, George determined as he held his cocked hat in one hand to shade his eyes against the glitter of the sea, was definitely going to be the one that reduced that barrel to a shower of splinters. It was far too small and too low in the water to make an easy target, but he knew from past experience that he had a very accurate eye.

During the exercises, the ninepounder had been well elevated. "Down," he said, "down"—and flapped his right palm. He could hear the captain of the gun knocking out wedges, and when he looked around the sturdy fellow had laid his cheek along the barrel and was squinting down to the end. "What do you think?" George asked, as he backed up to join him.

"A little more, sir," that worthy said, and George returned to the rail for another look at the target.

"You're so right, dear fellow," he said, and the adjustment was made. Finally the snout was pointed the way they both wanted, and the gun captain hammered in a quoin to hold it in place. Now came the even more fiddly and laborious task of wrenching the cannon about on a horizontal axis, while all the time the *Vincennes* was slowly bringing around her stern.

To George's irritation, and his gun crew's disgust, the other chaser had the first shot. He heard Captain Wilkes's shout, "Number six!"—followed almost instantly by a great boom and then a thud as the gun bounced back against its breeching. To the gun crew's satisfaction, however, the cannonball bounced along the water like a gigantic stone, skipping five times before it sank, missing the barrel by yards and sending it dancing up and down.

"Number four!"—and with another huge noise a carronade hurled its mighty ball—which soared high in the air and splashed down far, far beyond the target. A derisive cheer went around the decks.

"Number seven!" roared Captain Wilkes's speaking trumpet.

George's crew spat on their palms and braced their shoulders. "Take your time, my lads," he warned. The *Vincennes* was still bringing around her stern, and the heavy carriage had to be heaved some more to match the movement. While the gun crew fidgeted with impatience, and the whole ship watched and waited, the gun captain and George peered down the barrel by turns.

Then both ship and target were steady, and the cannon was aimed. "Cock your lock," George said calmly, back at his station at the rail.

The gun captain poured priming powder over the vent with the aid of a goose quill, pulled back the hammer, and turned his head to stare at George raptly, the string of the firing lanyard in his hand.

"Blow your match," said George, just as deliberately, and watched the slow fuse smolder red as the loader blew gently, just in case the flintlock did not catch.

"Watch for the weather roll—wait, wait for it—" His eyes slitted against the glare, George paused as the ship wallowed. "Stand by . . . stand by—FIRE!"

The hammer snapped, the flash ran through the breech to the cartridge, and the powder exploded with a mighty bang. The bag of grape shot out with the velocity of lightning, while the entire gun leapt backward with shocking force, jumping clear of the deck, and slamming up against the breeching. The air was filled with thick, stinging smoke.

"Stop vent and sponge your gun!" George roared, determined to reload and have another shot if the first had not demolished the target—but it wasn't necessary. The target had burst. All that was left was debris that briefly whirled and then disappeared down a vortex. Within seconds every last vestige of the butt had disappeared.

The noise, however, was going on and on. At first George thought his ears were ringing with the aftermath of the terrible explosion, but then he backed away from the gunport and looked around at his men. And all of them were pushing their fists in the air, their blackened faces split wide with huge grins, and cheering at the tops of their voices.

All he needed to crown his day, George decided, grinning like a fool himself while he and the gun captain shook hands, was for some masthead lookout to raise the dear *Swallow*.

And when supper was done, this ambition was satisfied, too. Signals jerked up on the main peak of the distant *Porpoise*. A sail had been spied, their lookout reported, silhouetted against a streak of silver on the westward horizon. Above the streak of light, the sky was darkening; but before nightfall enough of the shape could be seen to identify the vessel. More signals fluttered from the *Porpoise* lanyard, relaying the glad message that the brig *Swallow* had rejoined the fleet.

Eighteen

The crew of the *Swallow* was not nearly so jubilant, being too tired for much emotion at all. When the echoes of the cannon firing had registered, Forsythe had ordered a boat put down. Then they had towed the brig mile after mile, following the sound of the guns for hour upon hour. There had not been a breath of wind, and the sun had been white hot. It was early evening before the masthead lookout finally raised the *Porpoise*, and not until dark that Forsythe finally consented for the boat to be brought in again. After that, supper was at long last served.

When the steward tapped at his stateroom door, Wiki was lying on his bunk with his feet propped up against the back of that confounded locker, wishing fervently he could straighten out his limbs. He had gone down in the boat and taken one of the oars for two two-hour spells—not because Forsythe had ordered it but out of loyalty to his old forecastle mates—and now the broad muscles of his shoulders were stiff and sore. However, because of the way his berth had been shortened by that accursed locker, he could not stretch his bones to ease them.

He had investigated its contents long before, opening the outside door, set in the break of the quarterdeck, to find that it merely held shelves of folded signals. Now he stared at its back panel balefully, wondering if he could undo the screws that held it, and put his feet inside. The flags would serve as an excellent footrest, he mused. Someone else had had the same idea, he saw, because there were little glints where the brass heads of the screws had been scratched. Then the thought was interrupted by the tap at the door.

Though supper was ready, the steward was delivering a message. A boat from the *Porpoise* had arrived, asking the favor of the urgent attendance of the expedition linguister. As he passed through the saloon, Wiki grabbed up his coffee mug and took a couple of long, scorching, luxurious gulps. Then, after casting a regretful eye at the tasty-smelling dish of stewed salt meat, crumbled ship's biscuits, onions, and potatoes—lobscouse—on the table, he padded up the stairs to deck.

To his surprise, when he dropped down into the boat, it was to find that Midshipman Erskine was there. Instead of announcing his presence and coming on board, Erskine had sent one of the oarsmen with the summons, which seemed rather odd. Wiki did not know Rochester's erstwhile second-in-command very well, partly because he had spent so much time in the forecastle and partly because Erskine had been in charge of the deck the times Wiki had eaten meals in the saloon. What he had seen of Erskine he had liked, though. Rather prim and quiet in demeanor, Ernest Erskine had seemed older than his actual years, but he was hardworking, responsible, and patient, and had got along very well with the men.

As they pulled away, Erskine said rather wistfully, "How goes it with the brig?"

Wiki paused, thinking of Forsythe's temper, which veered about the compass like the wind. He was certainly a tyrant, quite merciless and often cruel, but when one expected him to fly into one of his vicious rages he was just as likely to act as if he couldn't give a damn. Added to that, he drank. Several times, he had terrified the crew by lurching onto the deck with his rifle in his hand, to carry out some target practice on the gulls that flew about the brig. Luckily, the midshipmen had been right—his aim was absolutely unerring, even when he was too intoxicated for coherent speech. Wiki still wondered if he was a murderer and was quite convinced that in other circumstances Lieutenant Forsythe would have been a pirate. Because of his strange attitude, the *Swallow* could have foundered—but, as he had demonstrated during the storm, there was plenty of crude courage, too.

So Wiki shrugged in the darkness and said dryly, "Interesting."

"I see." And Erskine sounded as if he did, indeed, understand quite a lot.

"And the *Porpoise?*"

"A smart ship. Captain Ringgold is a good man. But—"

It was Erskine's turn to pause. Wiki had already heard favorable reports of Lieutenant Ringgold, the master of the *Porpoise*, who had distinguished himself in the so-called "Mosquito Fleet," which had put down piracy in the West Indies. Cadwallader Ringgold sprang from a distinguished Maryland family but nevertheless was considered by the seamen to be a thoroughgoing fellow and one of themselves. However, it was obvious that Erskine greatly regretted leaving the *Swallow*—another indication, in Wiki's opinion, that Captain Wilkes was heading for trouble with his policy of shifting men willy-nilly about the fleet.

Wiki said next, "How did you fare in the storm?"

"Tore along with the lee rail buried in the foam." Then Ernest Erskine added, "The *Flying Fish* fared worse—flew through the darkness under just a fore staysail and a goose-winged trysail, but still she buried her hatches under water. The carpenter and the bo'sun were stationed each one by a mast, at the ready to cut away the weather shrouds and backstays and send the masts over the side to save the hull, if necessary. But in the end she come through with just the loss of the foresail and a boat, along with its davits. There's some alarm about the *Sea Gull* and the *Peacock*, though—we lost track of them entirely and haven't seen sight or sign of them since. But," he said bracingly, "the dear *Swallow* rejoined us, so we must hold hard to hope. Tell me, how did she weather it?"

"The first big squall could have easily caught us aback, but we were snugged down and ready," said Wiki, thinking it was best not to gossip, as the seamen would do enough of that when they got the chance. He looked about, thinking of the difference from the night of the storm. There was not a breath of wind to disturb the shimmering black surface on which they floated, and the atmosphere was close and warm. The sea was more like molten metal than liquid water.

The six oars of the gig dipped and rose rhythmically, the drops that spilled from their blades glowing with the cold fire of phosphorescence. There was a sudden swift flurry of the same eerie light as something cut through the water a few yards off, but then it disappeared so fast that it was possible to believe he'd imagined it. The lights of the *Porpoise* were bobbing closer, and all at once the hull was looming out of the night.

The boat touched the side, and an oarsman grabbed the dangling falls. When the boat stilled, Wiki reached up and gripped the rope that hung down from the gangway. Then he turned to look at Erskine, saying, "Do you know why Lieutenant Ringgold wants to see me?"

"One of our Kanaka seamen is acting strangely, and we're anxious to learn if there is anything wrong—he seems very distressed."

"Do you know his name?"

"Joe Rotuma."

His old friend, Wiki guessed with his eyebrows high, and clambered stiffly up the side to the deck. As he was technically a civilian, there was no shrilling of the boatswain's call as he arrived at the head of the gangway; and because he was a lowly seaman, he didn't head for the quarterdeck, either. Instead, he walked quietly to the forepeak, where the Rotuman was standing between the knightheads staring out at the shimmering, moonlit sea. It felt for all the world as if the gentle Kanaka had not moved an inch from the moment Wiki had first clapped eyes upon him.

This time the Rotuman did not turn as Wiki arrived. Instead, he seemed to be deeply lost in a trance, chanting softly and monotonously, *"Hitua, Hi—Hitua, Hi—Hitua Hi—"*

Ernest Erskine had followed Wiki. He whispered, "What does it mean?"

Wiki was frowning. "I don't know. I don't think it means anything. I've only heard it twice before—once at a funeral, and a second time when a Rotuman village was preparing for the arrival of a dignitary. I won't know till I hear the words that are recited at the end whether it signifies life or death. How long has he been like this?"

"Since the exercise with the cannon ended."

Hours, thought Wiki. He knew that the chant could be repeated for a while, but had never heard of it being kept up for so long. It was a strange rhythm in the night, almost like a distant drum. He felt at a loss to understand it, but then he was distracted by another flash of phosphorescence in the water. The swift glimmer faded, but another two trails appeared, farther off—and then a dozen streaks of icy radiance, moving in wide circles, but coming closer to the gun brig *Porpoise*. Then Wiki glimpsed a black triangle in the midst of one of the bursts of ghostly blue.

He whispered, "Sharks!" Now that he knew what was making the trails of cold fire, he could sense dozens of the predators circling the black mile-wide expanse between the *Porpoise* and the *Vincennes*.

"Dear God," said Erskine. His voice was shaky. He'd seen the same thing.

"Is the Kanaka frightened of them?" he asked. "Is he making a spell to cast them away?"

Wiki shook his head. "In his village the shark is an *'aitu*, a friendly spirit. All sea creatures are good, according to Rotuman lore. They don't believe that any *'atua*—devils—live in the sea."

"So what is he doing, for God's sake? *Summoning* them?"

Was he? A ghostly shiver chilled Wiki's warm skin. A couple of years ago—on an island in the Gilberts, not Rotuma—he had witnessed a calling of sharks.

The man with the magic to do such a thing was known as the shark-dreamer. For hours, as this fellow sequestered himself in his hut to dream up his sharks, Wiki, in the company of all the grown men of the village, had waited in the shallows of the lagoon. Each islander had had a sharp knife and a small shark-fishing canoe, which was loaded with nothing more than a paddle and a special shark-fishing line. The hook was a twig of the ironwood tree that had been bent and twisted inch by inch as it grew, and then cut, and lashed with a braid made of women's hair to a long, strong sennit rope that looped around the little canoe amidships.

Meanwhile, back in the village, the women and the children had been getting the ovens ready for the feast. The islanders had known without question that the sharks would come, but Wiki himself had not believed a word of it. The air, he remembered, had been utterly still—as still as it was this day. The lagoon had been a perfect turquoise, the sea, beyond the gray bulwark of the reef, a profound and glittering aquamarine. Even the birds had been still and quiet, so that the only sounds had been the ripple of water on the sand, and the quiet conversation of the village men.

Then, with shocking suddenness, the shark-dreamer had burst out of his hut with a horrible yell, and all the men had surged forward into the water with a roar, dragging their canoes behind them. "They come!" they had cried. "They come, they come!"—but Wiki had seen nothing, just the hard glare on the water and the fleeting blue backs of a shoal of mullet.

And then his sight had focused on the gigantic shark that had arrived at the gap in the reef, with a squadron of sharks lined up behind. As he watched, they swarmed through—tigers, their striped, writhing, graceful bodies shockingly beautiful, their evil gape-mouthed heads viciously brutish—and as they invaded the lagoon, the village men, armed just with knives, had dived into the water to fight them in single combat.

There had been method in it, as Wiki remembered. The

sharks had charged like bulls, with blind ferocity. Each waiting fisherman had flipped to one side at the last possible instant, shoving the knife along the shark's underside as the predator rushed past. Abruptly the water had been seething with blood and guts, and dead shark carcasses had begun to float up to the surface. Then the men had leapt into their canoes, to lower their shark-fishing lines. The sharks, which were fastened with the twisted ironwood hooks, had been forced to drag the boats along, each one with a man inside, until they had slumped, exhausted. Then the men had dropped overboard again to finish off the great tigers with their knives.

There had been a feast in the village that night, Wiki remembered now, and a great deal of shark meat had been dried for future meals. But had the shark-dreamer summoned them or had the sharks been chasing the mullet?

His mind jerked back to the present. Midshipman Erskine's hand was gripping his arm, his tight fingers bruising. The Rotuman's chant had come to a sudden end, with a long-drawn-out cry of, *"Lok pakura—Hi!"*

"What does it mean?" whispered Erskine. He sounded scared.

The words echoed in Wiki's mind, and the hairs rose on the back of his neck. "It means it was a chant for death."

The Rotuman was perfectly silent now, standing in the bows of the *Porpoise* and staring at the phosphorescent trails as they diminished, faded, and finally dissolved.

Nineteen

No one stopped George Rochester when he ordered a boat to be lowered from the *Vincennes*. No doubt, he thought, everyone expected him to steer for the *Swallow,* but the scuttlebutt was that Wiki was on the *Porpoise* with Erskine, so he ordered his boat's crew to pull that way instead.

Ernest Erskine met him at the gangway, his welcoming smile rather wry. They exchanged chat about the storm, and Rochester boasted about the prowess of his gun crew, while all the time he looked about curiously. The gun brig, while less than a hundred feet long, had a crew of sixty-five; and because the weather was so mild, most of the off-duty watch was on deck, so it was a bustling sight. The watch worked about decks and in the rigging, while the off-duty men sat about reading, sewing, or doing their laundry, while others were catching up on sleep in sheltered corners. Rochester thought that the gun brig had a good feel, the feel of a contented ship.

His old second-in-command had nothing bad to say about the *Porpoise,* either. The gun brig was a fast sailer, he told George, with a responsive helm—she was the fastest ship in the fleet. "Save for the dear *Swallow.*" Like the *Vincennes,* the *Porpoise* had had a poop cabin built for the expedition—though not as large, of course—and this had a stateroom for the sole scientific on board.

"Which scientific?" asked George. He was curious to know the name of the civilian who was thus comfortably accommodated on the *Porpoise,* while the scientifics on the *Vincennes* were so notoriously cramped for space.

"An astronomer," said Erskine.

"Ah," said George, remembering that Wiki had told him that Astronomer Burroughs had originally been assigned to the *Porpoise.* "But he's dead," he objected, also remembering the horrible moment when the astronomer's door had been broken down.

"You mean Burroughs? It's his assistant that has come over in his place. Sorry-looking fellow by the name of Grimes. He's an astronomer-proper now, not an assistant anymore."

"Great heavens!" said George, impressed with Wilkes's unusual magnanimity. "He's overwhelmed with delight, no doubt."

"I'll hazard he was even more gratified to get away from Astronomer Stanton," Erskine remarked unkindly. Like George, he had not enjoyed Tristram Stanton's company on the *Swallow.*

"I'm sure you are right, dear fellow," said George, and went in search of Wiki.

He found him on the fore hatch, squatting in a circle of six

Polynesians, playing cards. It was an animated game, with a lot of laughter and scores being kept, but George suspected that it did not involve gambling—because in the Pacific, or so Wiki had informed him, wagers invariably were in the form of pigs, an impossible currency here.

George paused, watching the group with his head tilted and his hands lightly clasped behind his back, ruminating how un-American his friend looked right now and how well he fitted in with this gathering of natives. Wiki was sitting cross-legged, scowling down at his cards so that his fine, black, swooping eyebrows were like horizontal question marks above his flat nose. Like the other Polynesians, he had stripped off his shirt, and his snaky hair hung loose about his shoulders and his broad, smooth, hairless chest. Then Wiki looked up, sensing George's inspection, and his face went triangular with the familiar creases of his grin, crescent-shaped blue eyes sparkling with delight.

"*E hoa,*" he exclaimed, and sprang to his feet, dropping his cards.

As usual, they locked forearms instead of shaking hands. "So at last you tracked me down," Wiki said and smiled.

"I was as impatient as a dog all the time the dear *Swallow* was out of sight." Then George nodded at the Kanakas, still squabbling happily over the cards, and jibed amiably, "Rejoined the realm of the savages, I see."

Wiki's grin widened. These Kanakas did look more like canoe paddlers than seamen in the service of the U.S. Navy, he conceded—but that was because they were such seasoned sailors. Traditionally, when a Pacific Islander was first shipped on a big American vessel, he couldn't wait to array himself in western sailor finery, exulting in stiff canvas trousers and shoddy frock shirts. Often, he wore his new outfit to bed.

Within a few weeks, though, the glamour wore off, and he would be back to bare feet—and be bare-chested, too, if the officers were prepared to turn a blind eye. It was not unknown for some to revert to draping the traditional *sulu* or *lavalava* about their loins, and it was a rare Polynesian who returned from a jaunt on shore without a wreath of bright flowers about the crown of his hat.

"Where do they come from?" asked George.

"Oh, there're a couple of Hawaiians—a Tahitian—a Samoan," said Wiki, with a vague wave of his hand. Then he added, "One is a Rotuman," and led the way to a place abaft of the foremast where they could hunker down against the stacked boats and chat in private.

First came the tale of the Rotuman and the sharks. Now the Rotuman was the most laughing and cheerful of the five card players—but George had learned long ago that though the Pacific Island nature might be dark and moody at times, it always bounced back to being sunny. Next, with ever-increasing alarm, he heard the story of Forsythe and the looming storm. "He left the deck without an officer on watch!" he exclaimed. "Is he mad?" he demanded, bright red in the face. "Thank God you were on board!" The account of the miraculous escape of the boatswain filled him with amazement. Then, with the description of the formal punishment of the two Samoans, at last Wiki silenced.

"He flogged them just because they were speaking Samoan?" George studied the card players again, listening to their loud chatter. They were talking in English, with some Polynesian words thrown in as a kind of punctuation—because they spoke different Polynesian dialects, he supposed, and English was their common language. However, Wiki did not give him a chance to comment, getting down to business by saying briskly,

"Well, did you have that talk with Jim Powell? Did he stick to that story about giving the note to Forsythe?"

George paused and then said rather defensively, "I couldn't find him."

"What!" Wiki frowned, looking annoyed. "But you did go to the sick bay?"

"Not for a while," George reluctantly admitted. "The storm was looming—there was much to do, and I couldn't get away, not without being asked awkward questions. But as soon as the decks had been cleared of wreckage, rigging fixed, and so forth, I sallied there first chance—and most impolite the surgeon was, too. What a pompous ill-conditioned fellow he is! Rumbled on about the ingratitude of a man he was only trying to save. Said that Powell quit the sick bay the instant everyone's back was turned and was apparently in hiding because no one had clapped eyes on him, despite a general call. So then," he went on, his tone becoming ingenuous, "I took a few surreptitious peeks in the officers' quarters."

"The—*what?* But why?"

"I thought he might have sought out a soft bed in preference to a hammock in the dank confines of the orlop. When I was a junior mid, I had a running battle with the second lieutenant," Rochester confided. "He was a stickler, I assure you! I was always finding cozy planks in quiet corners to snooze away my watch at night, and he always tracked me down and beat me. But as a kind of bet, he promised not to beat me if he ever didn't manage to find me before the end of the watch was rung. He must've been a sleepy shirker himself in his youth because he was an amazing dab hand at finding out where I'd hid myself, and so I got beating after blessed beating—but then I had a famous inspiration. He hunted here, and he hunted there, but the bell rang, and so he was forced to give up. When he went to his quarters for his watch below himself, he finally found me—curled up fast asleep on his own settee."

"And did he beat you?" Wiki inquired, with a distinct air of fraying patience.

"Of course not, dear chap! The second lieutenant might've been a beast, but he was also a gentleman of his word."

"Well, he should have," said Wiki flatly. "So did you find Powell's messmates to quiz them about his whereabouts?"

"I certainly did," Rochester assured him earnestly. "Though it was confoundedly difficult to find 'em. There are two hundred men on board that ship—sixteen messes, and he could've belonged to any one of 'em!"

Wiki frowned, reminded of how little he knew about daily life on a navy warship. All his experience had been on whalers and traders, and the only messrooms he knew were saloons like the one on the *Swallow*, which were the province of officers and passengers, the ordinary sailors eating in the forecastle or on the foredeck. He had supposed that navy men perched on their sea chests in just the same way, but now he wondered if they owned any, perhaps they had kitbags instead.

"Messes?" he said.

"Aye. Each mess is made up of twelve men, and they have their own special place to eat, on the deck between two guns—they even issue 'em a bit of canvas to spread on the deck for service as a tablecloth, along with a couple of wooden tubs for carrying the food from the galley. The purser is in charge of it all—another confoundedly rude fellow," Rochester complained. "He didn't want to divulge Powell's particulars in the slightest.

Then, when I finally and at long last found his messmates, the surly fellows would only say they reckoned he had lost the number of his mess—in the storm, most likely."

Lost the number of his mess? Wiki remembered the tin figures on the bulkheads of the gun deck and presumed that this strange saying meant that Jim had not turned up for meals. "But why did they never report him missing?"

"I don't think they noticed it for quite some time. They thought he was in the sick bay."

"And when you informed them he'd disappeared from there?"

"They seemed to know it already—had found out about it since, I suppose."

So someone from his mess had gone to visit him and had found that Jim had vanished—and yet still his messmates had not reported his absence. Why not? Wiki opened his mouth, but Rochester abruptly changed the subject, saying, "What are you going to do about Ringgold's idea?"

"What idea?"

"Haven't you been told? Erskine says that Captain Ringgold would like to request that Wilkes move you onto the *Porpoise*. He was very impressed with your performance last night, he says."

Wiki smiled wryly, remembering how relieved Ringgold had been that the Rotuman had turned back into a normal man, even though he did not have a shred of understanding as to what had happened.

"Tell him not to bother," he said. "My place is on the *Swallow*."

Rochester, predictably, looked relieved. However, he said gallantly, "If it's too dreadful on the brig with Forsythe in charge, old chap—"

"My sea chest is there." And the letter of authority. "But I must get on board the *Vincennes*."

"I'm sure there will be opportunities aplenty, old chap," Rochester assured him. "You're bound to be invited on board for something fancy in the eating way. Why, Wilkes himself has invited me to a feast next Saturday, along with some other passed midshipmen and a passel of scientifics—in hopes, I think, that the *Peacock* and *Sea Gull* will have rejoined us by then and there'll be something to celebrate, some quarterdeck alarm having been expressed about their welfare. I doubt that the wine will be plentiful, but the conversation should be amusing. Why, what do you want to do there?"

"I want to look for Powell—and I need to talk to that man who was Burroughs's assistant—Grimes."

"But he's right here!"

"What! On the *Porpoise?*"

"I thought you knew. Where the devil did you sleep last night? Surely not the fo'c'sle!" protested George, sounding as scandalized as if he himself had never consigned his comrade to the forecastle of the *Swallow*.

"In the house," said Wiki, meaning the cabin that had been built on the poop. Erskine had found him a small stateroom there. His eyebrows were high—it seemed very strange to think that the fellow he'd heard snoring on the other side of the partition could have been Grimes. Then he thought that it was even stranger that he had not seen him during daylight and wondered if the astronomer were avoiding him.

After George Rochester had headed off back to the *Vincennes*, the notion came to seem more and more likely. Wiki had unobtrusively but exhaustively searched the *Porpoise* for a couple of hours without finding hide or hair of the astronomer. When he finally located him, Grimes was in what Wiki would have considered the most unlikely place possible—the maintop. In fact, he'd only spied the gangly, hunched shape because he'd cast an eye upward to find Midshipman Erskine and ask for advice about where to look next.

When Wiki arrived on the broad platform at the top of the lower mast, the astronomer was perched on a folded sail with a sextant on his knee. He had evidently been taking observations because he was making copious notes, which made his being aloft more comprehensible. The glance he cast at Wiki as he came over the futtock shrouds, however, was not welcoming in the slightest; and, in an obvious attempt to discourage conversation, he busied himself with his note taking again.

Wiki stood watching him in silence a moment, one hand casually holding a lanyard as he swayed lightly with the slight roll of the vessel, wondering about the reason for the hostility. Though Grimes's demeanor was not as fraught with misery as the day he had questioned him, he still seemed hollow eyed and depressed—a sorry-looking man indeed.

Wiki said, "Perhaps you don't remember me, sir—William Coffin Jr."

"The sheriff's deputy," said Grimes ungraciously, without even looking up. "Of course I remember you—how could I not?"

"I wasn't aware until just now that you'd removed to the *Porpoise*."

"Captain Wilkes was kind enough to shift me to our—my old quarters."

Burroughs had originally been stationed on the *Porpoise*,

Wiki remembered. However, he also recollected that Grimes had said that both he and Burroughs had been jubilant at being moved to the flagship, so he asked in puzzled tones, "And you're pleased?"

"That's what I said, sir," Grimes snapped.

Wiki thought that wasn't what he had said at all and was tempted to snap right back. However, he kept a tight rein on his temper, contenting himself with insinuating, "If it's so pleasant to return on board the *Porpoise*, can I take it that you didn't find Astronomer Stanton an easy man to work with?"

Grimes's mouth tightened. For a moment, just as in that first interview, Wiki had the impression that he was going to break out into some kind of revelation. In the end, however, the astronomer merely said in precise tones, "Captain Wilkes promoted me from the station of assistant to fully rated expedition astronomer—an elevation that I find most agreeable, naturally."

"Then congratulations are in order, sir."

Grimes gazed distantly about at the water instead of meeting Wiki's eyes, while Wiki considered the averted head thoughtfully and wondered what Tristram Stanton thought about the promotion. In the distance a boat was putting out from the *Vincennes*. He could just discern a burly figure in the sheets and wondered if Astronomer Stanton was coming over for a consultation with Grimes. In a few moments, however, it became evident that the boat was heading for the *Swallow*, not the *Porpoise*.

Wiki said abruptly, seeing no other way of getting the man's complete attention, "There's a question I forgot to ask you back on the *Vincennes*."

Grimes frowned. For the first time his eyes flickered up to Wiki's face. "What?"

"I forgot to ask where you were when Mr. Burroughs ended his life."

Grimes stared. His face went red and then white, and he cried, "What the devil are you accusing me of?"

Wiki began to protest, "Nothing!"—but the thin man was gathering up his notebook and sextant with sharp, furious movements, stuffing them into a leather bag that he slung over his shoulder, before standing up and stepping over to the hole in the platform of the maintop that civilians used on the way up and down the shrouds, and which the sailors derisively called "the lubbers' hole."

His body began disappearing in angry jerks, as he shouted, "I was right here, Mr. Coffin—right here on this gun brig! Don't you realize I would have turned the whole world upside down to stop him if I had been there? And I don't believe it was suicide, neither! If you're so interested, why aren't you finding out the true facts instead of tormenting me?"

Wiki shouted, "Stop!" And to his amazement Grimes did stop, looking queerly like a half man, because he was through the hole as far as his waist.

Wiki took a deep breath and said, "Please tell me why you feel so sure that Mr. Burroughs did not commit suicide."

"Because he was happy! Because he had no reason for it!" Grimes cried. "Don't you understand? He was fulfilling a dream that he had cherished all the years I worked with him. He was a member of an illustrious scientific corps and on the road to scientific glory! Why should he commit suicide? Tell me that!"

Wiki opened his mouth, but it was as if a floodgate had opened, for the astronomer rushed on: "He hummed and whistled as he worked—he was doing exactly what he wanted most in the world. I tell you, he was happy! He even wrote poems in praise of his happiness!"

Wiki blinked, utterly taken aback by this strange revelation. "Poetry?"

"He was a gifted man, sir—gifted in more ways than science! And I found it—found the note in his very own writing among the equipment on the *Vincennes* only just the other day."

"What note?" Wiki asked swiftly.

"I told you—don't you ever listen? The poem, the poem!" And then, to Wiki's amazement, Grimes recited:

Wise men come in coveys, Scientifics abroad
And to hills of science, Lo! A royal road!
Some are dropping honey, Others dropping gall
But all is going well with me
All's well—all's well—all's well!

"Would a man who penned something like that put an end to himself, sir?" cried Grimes. "Think about it, think!" And then he was gone, leaving Wiki lost in startled speculation.

Twenty

*W*hen Erskine's boat delivered Wiki back to the *Swallow* late that afternoon, Lieutenant Forsythe was standing at the gangway rail and the two Samoans were on the foredeck deep in conversation. They all watched as the boat arrived, Forsythe's expression brooding, and the Samoans frowning fiercely. Some kind of situation had erupted while he'd been away, Wiki deduced with alarm.

Grabbing the gangway rope, he climbed up the side to where Forsythe was waiting. The lieutenant bared his teeth in a mirthless grin, while Wiki stood studying him warily, recognizing the telltale signs of one of Forsythe's vicious moods.

The southerner jibed, "You've come to take away your sea chest, I trust."

Wiki frowned, wondering if Lieutenant Ringgold had gone

ahead and asked for his transfer. "Has Captain Wilkes sent orders that I'm to move to another ship?"

"It's news to me that you need any goddamn orders, Mr. Coffin. Right now I need your room, not your company—so you'll oblige me by removing your worthless half-breed carcass. There're savages enough in the fo'c'sle, without havin' a cannibal at my table. So why don't you put your bone back in your nose and bugger off?"

Wiki's eyes widened and then narrowed into glittering crescents. Quite involuntarily, his shoulders braced and his elbows crooked, his hands shivering at the level of his biceps, on the verge of clamping into fists—but then he saw the flash of pleasure in Forsythe's expression and realized the lieutenant was spoiling for a fight.

It was like the night in Norfolk when he'd been foolish enough to rise to Forsythe's bait. Now, if he retaliated, it would give Forsythe the excuse he wanted to throw him off the brig. Wiki deliberately relaxed his taut muscles. Behind his forced calmness, his mind was racing. It looked as if Forsythe had a compelling reason to get him off the ship—but what could it be? Was he trying to fend off more questions about what he had been doing when Ophelia Stanton was murdered?

Probing for a reaction, Wiki said blandly, "But I don't have any choice—the investigation, remember. There are more questions to be asked."

Forsythe merely shrugged. "Ask whatever questions you bloody well want, but oblige me by getting it over and done with so you can get the hell off my ship."

Wiki's next thought was a still more disturbing one—that it involved the Samoans. He said sharply, "Was there some trouble with the crew while I was on board the *Porpoise?*"

"Nothing that I can't handle—and it's none of your god-damn business anyway."

"But it is, if it's something to do with the Kanakas."

"And what the devil gives you that strange idea?"

"Ask Captain Ringgold, if you need to check."

"Ah." Forsythe closed one eye and adopted a wise look. "So that's why you were sent for, huh? Is friend Cadwallader having some trouble with his Kanakas?" Then, when Wiki's silence had dragged on long enough for him to realize that he was never going to get an answer, he lifted his voice and shouted to the Samoans, "Do you have some kind of complaint to make to Mr. Coffin here? If so, here's your chance."

Both men looked startled, and then Wiki saw Sua's lips move briefly by Jack Savvy's ear. They both shook their heads and disappeared down the forecastle hatch. If there had been trouble, obviously they were going to handle it themselves—but not on board the ship. On the night of the storm he and Jack Savvy had not had time to introduce themselves at full length, but since then they had exchanged *whakapapa*, and Wiki had found that this warrior from the island of Savai'i was the son of a paramount chief. If the fleet dropped anchor there—which he believed was part of the navy's plan—then it was Lieutenant Forsythe who would find himself in trouble.

"That bein' settled," drawled Forsythe, "why don't you ask your goddamn questions and get going?"

Wiki said dryly, "Do you really want the whole ship to hear?"

"I've got nothing to hide, damn it!"

"No?" Then Wiki snapped, at the end of his patience, "So why did you tell me lies?"

"Lies!" shouted Forsythe. Then he looked around and lowered his voice. "I've told you no goddamn lies," he hissed. "That two-faced swab Jim Powell is the liar, not me—why don't you try badgering *him* for a change?"

"Yet you tried to convince me that your cousin Ophelia was suicidal—when the whole of Virginia knew she was planning to divorce her husband."

Forsythe went red in the face. "She *was* suicidal! Divorce was my idea, not hers!"

"*What?*"

"I told you! I had nothin' to gain by her death! But there surely was hope if she filed for divorce, because then the family money would be back where it rightfully belonged. You can ask the whole of Virginia if you like, because I was perfectly open about it. But she was besotted with the bugger. The more he treated her like shit, the more she was convinced the sun shone out of his arse. *I'm* the one who tried to talk some sense into her stupid skull. Right from the first time that string-shanked turd reduced her to a wet, weeping rag, I tried to convince her that divorce was the only answer. Why do you think the Stantons hated me so? It wasn't just that I kept on askin' her for money—which was money made by *our* family, not the bloody Stantons, remember! Why do you think the old bastard threw me out?"

"Dear God," Wiki said. "And yet you still live," he marveled. Remembering the snarl of animal-like hatred and fury that had twisted old man Stanton's face, he shook his head in wonder.

Then he was brought up short by the sound of the *Vincennes* firing a gun. When he looked over the expanse of water, the flag on the distant peak was at half-mast. Wiki's first confused thought was that the flagship was under attack—or that they were staging another live exercise. Then the faint echoes of three volleys clattered over the water, and he realized that it was a burial.

"Who died?" he involuntarily asked.

"Is that some more of your goddamn cross-examination?" Forsythe demanded savagely. "Wa-al, just for your information, I haven't the foggiest. It's just some poor bloody little tar on the *Vin* who lost the number of his mess."

Wiki went quite still, the conversation with George Rochester back in his mind, suddenly imbued with new meaning. He said softly, "What did you say?"

Forsythe didn't reply. Instead, his eyes shifted to look over Wiki's shoulder, and his expression became completely blank.

And a vaguely familiar voice from behind Wiki said in hearty tones, "The poor fellow lost the number of his mess—he slipped his cable—he's taken his *nunc dimittis*. Isn't it amazing, the words that navy tars employ to indicate departure from this world of life? It's as if even sailors—the most forthright of men!—can't bring themselves to simply say, *he's dead.*"

Wiki turned, to see the florid face of Wilkes's friend—the amateur philologist, Lieutenant Lawrence J. Smith, and wondered what the devil was going on. Before he could even start to ask, however, the steward's bell rang for supper, and Smith's hand grasped his arm, urging him toward the companionway stairs.

"The poor lad expired of the dysentery—a maintopman, they told me, and a capital fellow—a loss, a loss to his ship. You were surprised by the phrase 'lost the number of his mess?' "

"I've heard someone say something similar—just recently," said Wiki. "And I must confess I didn't know what it meant, not being a navy man, you see." *So Powell was dead.* The hairs on the back of Wiki's neck lifted as he remembered the Rotuman's eerie chant—and the glimpse of mortal terror in Jim's eyes as the surgeon and the loblolly boys had arrived to take him to the sick bay.

"There are a few other cases of the bloody flux on board the *Vincennes*," Lieutenant Smith rattled on as they arrived in the saloon at the bottom of the companionway. "Captain Wilkes confided to me that he's a trifle concerned for the general health of the ship, though the surgeon assures him the others will recover. Suspicions are that the saucy fellows stole a little pig from the pigpen and overindulged in their illicit dinner."

"I wonder how they cooked it," said Wiki absently.

He swung a leg over his usual bench at the foot of the table and sat down. Forsythe, his face still blank, arrived down the stairs and slumped into the chair at the head, while Smith perched on the bench where Passed Midshipman Kingman customarily sat. Wiki thought that he hadn't seen Kingman anywhere about the decks, and wondered again what was going on. He looked at Forsythe, but the southerner had his head down, moodily shoveling meat into his mouth that he had taken straight off the dish in the middle of the table.

"Bribed the cook without a doubt," said Smith, as he forked salt beef without a qualm. "The men save up their grog to trade for food or tobacco, or for bribing their fellows—the ration is far, far, far too generous! In fact there should be no grog issued at all! I truly believe, Wiremu, that the day that temperance rules the U.S. Navy will be a blessed one indeed."

"I'm sure you are right," said Wiki. What he could see of Forsythe's face was sour with disgust.

"Of course I am, Wiremu, of course I am right! The ration simply panders to depraved tastes. Did you hear about the man who almost met his end during that mishap aloft? That when he recovered his senses his first words were to inquire after his grog? And that the wicked fellow cursed the surgeon when he ordered that none should be given? Shocking, Wiremu, shocking!"

Wiki paused, wondering if Lieutenant Smith was aware of Forsythe's role in that mishap. Then he observed, "You use the Maori version of my American name."

"*Wiremu* for William? You told me that yourself, dear lad—yourself!—when you were a child, at the same time that I told you my hobby was words. It was then that I learned from you that word games were a popular pastime in your village back home. Tell me, is that still the case—that the New Zealand people keep their minds alert by playing with words?"

"Proverbs will always be part of the orator's craft, along with great knowledge of the traditional *karakia*," said Wiki, but his thoughts were not focused on the traditional chants. He asked, "Has it ever been known for naval officers to write poems?"

"But of course!" cried Lieutenant Smith. "In fact, I encourage poetical talent in my midshipmen! Not only does it serve to fill many hours of idleness at sea, but it keeps the mind alert. Indeed, every officer should apply himself to the pursuit. In the old days, you know, there was space in the *Naval Chronicle* for odes composed at sea. What a pity the custom has lapsed!"

Wiki wondered if Forsythe had ever been poetically inspired in his midshipman days, but instantly dismissed the thought as being even more unlikely than a versifying astronomer—something that was immediately confirmed by a muted snort of disgust from the head of the table, proving that despite all appearances Forsythe was still awake.

"What about scientifics?" he pursued. "Is it at all known for them to compose odes to science?"

"Of course! Attention to the arts as well as the sciences is the mark of a truly elevated mind. It was a mark of the greatness of the Renaissance."

"I see," said Wiki slowly, understanding with a sense of surprise that Burroughs might not have been so eccentric after all. Still deep in thought, he took up his fork. Silence descended as they ate—and silence was something that Lieutenant Smith found uncomfortable, it seemed, because it quickly became obvious that he was hunting for another topic of conversation.

His brow lightened. "Your escape from the rigors of the storm was truly providential, Wiremu. When we lost sight of three members of our fleet, we feared the very worst! When the *Porpoise* signaled that the dear little *Swallow* had rejoined the fleet, the relief was general, as a sign that soon, with the blessing of providence, we will be reunited with the others, too. It was a miracle, even, that you found us in the midst of the empty seas—and a great concern that the captains of the *Peacock* and the *Sea Gull* have not achieved the same as yet."

"Ah," said Wiki wisely, "but we were fortunate enough to hear the sounds of firing. We didn't know which way to steer, not until we heard the first explosions."

"Truly?" said the lieutenant, looking impressed. "Well, then, it was most fortunate that we were holding the exercise!" he exclaimed. "Which means you owe a particular debt to our good friend Astronomer Stanton."

At that Forsythe lifted his head to look at Smith, his expression surprised, and Wiki's own eyebrows were high.

"It's extreme' unusual for a scientific to be allowed to take any part in the routine maneuvers of the fleet, as you know," Smith expounded, looking gratified at their sudden attention. "But when Mr. Stanton observed to Captain Wilkes that the flat calm was a capital opportunity for exercising the guns, remarking at the same time that it would reinvigorate the crew after the stress of the storm, Captain Wilkes thought it a famous idea.

And when Astronomer Stanton suggested that it should climax with some live firing with a barrel as a target—which he volunteered to organize, with the cooperation of the cooper—accompanied by a competition to put the gun crews on their mettle, that was adopted as an excellent notion, too."

"Then I guess we were indeed very fortunate," Wiki conceded. However, he was frowning. This further evidence that Stanton had great influence with Captain Wilkes made him feel very uncomfortable.

"But, of course, the greatest blessing is that the *Swallow* survived at all—which she only did because of her captain's foresight, as Lieutenant Forsythe confided to both Captain Wilkes and me, after we pressed him for details. It is yet another testimony to the fact that whatever doubt or danger may beset us, the firm and gallant spirit that is characteristic of American navy officers will hold firm and prevail—as it will prevail, too, on the quarterdecks of the *Peacock* and *Sea Gull*."

Wiki put down his fork and glanced at Forsythe's blank expression. Then, deliberately, he turned to face Lieutenant Smith, contemplating him over the rim of his mug as he meditatively drank tea. So the burly figure he had glimpsed in the boat pulling from the *Vincennes* to the *Swallow* had been Forsythe—back from delivering a highly embellished and self-serving report of the *Swallow*'s adventures. Forsythe's jaws revolved stolidly, but the tension in the burly shoulders was perceptible enough to convey that he was unhappy with the way the conversation was going.

"Hearing Captain Forsythe's report of how he got the ship snugged well beforehand was an enormous pleasure to both of us," Smith enthused on, completely oblivious to the atmosphere. "We were quite convinced that without his prudence the first great gust would have brought the brig aback!"

So, Wiki realized, Forsythe had laid on the soft soap with a vengeance. And this was the reason, he mused, that the southerner had been so anxious to see him off the brig before Lieutenant Smith had a chance to engage him in conversation.

Feeling both amused and angry, he asked blandly, "And he also told you about the providential escape of the bo'sun?"

"Indeed, we heard about it—twice! We summoned the bo'sun to hear the details from his very own lips, and a stirring story he made of it, too."

So, Wiki understood, the boatswain had been in the party that rowed Forsythe to the flagship. He wondered what else the independent old fellow had told Wilkes. Very little, he thought—the old salt was too wise a sailor to stir up trouble with his superiors.

"Would you believe me, Wiremu," Lieutenant Smith was burbling on, "if I told you I once served on a ship where the exact same thing happened? The chap who was washed overboard was washed back again on the crest of the following wave, just as in your bo'sun's case. The captain ordered that he should be given a glass of grog, and the sailor—being a seaman—drank it down in a single draft; but after he had quaffed it he confessed that he couldn't understand why the old man had been so generous. When informed of his miraculous escape, he was astounded—it had all happened so smoothly and suddenly that he was quite unaware of having been overboard at all!"

"Great heavens!" exclaimed Wiki, suitably astonished. Then he observed, "I'm sure Captain Forsythe also talked about our debt to the Samoans in our crew."

Forsythe looked up. Wiki met his poisonous stare with a faint smile and then returned his attention to Lieutenant Smith. "Your Kanakas?" Smith asked. His eyes were blinking as he looked from Wiki to Forsythe, and he seemed rather at a loss.

"Aye," said Wiki, and smiled blandly. "They sensed the storm long before it arrived—as is common. More than once I've been on an American whaleship that was saved by the Kanakas' knowledge of the stars, the currents, the flight patterns of birds, and the winds."

"Fascinating," said Smith, after a small hesitation, his eyes still flickering back and forth between Forsythe and Wiki. "And these—Samoans gave warning of what to expect?"

"Well, I had to translate," Wiki amended. "They spoke their native language in their panic."

"Which is natural, I suppose," said Smith, sounding more doubtful than ever.

"I've since been informed that it's against regulations to talk in their own tongue. Is it really Captain Wilkes's policy that English should be the only language of the fleet? If that is the case, as the expedition's official linguister, I would be forced to make a strong protest."

"I've never heard of any such regulation," said Smith with a frown. "I can't imagine why there should be such a rule."

Wiki paused, again briefly meeting Forsythe's murderous look, and then murmured, "The reason I was given was that they might be planning mutiny."

"Well," said Smith. He darted little looks at Forsythe and Wiki again, patently aware of the tension in the room. His tongue tip touched his lips and then he said, "It is possible to see some logic in that, I suppose."

"But mutiny isn't part of *taha Maori*—the normal Polynesian way," Wiki objected. "In all the Pacific societies I know, the people are used to being subject to the rule of the chiefs, no matter how tyrannical those rulers might be."

"But once they become common sailors and liable to corruption and vice—"

Wiki waited for him to go on, wondering what kind of family the stocky little lieutenant came from. A lofty one, he thought, or else it would not be such second nature for him to despise the men who weighed the anchors, handed the sails, and hauled the ropes, straining their muscles to make his ships sail.

However, Smith did not finish the sentence, so Wiki went on reminiscently, "I once shipped on a whaler out of Sydney where the strangest form of discrimination was practiced. The forecastle had a line strung down the middle, with sheets sewn onto it to make a partition, and the white seamen lived on one side of it, and the others, the opposite. So the Kanakas talked together in a kind of Polynesian polyglot because that seemed to be what was expected of them—but it was just the usual sailor growl about the food, along with bold boasting about wild sprees in port. The white sailors didn't know it, but on both sides of the dividing line they were saying the same things."

"Exactly as I was saying about sailors' predisposition to vice—" said Lieutenant Smith, but he had lost all his heartiness. Instead of completing the sentence, he finished off his meal in what looked like a hurry. Then, with an obvious air of relief, he swung his legs around and stood up from his perch on the bench. Seizing his hat with its brave cockade, he popped it on his head, said, "Well, the watch awaits," and hurried off up the stairs.

Wiki had not heard the bell for the change of watch. He waited until the busy clatter of Smith's shoes had crossed the quarterdeck above their heads and then turned his frown on Forsythe to find the southerner glaring back.

"Interfering bastard."

Wiki ignored it. "What the devil is afoot?" he demanded. "What's he doing here?"

"Wilkes reassigned the prating arsehole to the *Swallow* as my second-in-command."

"Then Captain Wilkes is a shrewder man than most people would credit." Wiki paused for emphasis, and then said coldly, "If you ever punish a Kanaka for talking in his native tongue again, I swear I'll report you, not just to Lieutenant Smith, but to Captain Wilkes as well—and at the same time I'll make sure he learns that the *Swallow* was left without an officer on the quarterdeck when the storm was brewing."

Forsythe said nothing, but his expression was lethal. Unmoved, Wiki said, "So where is Passed Midshipman Kingman?"

"He's been reassigned to the schooner *Flying Fish*," Forsythe bit out, and stood up and slammed into his cabin.

Twenty-one

*N*ext morning, to the great alarm of Lieutenant Smith, the *Vincennes*, the *Porpoise*, and the *Flying Fish* were all out of sight, and the *Swallow* was sailing alone in an empty sea. Forsythe had taken full advantage of a brisk topgallant wind that had sprung up in the night, and, as the day went by, it became obvious that he was intent on putting as much distance between himself and the fleet as possible. The breeze increased to a gale, but still the brig was kept under whole sail, leaning over at a steep angle with the foam running along her lee bulwarks, her timbers groaning while everything aloft strained and vibrated.

"The ship is laboring," Lieutenant Smith protested in the middle of the afternoon.

Forsythe gave the hamper a glance. "Aye," he agreed. "We do have a smart press of canvas."

"The main topgallant is struggling hard. Don't you think—"

"It holds a good full, Lieutenant. Let it stand."

"But we must rejoin the fleet! Captain Wilkes is holding a feast for officers and scientifics on Saturday, and it's imperative that I attend!"

"Wa-al, he did not invite me," Forsythe retorted, and kept the canvas flying.

As soon as night had fully fallen and Forsythe had left the deck for his four hours below, Smith sent the watch aloft to take in sail. The hands complied with alacrity, having felt some alarm themselves. However, the instant the fast thud of the hull through water slowed to something more sane and rational, Forsythe came storming up to deck to countermand the order. Lieutenant Smith obeyed, but when Forsythe came up at midnight, again he begged him to reduce sail. Men were standing at every belaying pin, holding halyards by a single turn, ready to let go and clew up the straining canvas.

"Let it stand," said Forsythe.

Still the gale strengthened, but still he kept every stitch of canvas flying. Halfway through the next morning, when the fore topgallant tore out of its bolt-ropes and disappeared downwind like an errant kite, he simply sent up another sail in its place. When that one ripped, he set the watch to clewing up the remnants and ordered the old boatswain to go aloft, with two hands to help, and mend it in place. It was wild and dangerous work and took all of two hours, but after that the sail held. No one could fault Forsythe's seamanship—when he was paying attention to his ship—but nevertheless Wiki felt that the southerner was simply taking out his evil temper on the gallant little brig.

When Wiki arrived on deck the morning after that it was to find to his surprise that though the brig was still under a full press of sail, Forsythe had ordered a change of course. No one offered an explanation, so Wiki went aloft to see if there was anything in sight that would account for it. His curiosity was soon satisfied. Five miles ahead, a homeward bound whaler was dashing along on the breast of the wind, obviously anxious to get her valuable lading onto the New Bedford market. She was a magnificent sight, low down in the sea because she was full to the bung-hole with oil, but nevertheless flying along like a racehorse, with studding sails alow and aloft.

The brig *Swallow*, having altered course, was following fast in her wake. For a long time Wiki wondered why, but then, as an hour ticked by, it became increasingly evident that Forsythe was determined to overhaul her—for no reason other than simple bloody-mindedness, it seemed. The Yankee whaler captain, equally stubborn, was determined to outrun the brig. Instead of taking in sail in response to Forsythe's signals to heave to for boarding, he found another sheet of canvas and sent it up as a royal to the main, meantime keeping doggedly to his course.

The chase was both exciting and spectacular. Wiki stood on the waist deck, holding on to the lee shrouds of the foremast with the wind lashing his hair about his shoulders, watching the flying spouter with fascination, and wondering why the old ship was so obviously determined to defy the navy and show the *Swallow* a clean pair of heels. Then he bit back a grin, abruptly remembering George Rochester's little yarn about the merchantman who had done his utmost to run away from the brig in Chesapeake Bay because he had mistaken her piratical lines for the real thing. This, without a doubt, was the explanation for the whaler's recalcitrance.

Relentlessly, despite the whaling master's magnificent ship handling, they came up with her. Even then he refused to heave to in response to their flags, kicking up his wake instead, so Forsythe fired his rifle, felling an innocent gull as a signal. There was still no response, the old spouter skipper obstinately maintaining his pose of being both blind and deaf, so Forsythe ordered one of the stern chaser cannon charged, and a shot fired across the whaleman's bows.

Lieutenant Smith was nothing short of appalled, and vociferous about it, too, but mountain man Dave was more than happy to rouse up the gun crew that belonged to the starboard chaser. "Cock your lock, blow your match, watch the weather roll, stand by," he cried—

"A-n-d . . . FIRE!"

Luckily, his aim was true. There was a huge explosion, the cannon carriage screeched backward across the complaining planks, and the cannonball whistled across the bows of the whaleman, before plunging to the depths far beyond.

Where signals and musketry had failed, this demonstration of firepower worked. The spouter captain hastily backed his fore and mizzen topsails, and waited for the *Swallow* to come down. The brig luffed up and rounded to with a flourish, and then, as sail was taken in, she slowed. Wiki felt her sink lower in the water, the deck leveling and steadying, and then the *Swallow* lay still. No sooner had their wake stopped catching up with them, than Forsythe barked out orders to put down a boat. Then he looked at Wiki, who was studying the whaleship very thoughtfully indeed, and snapped, "You're coming with us, Mr. Deputy Coffin."

Wiki lifted his brows. "Why should I want to do that?" he inquired.

"Because you have a letter to deliver—right? She'll be in New Bedford in three or four weeks, and if you ask very nicely she'll send it along to Portsmouth, Virginia. And then," Forsythe said, his expression both vicious and smug, "your job will be finished. You can take a little vacation—on board another ship."

"What job?"

"Don't pretend to be thick skulled when I know a damn sight better. The sooner you get quit of that damned report that you've been so busily concocting for the sheriff, the better. That done, Mr. Deputy Coffin, you can pick up your sea chest and move—if you can find a ship where an interfering bastard Kanaka might be welcome."

Wiki looked at Forsythe curiously. He found it surprising that the lieutenant had even noticed that he had been writing his report of the investigation, because he had been forced to work on it in his stateroom. While it would have been a great deal easier to spread out the sheriff's instructions and make notes on the saloon table, the saloon had been far too public for coherent thought—because when Forsythe was on deck, Lieutenant Smith was below. And Lieutenant Smith could not cope with silence, not when he had a captive audience.

The first time the lieutenant had sat down for cozy conversation—pushing Wiki's papers to one side to give himself more room—he had announced that his intention was to watch Wiki closely. "Something of human nature can be learned even from a savage, only think!" he had enthused. However, as Wiki had swiftly found, all he wanted to do was rattle on, regardless of his listener's fraying patience. So, to avoid Smith's constant self-absorbed chatter as well as Forsythe's boorishness, Wiki had kept to his stateroom, where he had carried out his thinking lying on his back with his feet propped up on that accursed locker panel.

When he wrote, he had seated himself on the edge of his berth with his notepad on his knee.

Now he studied Forsythe warily and prevaricated, "But I haven't finished yet."

As it happened there was only a name to be inserted in a key sentence. Itemizing his observations had helped clarify his thoughts, and now he was certain he knew who had murdered Ophelia Stanton. The precise progress of the events that had followed the killing still evaded him, but he sensed that the puzzle was on the verge of being solved—that if he asked the right question of the right person, or someone inadvertently revealed just one more fact, he would have the whole answer.

"Then get it done," Forsythe snapped. "You've got five minutes."

Wiki's eyes narrowed at his tone, but then he abruptly thought, *Why not?*

Without a word he went below, and wrote down the name of the murderer of Ophelia Stanton in the appropriate place—and filled in the same gap in the copy he had made to give to Rochester to hand on to Captain Wilkes. Then he swiftly shifted into his cleanest dungarees, wound up his hair into a knot on the top of his head, stabbed it with a quill to keep it in place, put the folded and addressed report to the sheriff in his pocket, went up on deck, and nodded curtly to Forsythe.

Forsythe had changed into the kind of uniform Wiki had been accustomed to seeing George Rochester wearing on formal occasions—lieutenant's blue claw-hammer coat, gold buttons and lace, proud epaulette on the right shoulder, lieutenant's fore-and-aft hat. Obviously, Wiki meditated dryly, Forsythe was going to board the whaler in the full gold lace and glory of a commanding officer of the U.S. Navy, in order to exact revenge for the run the old spouter had given him.

Ominously, the southerner's expression was more complacent than ever. However, he simply called out, "Prepare to lower," and stepped into the boat as it swung in the davits, standing easily in the middle as the two hands who were already there worked the falls to make sure it touched the water evenly. Wiki waited until it had settled, and then jumped down, along with the rest of Forsythe's boat's crew.

The sun was high in the sky, turning the chunky hull of the whaleship into dense black shadow as they approached, and pointing up the tops of the masts so that they shone orange in the warm light. She was a well-kept ship, Wiki observed—he could see figures at work in the rigging, taking advantage of the pause in the onward rush of passage to take down a sail and bend on a new one. Seabirds fluttered and swooped about the broad stern, quarreling over the widening patch in the sea where a man in a white jacket had emptied a pail of garbage. As the boat pulled close, they rose in a screaming flock, and the sun on their wings made them look like flying bits of paper.

Like many Yankee whalers, this ship had a hurricane house built over the stern; and Wiki, craning his neck to look upward, could glimpse the man at the helm in its sheltering shadow. As they came around the starboard quarter he saw a stumpy figure standing foursquare and brace legged on the roof of this house—the captain, without a doubt, and probably in a fuming mood as well. As they neared, he came to the rail-less edge, and glowered down at them with his thumbs hooked in his braces.

Forsythe bid the crew to still the boat by stirring with their oars, lifted his voice, and shouted, "Ship ahoy!"

The spouter skipper shifted aggressively from one boot to the other, but though the answer was grudging, it was clear. "*Mandarin* of Nantucket, Captain Israel Starbuck, three thousand eight hundred barrels of sperm, last port Lahaina, bound home."

Wiki was impressed, thinking that three thousand-eight hundred was a cargo old Starbuck must have enjoyed reporting, because it meant that he had done very well with a ship of this size. On the New Bedford market, he could probably rely on a gross return of more than one hundred thousand dollars. That their last port was Lahaina, Maui, was less surprising. While the Bay of Islands, New Zealand, was the most common choice for whaling masters who wanted to reprovision their ships for the homeward passage, the ports of the Sandwich Islands were becoming more popular.

Forsythe introduced himself, his ship, and his mission in equally formal style. Old Starbuck did not bother even to pretend to be politely interested and refused to be impressed by the uniform. Instead, he snapped irately, "I'd like to know what gives the navy the goddamn right to chase a peaceful merchantman about his ordinary work, and bring him to with a shot across his bows."

"Permission to come aboard?" said Forsythe blandly.

"And what happens if I say no, sir? You blow me out of the goddamned water?"

However, Captain Starbuck stepped back, disappearing from view in a tacit invitation to come on board. The boat pulled around to the gangway where there were falls awaiting, and the man in the bow hooked on. Then Forsythe reached up, grabbed a rope, and clambered up the side, jerking his head for Wiki to follow.

When he arrived on deck, Wiki looked about curiously. The deck planks were weatherworn, and scarred and chipped with much chopping of blubber, but they shone white with much meticulous scrubbing. The double-ended, graceful whaleboats had been freshly painted before they were chocked up tight to the sides of the ship, and the masts and yards were equally neat, varnished and slushed, with the tips of the yards painted white. But that, he meditated, was typical of old Israel Starbuck, a captain he remembered as being house-proud—a thorough, outstanding, farthest-limit skipper, who was determined to have the cleanest, most grime-free establishment on the whole wide ocean. In fact, gossip had had it that when his ships were refitting he spent twenty hours of every day on board, just to make sure that there were no slackers in the gangs. Wiki had even been told that he ran his home in the same shipshape fashion, demanding that his domestic help should turn out just like his watch at sea. If his wife despaired because the cook became mutinous and all the maids deserted, old Starbuck paid no notice because it was just part of his usual disciplinary warfare.

Now, on board the *Mandarin,* the only neglect was the tryworks furnace with its blackened bricks where the whale oil had been rendered from chunks of blubber, but Wiki knew that shortly the great cauldrons would be taken out, scrubbed until the metal shone, and then set aside, after which the tryworks would be torn down and the bricks hove overboard, in one of the rituals peculiar to American whalers, in celebration of nearing home. Meantime, there were men busily at work all about the decks and the rigging. Wiki recognized a few, and lifted his eyebrows and nodded. Then, he turned to study Captain Starbuck—and found the old skipper studying him right back, his bristling eyebrows hoisted high and a riveted expression on his deeply weathered face.

"Well, well, well," the old fellow exclaimed. He had an air of suddenly enjoying the situation much better than he had expected. "Strike me blind if it ain't Wiki Coffin, the same damn rogue who absconded from this ship in Callao."

Twenty-two

Though the smell of old whale oil rose to meet him as he descended the steep stairway, and the room itself was gloomy, the saloon of the *Mandarin* was as scrubbed and neat as Wiki remembered. A red-and-pink cloth covered the table; and the bottom of the mizzen mast, which protruded through the forward end of the saloon, was encased in highly polished wood. Out of sheer habit, Wiki seated himself on the starboard bench, in the same place where he'd eaten his meals for five reasonably pleasant months.

"Best seaman I ever shipped, without a lie," Starbuck informed Forsythe, meantime dispensing brandy with a lavish hand. The discovery that one of his old hands—albeit a confounded deserter—had come to call had mended his temper considerably. "Picked him up on the beach at Pitcairn," he recalled.

"What ship did you jump from there, huh?" he inquired of Wiki. "I did hear tell that Jed Luce of the *Concerto* was putting the word around the ports that he wanted to talk to Wiki Coffin real bad."

With a broad wink, he placed a full tumbler in front of Forsythe and another in front of Wiki, and then set himself down at the head of the table with a great creaking of the chair. Forsythe, without bothering with any kind of salutation, disposed of half the contents at once, and smacked his lips appreciatively. Wiki nodded thanks, but let his drink alone.

"Gave you second mate's berth; would've made you first officer if anythin' had happened to Tobey," said Starbuck, slapping down his own glass after absorbing a hearty slurp. "What did you want to go and jump ship in Callao for, huh? Not that he stole nothin' from the ship," he reassured Forsythe, who was watching Wiki very thoughtfully. "Dived overboard at midnight just like a goddamned Kanaka, and swam off to shore. What the devil did you want to go and do it for?" he demanded of Wiki.

Wiki smiled, lifting his brows in recollection. He had indeed stolen something—one of the cooper's small tubs, which he had filled with his clothes and a few prized possessions, and floated to the beach. However, he chose not to reveal this, shrugging vaguely instead.

"Didn't I treat you good, young man?"

"You did," allowed Wiki. Starbuck had a fist like a rock and could be merciless with boneheaded greenhands; but if a man worked well and willingly, he got good treatment in return.

"So why did you jump, huh?"

"Because of a girl?" Wiki hazarded. "Or maybe because you were headed for the Callao sperm whale ground?" He had jumped so many ships, it was hard to sort them out.

"That could be so," the old salt allowed.

Then that accounted for it, Wiki meditated. Usually his immediate reason for jumping a ship was because he had no ambition to reach the next destination. The prospect of bucketing about for months on the notoriously rough Callao ground, along with all the hunting, killing, and cutting up of sperm whales that it involved, had not been attractive in the slightest. The whaleships stayed on the ground as long as the season lasted, calling in at the uninhabited Galapagos Islands to collect huge tortoises that ambled the decks until killed for food, so there weren't even liberty times in port to leaven the monotony. Quite apart from all that, however, was the overriding fact that he just plain disliked the whaling business.

"But why South Americky?" Captain Starbuck demanded. "Did you think to make your fortune there? I've seen it happen before," he informed Forsythe. "First good look at South Americky, and any resourceful Yankee sees the natural possibilities, even a Kanaka Yankee like this one—he thinks what a little hard work and ingenuity could do, and off he goes to make his fortune. I've seen captains do that, as well as common seamen, but it all comes to the same in the end. Every single manjack loses his money and is forced to move on, sore enough for certain. Is that what happened to you?" he demanded, swiveling his stare to Wiki.

Wiki, who by sleight of hand had managed to exchange his full glass for Forsythe's empty one while Starbuck wasn't watching, shook his head. There had indeed been a girl, he remembered, but when he'd arrived on shore in Callao it was to find she had married since he'd called there last. Then he had heard that the ship where Rochester was serving was lying at anchor in Valparaiso, and so he had shipped for the run south as the third mate of a coaster. He'd found George Rochester on the bark of war

Acasta, and George, providentially, was at a loose end. The ship was refitting for the West Indies station, which involved a lot of waiting about and killing time. So they'd bought brown riding clothes and—after bargaining for two tough pinto horses with slit ears and the cartilage between the nostrils divided to give them better wind—had headed out into the hinterland plains, with nothing but their bedrolls, a small sack of big silver Chilean dollars, and their guns.

It had been one of their best adventures. During the long days on the southern plains, they had watched the wild horses play; and when the sun lowered, turning the sky to a luminous indigo, they had watched long lines of pink flamingoes rise from the lakes, their wings translucent in the golden light. After about a week, they had joined a roaming band of gauchos and had learned to hunt with bolas. About the campfire at night, they had sipped the aromatic tea called maté through hollow stalks from a common gourd that was handed around, and traded yarns of the sea for tales of the pampas. Then it had been time for George to return to his ship, so Wiki had kept him company as far as the port. There he had signed articles on a homebound California hide-and-tallow trader, and after a long and tedious passage he had arrived in Boston in time to get a message from his comrade suggesting the exploratory expedition.

So Wiki grinned reminiscently at Captain Starbuck as he said, "I didn't try anything in South America, save take a look at the scenery. And then I went home and made up my mind to explore the Pacific with the navy."

"But why the hell should you do anything like that? I thought you had more brains."

"He didn't join," remarked Forsythe. "He's a civilian."

"Ah," said the whaling master alertly.

"He ain't bound by navy articles."

"Aha!" said Starbuck, and swiveled around to stare at Wiki. "I can't offer you more than fourth mate's berth right now, the whaling being over," he said swiftly, "but I'll ship you as first mate next voyage and be right glad to do it. What do you think of that plan, huh? Four months in New England to get acquainted with your folks again—on account of I heard that your father be back in Salem—and then it's the Pacific for you and me."

Wiki said, "But—" and stopped, as a shout echoed down from the deck.

Without a word Forsythe drained the brandy glass and went up the stairs to investigate.

When Wiki started to rise from his seat to follow, Captain Starbuck detained him by barking, "Why not?"

"I signed on as the expedition's linguister—to translate Spanish, and the various Pacific languages—so I'm committed, even if I haven't signed articles. And," Wiki went on, fishing the package for the sheriff out of his pocket, "I have a job to do—an investigation, which means I have a favor to ask."

"Favor?" Starbuck echoed blankly.

"Aye. It would be a considerable help if you would get this on the way to Portsmouth, Virginia, as soon as possible after you make home."

Starbuck took the packet and turned it over in his huge gnarled hands, scowling down at the address. Then he looked up and said aggressively, "What's all this about, young man? Just what the devil have you been up to?"

"There was a murder in Virginia before the expedition sailed, and the sheriff strongly suspected that the man behind it was with the fleet, and so—" Wiki paused and then said wryly— "he appointed me a kind of sheriff's representative with the expedition—a deputy, if you like—with instructions to keep on with the investigation."

"You?" said Captain Starbuck, and guffawed, as derisive as Rochester had been. But he was greatly interested as well, Wiki saw. The old man enjoyed mysteries, he remembered. Starbuck carried more than a hundred history books with him on voyage; he had willingly allowed Wiki to read them, and then had discussed the puzzles of the past with enormous animation, his mind tugging at old conundrums like a thrush at a snail.

So Wiki told him all about it, starting with the discovery of the body and going on to the theory that someone had posed as Stanton in order to get into the plantation house. Having piqued the old skipper's curiosity, Wiki was not allowed to stop there, and so he went on to describe the discovery of Burroughs's broken-necked body and the seemingly insoluble mystery of the note.

It flowed remarkably easily. Back when he was second mate of the *Mandarin*, he and Captain Starbuck had paced the deck together during many a night watch, the Nantucketer being an incorrigible and entertaining spinner of yarns. The recounting took not a few minutes, but Captain Starbuck listened with deep attention throughout.

"Well, it sure do look to me as if the woman's husband is the prime choice for the feller who put the body in the boat and then tried to sink it with those shots," he observed at the end, "especially as the servants were so positive they saw him."

"It's physically impossible. Many men have testified that he was at Newport News at the time."

"Unless a powerful lot of fellers were makin' a big mistake, there's no getting around that, that's for sure," Starbuck agreed. Then he said, "What about this Burroughs feller? You reckon he was the one who posed as Stanton to get into the house and take Mrs. Stanton away—maybe because he was bribed?"

"When he committed suicide, it seemed to bear it out. Everyone who knew him has said how proud he was of his reputation. He put his head in a noose because he was on the verge of being exposed—or so I thought, for a while."

Starbuck was looking at Wiki very alertly indeed, his little eyes bright and shrewd. "But you don't believe that anymore?"

"In my report to the sheriff," said Wiki, nodding at the packet in Starbuck's hand, "I've told him how strongly I doubt it. Everyone who knew him seems to think he was too contented with life to end it all. He even wrote a note telling the world how happy he was."

"A letter?"

"A poem. An ode to happiness."

Starbuck snorted, for a moment sounding like Forsythe, but then said abruptly, "It sounds to me like someone knocked him on the head, broke his neck, and strung him up to look like he put an end to hisself. What do you reckon about that idea, huh?"

"It fits," said Wiki, and nodded emphatically. "Quite apart from the poem, the ceiling simply wasn't high enough for the drop to break his neck when he kicked over the chair. If it *was* suicide, it's much more likely he would have strangled to death—and not very quickly, either."

"So who do you reckon snapped his neck?"

"The obvious candidate is Tristram Stanton. When George Rochester arrived at Burroughs's door, Tristram Stanton was hammering on it, on the verge of breaking in—but George had been with Wilkes quite a while before that. Stanton had plenty of time to kill Burroughs, fashion that noose and string him up, and then get outside the door to put on a show of having to break it down."

"The door was locked?"

"The key was never found. Astronomer Stanton reckoned that Burroughs threw it out the sidelight."

"And no one searched Stanton's pockets?"

"Of course not."

"H'm!" Starbuck grunted. "It does seem logical that he would've wanted him out of the way. This Burroughs fellow knew too much by far."

"Aye," said Wiki. That had been another of the suggestions he'd made in the sheriff's report. The hard part, he mused, was proving it.

"And this unreliable man, Powell—what do you reckon about him and the note he told you he delivered to Forsythe?"

"He tells so many lies it's impossible to know when he's telling the truth," Wiki said, letting his frustration show. "And now he's disappeared. His messmates reckon he lost the number of his mess—which means *'dead'* in navy language."

"What?" said Starbuck, looking more alert than ever. "You mean to say that he's been murdered, too?"

Wiki remembered the fleeting look of terror that he had glimpsed in Powell's bloodshot eyes and nodded grimly. "Though there is the chance he went overboard in the last big storm," he amended. "At least, that's what his messmates think."

"H'm," Starbuck grunted, and then said abruptly, "This was on the *Vincennes?*"

"Aye."

"And what's the complement?"

"About two hundred men, all told."

"And no one would've noticed him going over? That's a bit hard to believe."

The whaling master was right. Wiki remembered the panic as the boatswain of the *Swallow* had floated out of reach on the tossing waves, and the way the men had watched the sea as if mesmerized, as the immense billows rolled in from the night. Even though the brig—one-eighth the size of the *Vincennes*— had just seventeen men on board, it was impossible to believe that someone could have fallen overboard unnoticed.

"Nope," said Starbuck roundly, "he's been put out of the way." He pursed his lips judiciously and said, "Even then, there's the problem of his corpse. It ain't that easy to get rid of a body at sea, you know, accidentally or otherwise. Lubbers might think that a body could be slipped overboard while no one was watching, but you and I know that bodies float. Three voyages back," he said reminiscently, "a couple of my Portugee greenhands got into a fight, and one knifed the other and tipped him over the rail. And do you know what? The body got caught on the rudder. We couldn't work out what was up with the ship, not until we looked over the taffrail and saw an arm poking up out of the water."

Wiki grimaced. "What did you do with the murderer?"

"Handed him in at Talcahuano. He was hanged, I do believe," Starbuck said carelessly, and then looking animated went on. "So where do you think the corpse might be stowed, huh? One would think it would have given away its presence by now," he ghoulishly observed. He picked up the brandy bottle and pointed it questioningly at Wiki's empty glass, bristling eyebrows lifted.

Wiki looked down at the table—saw Forsythe's empty tumbler, and abruptly realized that the southerner had never come back. "My God!" he exclaimed. "Where is he?"

"What? Who?"

"Forsythe!" Wiki swung his legs around, leapt off the bench, and sprang up the companionway—and arrived on deck just in time to see the brig *Swallow* putting on the last of her sails. Even as he watched, the topgallants snapped taut with wind.

"He's marooned you!" Starbuck exclaimed, arriving at Wiki's side. He looked as if he was on the verge of a highly entertained guffaw. "So I get you as fourth mate," he observed merrily.

"But I have to get back on board!"

"Why? Do you reckon he's the imposter?"

Wiki shook his head. For a long time he had indeed considered Forsythe a prime candidate, especially after Powell had claimed to have delivered the note to him. Since then, however, the southerner's own actions had convinced him that he'd told nothing but the truth.

"It was his idea to mail the report to the sheriff, along with his testimony," Wiki said, the hasty words spilling out. "He's not likely to do that unless he's innocent."

"So why is he so anxious to get quit of you?"

"Because he dislikes Kanakas, and he dislikes me interfering with his mistreatment of them."

"He don't like Kanakas? How odd!" exclaimed Captain Starbuck, who—as Wiki knew well—didn't care if a man was brown, black, white, or brindle, just so long as he had sharp eyes and broad shoulders. "Well, then," he said briskly, "I most surely don't want to lose you; but seein' as you're determined, the least I can do is get you there, it being my own fault for holding you up." And he spun on his heel, shouting, "Clear away the starboard boat!"

Men dashed up to the roof of the hurricane house and released the cranes that supported the bottom of the boat, so that it was swinging loose from the davits. Two of them jumped into it, and then swiftly worked the falls so that it lowered with a single splash. Three more scrambled down the side of the ship, Wiki with them. Then, as he braced himself to jump, he found that Captain Starbuck was close behind.

"Are you sure?" he said.

"Wouldn't miss it for the world," replied the old salt with a savage grin and gripped the steering oar.

Three minutes had elapsed. The *Swallow* was still just a couple of ship lengths off, but gathering speed fast as she headed downwind.

"Take oars," snapped Captain Starbuck. The five oarsmen picked up the rhythm at once, bracing their legs and feet, and hauling mightily.

"Step mast." The wind gusted, whipping Wiki's hair out of its knot and lashing it about his face, so his eyes streamed as he manhandled the long mast into the step and locked it in place with a fid. The sail snapped and then roared full, and the whaleboat lifted and danced across the waves.

Starbuck's steering oar dug deep, bending like a newly cut willow as he brought them around to the curling edge of the fleeting wake of the brig, so that the seethe of the water was in their favor. "Spring to it, boys!" The boat surged strongly with the double force of muscle power and the sail.

Then Wiki felt the wind drop. The boat sail fluttered and sagged. As the canvas slapped and flopped, he glimpsed the same tremble in the *Swallow*'s sails. "Pull!" cried Captain Starbuck—and they were catching up as the brig lost way, running by momentum alone in the sudden calm. Pull by pull the boat was drawing closer—close enough for Wiki to discern two figures on the quarterdeck, one much shorter than the other, and doing a lot of gesticulating. Lieutenant Smith arguing strenuously with Forsythe, he thought, and tautly grinned.

Then the wind flicked up. The *Swallow* fled on. She had lost much of her lead, though—and now they were gaining still more, slowly but surely, with the extra power of the oars. Suddenly, they were level with the taffrail. It was time to take down the mast, as the hull of the brig stole their wind. Still the long oars dipped and swung, bringing them farther along the *Swallow*'s starboard side. Standing in the back of the boat, leaning powerfully on his steering oar, Captain Starbuck kept them just outside the hollow of green water that rushed and swirled along the *Swallow*'s hull. Then, as he rapped out orders, they ventured closer.

The whaleboat began to dip and sway sickeningly with the conflicting forces in the inner edge of the wash—one unwise bump, and the light cedar planks would be stove. Wiki stood up, balancing precariously. A rope banged and scraped as it dropped over the rail. Looking up, he saw Sua's broad brown face, his huge fists gripping the rope, ready to haul him on board. Wiki reached out, grabbed, and missed. The boat swept outward, and he seized his balance by bracing his palm on the nearest oarsman's hat.

Then he was standing steady again. Starbuck snapped, "Pull three, stern two!" The boat spun round in a tight curve, arriving close alongside again—and the *Swallow* was losing way at long last, as some sense prevailed on the quarterdeck and clew lines were released. Wiki waited, gauging the moment, then launched himself into space. His wildly flailing fist hit the rope and gripped, the other came up above it in an equally tight grasp, and he was being drawn upward. He kicked powerfully at the planks as he rose, and then Sua heaved him over the gangway, and he was standing on the deck.

"*E hoa,*" he said to the Samoan and clapped him on the shoulder. Then Wiki looked over the side at Starbuck and his men and formally saluted them. After that, deliberately, he turned and headed aft, where Forsythe was waiting at the break of the quarterdeck, his arms folded, his expression aggressive.

"Bastard," said Wiki, but did not feel as if he really meant it. The exhilaration of the chase was still buzzing through his veins, and all about the decks men were cheering—cheers that were echoed by hails of triumph from the whaleboat.

At that perfect moment there came a great cry from the lookout, "Ship ahoy!" The *Vincennes* had found them, drawn by the sound of the shot they had fired across Captain Starbuck's bows. As the brig changed course to meet her, they could see she was now tagged by three ships—the *Porpoise*, the *Flying Fish*, and the *Sea Gull*. The second schooner had joined the fleet and only the *Peacock* was missing.

Twenty-three

*I*t was truly wonderful," Lieutenant Smith enthused, "to see what a difference the firing of a cannon can make! No sooner had the echoes faded than this personification of Yankee republicanism backed his fore and mizzen , topsails and graciously permitted us to speak his ship."

It was late Saturday afternoon, and Captain Wilkes's feast was in full and rowdy progress. When George Rochester had come along the main deck on his way to the afterhouse, the scene had been wonderfully tranquil, the other ships of the expedition fleet lying aback like gulls sitting on their own reflections. Because the weather was so mild, the sailors had taken their supper on deck, and were now quietly preparing for the dogwatch. In the big saloon of the *Vincennes*, by contrast, it was noisy in the extreme, in a jolly celebration of good food, good wine, and much gossip. The *Peacock* might still be among the missing, but the return of both the *Sea Gull* and the *Swallow* was something to celebrate, and so Captain Wilkes had turned out to be an unexpectedly jovial host.

Lieutenant Smith, his red face shiny with delight that he had been able to keep the appointment and attend the party, was the life and soul of the table. His account of the prowess of the *Swallow* was racy and exciting, drawing grunts and comments of appreciation, along with much laughter at the besting of the independent old blubber hunter. As George meditated with some amusement, many of the men sitting about the big table might not even be aware that it was actually Forsythe who had command of the brig. Throughout Smith's account the overriding impression he gave was that the brig had sailed like a bird simply because he, Lieutenant Smith, had been in charge of the quarterdeck, and that it had been his idea to force the whaleman to back his headsails—by firing a shot across his bows, for God's sake! That, George could believe of Forsythe, whom he did not consider quite sane; but he thought he knew Smith well enough to predict that the only part he would ever play in anything so rash was to make a verbose and nervous fuss. However, not only was the chubby lieutenant telling it as if he had been totally in charge, but Wilkes appeared to believe him, smiling with obvious enjoyment as he listened.

George took no part in the conversation himself. Just as at the banquet at Newport News, he had been placed well below the salt, right at the bottom of the table, with a junior midshipman on either side of him. Both these young men were poor company, being so overwhelmed by the honor of being there that they were distinctly tongue-tied, and making up for their silence by drinking rather a lot of wine. Fourteen assorted scientifics and officers sat seven to each side. At the far end, Captain Wilkes presided, with the highly exhilarated Lieutenant Smith on his right, and Astronomer Stanton on his left. All three gave every appearance of enjoying themselves in famous fashion, thought George, though it was Smith who was dominating the conversation, while Stanton was focused on the decanter.

"And no sooner had we boarded the smelly old spouter," Lieutenant Smith cried, "than the skipper—Israel Starbuck was the fellow's name—calculated to kidnap young Wiremu, on account of the fact that the lad had jumped from his ship in Callao!"

Wilkes frowned. "He kidnapped one of our men?"

"The old rogue sent back our boat without our linguister!"

"You call him Wiremu?" Captain Wilkes queried, looking baffled.

The answer was lost in the hubbub as men called out in amazement at the sheer sauce of the Nantucketer, but George had heard enough to guess what had happened. *Ye gods*, it was Starbuck of the *Mandarin!* Wiki must have been uncommon' embarrassed to find himself on a ship he'd quit without the proper good-byes; and George could imagine, too, that Starbuck would have been glad to recapture him because he was such an outstanding seaman. But to kidnap him against his will! Was Wiki lost to the expedition—was he homeward bound on a whaling ship? The thought was horribly depressing.

Then George was sidetracked by one of the junior midshipman—the fellow named Keith who had been so helpful with the cannonry routine. Midshipman Keith was nudging him with an elbow and jerking his chin at Lieutenant Smith. George blinked, and then saw that Smith, having finished his yarn, was endeavoring to get his attention. He had a packet in his hand, which he was waving. Seemingly, he had something to give him, once the feast was over. Well, Rochester meditated, that would be a while. The feast had only really got going, and would probably go on for hours longer.

It was all rather a lot like the banquet at Newport News. Keith, having got up his courage with his fourth glass of wine, was roaring some midshipmanlike joke in his ear, but George, who was surreptitiously studying Astronomer Stanton's burly form at the far end of the table, paid him scant attention. He'd almost forgotten how ape-like the scientific looked—the small, deep-set, glittering eyes, the meaty forehead mostly hidden by a flop of dark hair, and the round ears that protruded from the bushy sideburns.

Seeing him now brought a strong and unpleasant reminder of the astronomer's unfriendly presence during those days of passage on the *Swallow*—but, George mused in some perplexity, it did not remind him quite so much of the banquet at Newport News. Instead, there was a nagging sense of something different about Tristram Stanton's appearance now from the way he had looked back then.

Again, George was distracted. Midshipman Keith had commenced an earnest discussion of the relative merits of nine-pounder cannon and twenty-four-pounder carronades, and the bottom half of the table had become rowdier than ever, as the argument was swiftly and energetically pursued. George did not have much in the way of comment to offer, but that didn't matter. Despite his youth, Keith was the old-fashioned sort who liked his roar and thunder, and so the cannon were his preference, and the bigger the better—an opinion that was hotly challenged, most of the officers being vociferous in their defense of carronades.

"Smashers are safer!" someone declared. *Smasher,* as George Rochester knew very well, was common cant for the carronade, a much lighter, shorter gun than a Long Tom of the same caliber, mounted on slides instead of wheels, and throwing an enormous ball for its weight.

"Much less unwieldy," another man agreed. "And not so likely to run amuck."

"More economical, too," a passed midshipman pointed out, and then, with a superior air, reminded the junior mids that the gunpowder required to charge a carronade was only one-twelfth the weight of its ball, as opposed to the Long Tom's one-third.

"And much faster to reload!" cried a lieutenant, going on to elucidate that a carronade saved the crew an uncommon lot of hauling on the train tackle, being short enough to be reloaded at the end of the recoil.

"But it's a short-range weapon!" Keith argued. "You have to admit that you can't beat a Long Tom for putting the fear of God into the enemy at a distance!"

"Aye," said a junior lieutenant, who was nodding energetically in agreement. "You most surely can't use a carronade to put a ball through the enemy at the range of half a mile."

"Or to fire a shot across his bows, either," quipped somebody else, and the whole bottom of the table burst into a roar of laughter, accompanied with pounding of fists and the quaffing of much wine. Lieutenant Smith had heard it, it seemed, because he gave a jocular salute with his glass, and Captain Wilkes's perpetual smile widened, on the verge of a grin.

This was followed by a babel of debate, to which Rochester still made little contribution. While he listened distractedly to the two junior mids, he was shooting puzzled little glances at the head of the table, still trying to pin down what was different about Tristram Stanton's appearance. He wondered if there was anyone at this table who had also been at the feast at Newport News, so he could compare notes, but then belatedly remembered that all the other guests had come from the *Relief* and the *Peacock*, and, of course, neither of those ships was with the expedition right now.

When he returned his puzzled gaze to Stanton's heavy, hair-framed face, it was with a little jolt in his stomach, because it was to find that the astronomer was staring at him. The eye contact was very brief because Rochester quickly looked away. Pretending that his scrutiny of Stanton had been very casual, he put on a show of being deeply involved in conversation with Midshipman Keith—but still he wondered about the difference. Was it that Tristram Stanton had been the life and soul of the party in Newport News—as if he had had something to celebrate, George remembered—while this time it was Lieutenant Smith who dominated the head of the table? Perhaps, he thought, but the contrast in mood did not quite explain the nagging doubt in his mind.

Then, all at once, he had it. George almost laughed aloud, because it was such a minor detail, and yet explained so much. It was the way Tristram Stanton dressed his hair! At the banquet, Stanton's hair had been sleeked back with some kind of oil. George remembered how it had reflected the light of the candles, gleaming as Stanton had enthralled the gathering with his account of the trials and tribulations of Thomas ap Catesby Jones in the early days of planning the expedition. Today, Stanton's hair dangled thickly over his forehead and reflected no light at all. George felt almost silly that it had bothered him so much when it had come down to something so trivial as the way a man dressed his hair.

Telling himself not to be such an overimaginative fool in future, he lent a much more attentive ear to young Keith, whose conversation had moved, coincidentally, from the armament of the flagship to the man who had ordered, not only that the guns should be reduced in number, but that most of the cannon should be replaced with carronades—Thomas ap Catesby Jones himself, who, according to Midshipman Keith, had been very badly advised when he managed the armament of the expedition. It was a great tragedy to him that of all the wonderful, weighty, twenty-four-pounder Long Toms the *Vincennes* had originally boasted—twenty-two of the marvelous brutes!—only two remained, the rest having been taken away to be replaced with eight—just eight!—of the despised carronades. And the rifles supplied to the company were old, old, old—manufactured in 1819!

Again, the argument was taken up with a will. Midshipman Keith, having strong feelings on the subject, was prepared to expound on them for as long as people would listen, obviously—and the bottom half of the table was as enthusiastically engaged as ever, Rochester noted. Instead of taking part, Wilkes and his two cronies at the top of the table were sharing a joke, judging by Lieutenant Smith's loud laughter. As Rochester watched, Tristram Stanton drank deeply from his wineglass and replenished it from the decanter.

"But the Hall breechloader was an excellent choice!" a lieutenant four places up the table was declaring. "The Hall was the first rifle made with guaranteed uniformity, with interchangeable parts. It's no wonder at all that the navy chose it as the standard military weapon, and only natural that the expedition should be armed with it, too."

"But surely vintage weapons are not appropriate for a modern expeditionary force?" exclaimed Midshipman Keith, who evidently harbored images of the exploring ships being stormed by squads of rabid cannibals. "The savages of the Pacific are well armed with muskets—provided as trade by the mariners of our own country! Whaling masters distribute arms freely in exchange for provisions and water!"

This, George saw, had caught Captain Wilkes's attention, because he put a hand on Lieutenant Smith's arm to silence him so he could listen. And rightly so, George thought—this was a topic of importance to the expedition.

"Well, naturally it would be better if the natives accepted tobacco or trinkets—or grog—instead," a geologist's assistant was commenting. "But they insist on guns, so the American mariner has little choice—unless he's blind and foolish enough to seize the provisions by force and steal the water. And that would auger ill for the next American who drops anchor in that place."

"Granted," said someone else, judiciously. "But the midshipman is right. For whatever reason, the savages we'll be dealing with are armed, and so we should be prepared for attack."

"But they are armed with muskets, not rifles, remember," the surgeon of the *Flying Fish* objected. Evidently, thought George, he was a sportsman who knew his guns. "And that makes a great deal of difference, I think."

"Indeed it does," the knowledgeable lieutenant assured him. "A Hall rifle will outdistance even the best musket—and the savages of the Pacific don't have those, believe me. The American spouter skippers buy their trade muskets in New York by the hundred, at the rate of four dollars each! But quite apart from that, even if their muskets did happen to be prime quality, and were wielded by great marksmen, the Hall carbines will drop them on the beach before any of our men were in musket range. That, sir, is how the Revolutionary War was won—with snipers armed with rifles, who picked off Loyalist officers even though they were surrounded by battalions of soldiers with muskets. It was partly due to the fact that the Revolutionary leaders refused to let their troops march like automatons to meet enemy fire, but mostly because of the rifle's longer reach."

"So Commodore Jones chose well, you say?" queried Midshipman Keith.

"Assuredly he did."

"Then three cheers for Commodore Jones!" the midshipman cried, and other midshipmen, as drunk or drunker than he was, joined in the chorus of hip-hip-hip-hurrahs.

Captain Wilkes was shaking his head, not looking at all impressed. Rochester remembered that Wilkes had been an unpopular replacement for the flamboyant Thomas ap Catesby Jones. Lieutenant Smith had his mouth a little open, as if he hadn't quite caught up with the conversation. It was Tristram Stanton who startled them all by thrusting his fist in the air and shouting out, "I have not yet *begun* to fight!"

Then he looked around, as if he expected people to laugh. Instead, there was an awkward little silence. Someone coughed. Then the babel started up again in a hurried kind of way, as Wilkes's guests politely pretended that the tremendous gaffe had not been committed. Tristram Stanton was staring around the table, his jocular expression puzzled at first, and then turning to stone as Lieutenant Smith whispered something in his ear. Slowly, he looked at George Rochester.

George stared back numbly, unable to drag his gaze away. A sick, cold knot had taken hold of his stomach. It was a long moment before he became aware that Midshipman Keith was asking something. He turned his head stiffly, and said, "I beg your—"

"Are you feeling quite fine, sir? You've gone dead white."

Rochester said numbly, without even knowing what he was saying, "It's not the same man."

"Aye, sir, it is most remarkable, I agree, that anyone should confuse the great John Paul Jones with Thomas ap Catesby Jones; but, after all, Mr. Stanton is only an astronomer."

Rochester shook his head, saying to himself, "I must tell Wiki he's not the same man—" Then he abruptly remembered where he was, and stopped.

"Sir?"

"Nothing," said George very clearly. "Forgive me, I was rambling."

Regaining self-control had been an effort so huge it felt physical. Afterward he had no memory of getting through the rest of the feast, save that somehow he managed to make conversation and eat and drink like an unworried man. The urge to get up and leave was almost overpowering. If he hadn't been so doubtful that Wiki was still with the expedition, and if he hadn't been so anxious not to make himself conspicuous, he might not have been able to stop himself from standing up without a word of excuse and heading for the deck to find a boat to hurry him over to the *Swallow*.

At long, long last the final toast was given, and the last plate cleared away. Wilkes, thank God, did not include him in the invitation given out to a favored few to remain at the table for port, madeira, and nuts. "Sir," said Midshipman Keith, following closely as Rochester strode swiftly down the passage to the door that led to the night-swathed deck. "May I ask a question?"

Rochester said distractedly, "What?"

"I keep on wondering—about the man."

"What man?"

"The man—h'm!—who was not the same man. That is, if you were not talking about John Paul Jones." Keith, obviously, was regretting giving rein to his curiosity.

"I haven't the slightest notion what you're going on about—but I need a boat," George said curtly. "Can you get me a boat's crew?"

"Of course, sir." And Midshipman Keith ran off forward, probably glad to get away.

The others who had left the saloon had dispersed, and so Rochester stood alone in the shadow of the mainmast, sunk in churning thoughts. The deck was very quiet, the men who were on watch having taken their positions at lookout, and the others all below at rest. There was no moon, but the bright stars turned the black surface of the sea into shimmering satin. Above him, the sails bulked shapeless in the night.

He heard quick footsteps coming from behind. *Midshipman Keith*, Rochester thought, and turned quickly—not in time to evade the blow completely, but enough to avoid the full force of the cudgel on his head. Because of that, it did not kill him. Instead, the world swung sickly with the jolt of awful pain, and then he fell senseless to the planks.

Twenty-four

*I*n the morning, Lieutenant Smith had still not returned, with or without George Rochester. Wiki had been on deck since dawn, when the watch on the *Swallow* had been roused up to wash the decks. On the other ships the same routine was being followed, the echoes of whistles and shouts drifting over the expanse of glittering water where the small fleet was laying serenely aback. However, there was no sign of a boat putting out from the *Vincennes*. Wiki paced back and forth, feeling deeply worried. He had entrusted Lieutenant Smith with the copy of the report to the sheriff, asking him to give it to George Rochester to read, add any extra information that he might have gained in the meantime, and then hand on to Captain Wilkes at the first good opportunity. Now he wondered if his faith had been misplaced.

Below decks, the saloon was empty, so Wiki breakfasted alone. Forsythe had seized Smith's absence as an opportunity to get roaring drunk and was still sleeping off the binge. After drinking two mugs of the steward's excellent coffee Wiki went into his stateroom, shut the door, and sat on the edge of the berth in his thinking position, forearms on thighs, hands loosely linked between his knees, scowling down at his feet.

The more he thought about the flash of fear he had glimpsed in Jim Powell's eyes, the more sure he became that the seaman had been murdered. There was reason enough for it, particularly if that was not the first time Powell had let slip that he'd opened the note before he delivered it. So, Wiki wondered, if the crowd had not suddenly arrived in the doorway, what would Powell have said? Would he have confirmed what Tristram Stanton had told the sheriff—that it was a message to his wife that made it brutally clear that he was determined to sail? At the time the ultimatum had seemed to provide a plausible reason for suicide, so did the fact that Ophelia Stanton had *not* killed herself make his story less convincing?

It did seem an odd kind of message for a man to write in the middle of a banquet, Wiki mused now. Surely, if Stanton had been as exhilarated and ebullient as George had described, he would not have been in the mood to be so deliberately cruel. The astronomer had certainly scribbled something, though, so what else could it have been? Wiki abruptly thought that maybe Jim had still tried to let him know what he had read, but in a crafty fashion. While the sick-bay attendants had been carrying him away, the seaman had been drunkenly crooning a little song— *All's well, all's well*—which was the same as the last line of Burroughs's ode to happiness. Was Powell's burbling as drunken and meaningless as he had thought at the time, or could something be read into the coincidence?

Grimes had claimed he had found the poem discarded in some astronomical equipment. Presumably it had been dropped while Burroughs was working on his observations. Surely, Wiki mused, there was no connection between the poem and the message, and Powell had been merely maudlin with his grog—but still he hunkered down to haul out the boxes Stanton had left stacked beneath the berth when he'd moved over to the *Vincennes*. They were alongside his sea chest, but hadn't inconvenienced him, so Wiki had paid them scant attention before this. Now he heaved out the wooden cases with a growing sense of excitement, thinking that maybe, most ironically, the last clue to the mystery of Ophelia Stanton's murder had been stowed under his bed all the time.

But the boxes held nothing but racks of lenses, telescoping spyglasses, and other instruments. Obviously, Stanton had left them behind in reserve because they weren't currently needed. There were no papers at all, let alone anything significant. The disappointment bit unexpectedly keenly. Wiki kicked the boxes back into place, threw himself onto the berth, and stared at the back panel of the locker balefully.

The morning sun glinted on the scratches in the brass screws where someone had worked them loose in the recent past. Why? In order to replace the panel? Stanton had slept in this room while the *Swallow* was on passage to join the fleet, so there was a good chance he had broken the panel one night. Tristram Stanton was a big, heavy man, a couple of inches taller than Wiki himself, and so would have been even more irritated that the locker intruded so on the length of the berth. It was easy enough to imagine him giving the panel such a hefty kick that it needed replacing. On yet another impulse, Wiki got up, heaved the mattress aside, and set to work on the screws.

It didn't take long at all. Within a couple of minutes all the fastenings were free, and the panel was held only by its tight fit in the frame. Levering with his sheath knife, Wiki pried it loose, to reveal the backs of shelves that were piled deep with folded flags—and a long box that had been wedged into a space created by shoving the shelves a few inches forward. Wiki tested the weight of the case by lifting it a couple of inches, and then braced himself and heaved it out. Then he laid it down on the bottom boards of his berth.

The long box was locked but easily broken open. Wiki inserted his knife into the gap between the bottom and the lid and levered hard. With a loud crack and some splintering the lid swung open, to reveal a fully equipped gun case, expensively lined in velvet. A matched pair of fine rifles rested in padded grooves, along with all the usual appurtenances, such as powder horns, brass cappers, and so forth, all in their own special niches. For a long moment Wiki stood there staring, feeling numb, the hairs on his neck lifting and ruffling in a long shiver. Find the rifle and you find the killer, the sheriff had said with great confidence—and here on the brig *Swallow,* in the midst of the Atlantic, was the gun he sought.

Carefully Wiki picked up one of the rifles, running his hand over the beautifully crafted stock and then lifting it to his shoulder to squint down the smooth double barrel. The two were an exact pair, so Wiki had not a notion if he was holding the same gun the sheriff had so reverently hefted in Tristram Stanton's study or the one that had been hidden on the riverbank after the attempt to sink the boat. It made no difference. Without a doubt, these were Tristram Stanton's guns, and it was Tristram Stanton who had hidden them here.

Wiki heard a grunt and then a curse in the saloon as a chair was knocked over. Swiftly, he returned the rifle to the case. Then, without bothering to put things back the way they had been, he opened the stateroom door.

Forsythe, having picked up the chair, was slumped into it and had his hands wrapped round a mug of coffee. He looked, Wiki meditated, like the last three days of a misspent life. The eyes he briefly lifted were bloodshot and yellow, and he smelled vile too, of old sweat and a foul stomach.

Wiki sat down, reached out for the coffeepot and his mug, and said abruptly, "I have to get over to the *Vin*."

Forsythe grunted, "Well, you can't."

"Why not?"

"As you might've noticed, Mr. Deputy Coffin, we're a two-boat ship—as you *whalemen* call it—and one of the boats was taken off by Lieutenant Smith, who has not seen fit to return. I refuse to be left with no goddamn boat, so you can't go until he gets back."

Wiki thought that made a lot more sense than many of Forsythe's decisions. However, it seemed that the southerner was curious despite himself, because he demanded, "What the hell d'you want to go there for anyway?"

"I need to see George Rochester first and then Captain Wilkes."

Forsythe paused and then jibed, "And I don't suppose you're going to condescend to tell me why."

"I asked George to try and find out what Jim Powell got up to after he was taken to the sick bay."

"Why, for God's sake?"

"Because I believe he's dead."

"Because he lost the number of his mess?"

"Aye." Wiki lifted an eyebrow at the unexpected shrewdness.

"And you want to know how it happened."

"Exactly."

"And, no doubt," Forsythe said sarcastically, "you reckon he's been murdered."

Wiki kept his tone neutral. "No one has reported finding a corpse—not yet."

"Well, for once you can't blame me for whatever foul crime you're brewing up in that glob you call a mind. I haven't clapped eyes on the little bastard since you carried him down from the maintop."

Wiki didn't bother to hide the contempt in his silent stare.

"So who d'you reckon murdered him, then?"

Without even knowing he was going to say it, Wiki said, "Tristram Stanton."

And his instinctive answer was right, he suddenly realized, because of something that had been unconsciously nagging him all along—that, while it had been Forsythe's name Powell had given, it had been Tristram Stanton, not Forsythe, who had arrived in the doorway with the rest of the crowd. It was the sight of the astronomer that had triggered the flash of mortal fear in Powell's expression. Jim had swiftly changed the name he was on the verge of revealing, but for him it had been too late.

"Stanton killed Jim Powell?" Forsythe seemed more entertained than surprised. "Why the hell would he want to remove a lying little swab like Jim Powell from the face of the earth?"

Because he knew too much, thought Wiki, *and could not be relied upon to tell glib lies the whole of the time.* Also, Jim had boasted about reading the note—the note that Stanton had scribbled at the banquet table and supposedly sent to his wife.

Instead of answering, however, Wiki took a long swallow of coffee. Then he observed, "You were wrong about your cousin turning a deaf ear to your talk of divorce."

"And what makes you so sure of that?"

"As long as her husband was around, she had some reason to threaten to do away with herself. Once he had sailed away, talking suicide wasn't going to bring him back. She would've divorced him just for revenge, probably—not because it was the sensible option you recommended."

"The poor bitch was never sensible," Forsythe said moodily. He was staring down at his breakfast plate, which held congealed baked beans, untouched.

"Suicide would have suited the Stantons first rate, but they couldn't rely on it, and so killing her was the only safe way out. There was too big a chance she'd go to a magistrate and start proceedings after Tristram Stanton had sailed."

Forsythe lifted his head, his expression brooding. "Wa-al, if that was the motive for murdering her, it surely lets me off the hook—and puts Tristram Stanton fairsquare in the dock. So how do you reckon he did it?"

Wiki shook his head. "He was at Newport News, remember."

"So who did it, then?"

"The old man—Tristram Stanton's father."

"The old bastard?" Again, Forsythe betrayed no surprise.

"Aye. He was the one with both motive and opportunity—he and Ophelia dined alone together that night. Sometime during the meal he slipped opium into her food or drink—or possibly he foxed her that he was giving her some ordinary medicine; something like that. That was why she didn't make a fuss when someone came into her bedroom to take her body away. By eleven, she would have been deeply unconscious, on the verge of dying, probably. An empty pill bottle was tucked into her bosom to make it look like she'd done it herself, but it was the old man who poisoned her, I'm certain of it. The whole point of taking the body away and disposing of it in that elaborate fashion was to divert suspicion from him."

"Jesus," said Forsythe. He squinted his eyes in thought and then nodded. "Figures," he said. "And you put this in the report to the sheriff?"

"I did."

The southerner let out a grunt of mirth. "Sure would like to be a fly on the wall when he issues the warrant," he commented. "So what about the man who came to her bedroom?"

That was the crux of the matter. There were several good reasons to think that it had been Forsythe himself, Wiki mediated.

He said softly, "How did you pay your mess bill, Lieutenant?"

"It's *Captain* to you," Forsythe snapped without a pause. "And paying my mess bill had *nothin'* to do with Ophelia."

Then to Wiki's great surprise he barked with laughter, slapping his thigh and saying, "It's too good a joke not to share—it was Tristram Stanton himself who donated the necessary to pay off my accounts."

"*What?*"

"Not that he knew about it," Forsythe confessed, with a reminiscent grin.

"So what happened?"

"I was mindin' me own business on the wharf at Portsmouth when Astronomer Burroughs toddled along totin' a parcel. He had the confounded sauce to instruct me to deliver it to Stanton, and while I was learnin' him that lieutenants are not to be ordered around like common little swabs of junior mids, who should arrive but Tristram Stanton himself. I told him to take his own bloody parcel, and he told me to keep it. So I did."

"And there was money inside it?"

"Not to first appearances. It was a suit of clothes—a good suit, fine black broadcloth coat, white vest, shirt, stock, good black breeches. The best surprise, though, was what one of the pockets held—a draft for a thousand dollars, to be cashed by the bearer, and signed by Astronomer Burroughs himself."

Wiki was sitting very still, scarcely breathing. "Can you think of any reason Burroughs would borrow a suit of Stanton's clothes and be so extremely grateful for the loan?"

Forsythe shrugged heavy shoulders. "Beats me. As far as I knew, they was enemies, but they must've made up when I wasn't noticin'—and the two of them was about the same size. Did you know they were cousins? Burroughs was as rich as Croesus, but no one would never have noticed it, because the silly swab went around in rags. He must've borrowed 'em for some grand occasion—he still had his hair all slicked back with that head oil smart folks use. What d'you call it? Macassar? Mebbe you're right, and the thousand was a little present to thank Stanton for his kindliness—but it was a present that Tristram Stanton didn't know about and was sure appreciated by me. I had it cashed before the day was out, and so I sailed out of debt."

He reached for a ship's biscuit, which he dipped into the baked beans and then noisily crunched with his mouth open, all the time grinning at Wiki.

Wiki said carefully, "Was this before or after Ophelia was murdered?"

"It was a couple of hours after all the fuss and commotion when you salvaged the boat with her body inside. You never saw us, but we could see you—being hauled along the waterfront to the prison."

"And Stanton was on horseback?"

"Right again, clever Mr. Coffin. I guess he had come straight from where you landed the boat. He looked altogether as if he'd been ridin' bloody hard, and through mud and water, at that."

Mud and water. Wiki stared down at his mug, turning it between his palms, remembering how Tristram Stanton had looked when he had galloped out onto the riverbank to find a crowd gathered about his wife's corpse. He had been smartly and fashionably dressed but spattered with mud from top to toe, his knee-high boots badly water stained. Had he been wading through water, or had it all been thrown up by the horse's hooves?

Because he was hatless, Stanton's brown hair had flopped over his broad, meaty forehead and heavy eyebrows. It had certainly not been oiled, and yet when Stanton had arrived in his study that same afternoon, his hair had been greased and slicked back—why? Because when he had encountered Forsythe and Burroughs on the wharf, he had seen that Burroughs had dressed his hair that way, and he needed to keep up a deception?

Forsythe's harsh drawl jerked Wiki out of deep thought. "You want to see 'em?"

"What?"

"The suit of clothes."

Wiki exclaimed incredulously, "You've still got them?"

"Yup." The tone was complacent. Forsythe scraped back his chair and retreated to his cabin, coming back with a canvas kit bag, which he tossed onto the table. Out came claw-hammer coat, vest, trousers, white shirt, white silk stock, and black breeches. There was an oily stain on one fold of the stock, where it had rubbed against Burroughs's greased hair. Otherwise the clothes were clean, though very crumpled.

"It's no good going through the pockets," Forsythe said with a sardonic grin. "They've been well overhauled, I assure you."

Wiki was shaking his head in bemusement. "I can't believe you didn't get rid of them."

Forsythe flushed at his tone and snapped, "He's my size, and I ain't rich enough to be proud. After all, they were bought with *my* family's money."

Wiki said flatly, "You're a fool."

"*What?* Why, you half-breed bastard, what the hell gives you the right to talk to me like that?"

Forsythe slapped his fists down on the table, shoving himself headlong out of his chair; but Wiki, though he stood up, too, his eyes narrowed dangerously, merely put up a hand.

"Oh, it was probably a spur of the moment inspiration on Stanton's part," he said. "But it was an efficient trap, and there was a big chance it would have worked."

"What the hell are you talking about?"

Wiki said patiently, "The man who came to the house to collect Ophelia's body posed as Tristram Stanton—and got away with it because he was wearing those clothes."

Forsythe scowled this over, and then his eyes widened. "But it was John Burroughs who borrowed 'em!"

"Exactly."

"So you reckon John Burroughs was the man who went to the house to collect Ophelia's corpse, stow it in that rotten old boat, and then shove her off into the river?"

"Aye."

"Then you're the one who's a fool," Forsythe said flatly. "I don't believe for a bloody instant that Burroughs had the guts to do anythin' so daunting."

"Where sailing with the expedition was concerned, he was brave enough," Wiki pointed out. "He was prepared to pay his cousin money to put in a good word with Captain Wilkes. Instead, the Stantons asked him to collect Ophelia's body. And, to make it easier for him to get away with it, they gave him this set of clothes."

"So these clothes are proof of that? You're bloody jestin'!"

"I'm not," said Wiki. "It must have been a nasty moment when Burroughs tried to return the suit so publicly. Being a quick thinker, though, Tristram Stanton took the chance to plant the evidence on you. If he's ever accused, he'll simply suggest that your sea chest be searched. You'd have a very hard job explaining those clothes away."

"Is that so?" said Forsythe. He was staring at Wiki, his eyes very narrow. "He was plannin' to see me swing for Ophelia's murder, huh?"

"If necessary." Wiki paused, and said, "There's something else on board this ship that would incriminate you, too."

"Jesus lord," said Forsythe, and jerked out a grunt of disbelieving mirth. "So what the hell else have you got for me, Mr. Deputy Coffin?"

"Come and see." And Wiki led the way into his stateroom.

It was odd, he reflected, how much like the sheriff Forsythe looked as he lifted one of the rifles out of the box. There was the same air of professional admiration, though his expression held rank envy, too. "A Leman turn-barrel rifle," the southerner said, as if to himself. "I've heard of 'em but never seen one before."

"The sheriff called it a revolving rifle," said Wiki, watching him. "You fire one barrel, turn it, and then fire the other, so you can get off two shots in quick succession."

"Nice, very nice," said Forsythe, and set the rifle back in the case. Then he picked up its twin, and inspected it in the same judiciously appreciative manner. Peering down the barrel with one eye half shut, he said, "So what have these rifles to do with incriminatin' me?"

"One of them was used to shoot holes in the boat that was floating off with Ophelia's corpse."

"What—they shot her as well?" Forsythe exclaimed. He shook his head, his expression sour. "They sure was set on makin' her as dead as last week's mutton, huh? Poisoning was not enough, so they snapped her neck and shot her in the bargain."

"I didn't say she was shot," Wiki said. "And I think breaking her neck must have been an accident, because it turned out to be such a big problem. Stanton had organized the scene to make sure of a verdict of suicide—he probably even calculated the tides, so that the boat would be sighted before it sank. But when her neck was broken, it was obviously impossible to believe that she'd done it herself, which led to a lot of panic."

Forsythe grunted, thinking this over. Then he asked shrewdly, "Who panicked?"

"A maidservant testified that she saw Tristram Stanton running down the stairs about three in the morning, carrying one of these rifles. But it must have been Burroughs."

"So these guns are Tristram Stanton's." Forsythe's lips pursed in and out, but he did not seem unduly surprised.

Wiki said, "When I was at the Stanton house with the sheriff's party, we saw one of these guns on display in his study—just one. Tristram Stanton told the sheriff he had bought the pair to bring along on the expedition. The other one was missing. He left it to us to work out that it had been stolen."

"By Burroughs?"

"It must have been Burroughs," Wiki said, though there was an uncomfortable nagging in the back of his mind that something critical had been missed. "As I said, he panicked. The boat was floating out of reach, so he galloped to the house, grabbed one of those rifles, and then raced back to the riverbank, hoping to sink it with a couple of well-placed shots before anybody noticed. It was an act of desperation, and because I was there it didn't work."

Forsythe scowled, slowly taking this in. "So how did these guns get into this room?"

"Somehow, Stanton must have managed to retrieve the gun from wherever Burroughs had hidden it. It seems obvious that he sent the gun case on board with his astronomical equipment. Then, while we were on passage, he hid it. And it has been hidden here ever since." Wiki jerked his chin at the back of the signal locker.

Forsythe lapsed into silence, frowning this over. Then he shook his head again. "Men who knew him would find it bloody hard to believe that John Burroughs had that kind of guts."

Wiki opened his mouth, but no words came out, because the nagging thought had abruptly materialized. The top hat, he thought—the top hat that had been left on Tristram Stanton's desk. There had been no trace of hair oil on the inside of that hat.

Which meant that John Burroughs—who had dressed his hair with oil on the night of Ophelia Stanton's murder—could not possibly have worn it.

Twenty-five

A hail echoed down from the deck above, and then Wiki felt the bump as a boat hit against the starboard side of the brig. He spun on his heel and sprinted eagerly up the companionway. To his great disappointment, however, Lieutenant Smith was alone.

Wiki demanded, "Where's George Rochester? Did you give him the packet?"

"I don't know where he is, and no, I did not give him the packet," the tubby lieutenant said testily. "That's why we've taken so long. The whole ship is searching—we've lost him!"

Wiki's pulse started hammering with alarm. "What do you mean, you've lost him?"

"He vanished in the night. There's a general search, but we can't find him anywhere."

My God, thought Wiki. His thoughts were tumbling over each other with incipient panic. It was like a horrible echo of the disappearance of Jim Powell, only happening faster.

He looked over to where the flagship floated on the dead calm a half mile away and said tensely, "I have to get over to the *Vin*."

"Well, you can't."

"What?" Lieutenant Smith had sounded so disconcertingly like Forsythe that Wiki flinched.

"It's simply not possible, not right now," Smith pronounced.

"Why not?" Wiki demanded.

"Because they are beating the drum for quarters."

"I beg your pardon?"

"There is general upset and confusion over the disappearance of a man who is a popular officer and one of our own, and as it is a flat calm it was considered a live exercise of the cannon would boost the men's spirits in this time of distress."

Oh, dear Jehovah, Wiki thought as he stared with narrowed eyes at the distant flagship, they were playing games instead of keeping up the hunt. Was this the value Captain Wilkes placed on a man who was lauded as a popular officer?

He spun round and snapped at Smith, "Did you see him at *all?*"

"Of course I saw him," Smith said angrily, flushing at his tone. "I saw him at the feast."

"Then you must've talked to him, surely!"

"How could I?" Smith turned with a sniff, heading for the companionway. "He's just a passed midshipman, you know."

Wiki pursued him, anger making his movements jerky and fast. "And what the devil is that supposed to mean?" he demanded.

"That's no way to talk to me, young man. It means that I

was at the top of the table with Captain Wilkes and Astronomer Stanton, and he was right down at the bottom with the other midshipmen, where he belongs." Then Lawrence Smith added peevishly over his shoulder as he rattled down the stairs, "And an infamously noisy lot they were, too. Shouting, arguing, cheering—a disgraceful performance, truly."

They arrived at the bottom of the stairs. Wiki put a hand on the lieutenant's shoulder and spun him around, but still the choleric little eyes refused to meet his urgent stare. "What about after the feast was over?"

Shrugging Wiki's hand away, Lieutenant Smith went over to the table and rang the little bell he kept specially for summoning the steward. "As the midshipmen and junior lieutenants were leaving the table," he said loftily, "Captain Wilkes included me in the gracious invitation he extended to a select few of the officers and scientifics to stop behind for a few circuits of the decanter—and you couldn't possibly expect me to offend our commander with a rude refusal just on account of your friend! Then when it was over the hunt was up; and it was generally reported that Rochester was nowhere to be seen."

Wiki said softly and dangerously, "So you were drinking madeira with Captain Wilkes while George Rochester was in trouble. You didn't even try to give him the packet—and yet you had made your promise to me, as an officer and a gentleman."

Smith did not even bother to pay attention to his words, let alone take note of the tone. Instead, turning away from Wiki as the steward poked his head out of the pantry, he ordered a pot of fresh coffee and for his private box of cake to be produced. That communicated, he condescended to look at Wiki again, his eyebrows lifted.

"While I sincerely regret your friend's mysterious disappearance, Wiremu," he enunciated, his tone elaborately patient, "you must accept the plain and simple fact that I was unavoidably detained at the time."

"*My God,*" Wiki hissed. It took a physical effort to restrain himself from lifting his clenched fist. Then he registered a movement behind his shoulder.

Forsythe was standing in the doorway of Wiki's stateroom. He said nothing but surveyed Lieutenant Smith with his lips turned down, his expression sour. Beyond him, Wiki could see the gun case, still open, with both the rifles inside.

Wiki said to him in a rush, "George Rochester went missing in the night, and instead of organizing a decent search they're exercising the cannon."

"But there has been an intensive search already—and the exercise is more appropriate than you think," Lieutenant Smith protested before Forsythe had a chance to open his mouth. "It reflects the subject of debate at the feast last night. We thought it an excellent idea to demonstrate that our armament is amply sufficient for our purposes."

Wiki scowled. "Debate? What debate?"

"The midshipmen and junior lieutenants were discussing the disadvantages and merits of cannons compared with carronades. At the tops of their voices," Smith added with disapproval, and stopped to seat himself at the saloon table as the coffee and the cake box arrived. Then the steward was sent off again, for a napkin, a table knife, and a fork. As Wiki watched with rage and frustration boiling inside him, the lieutenant concentrated on cutting a generous portion of cake, which he slid onto his plate. Then he used the knife to slice the piece up precisely, before picking up a fork.

"You were saying?" said Wiki dangerously.

"The midshipmen became unduly heated on the topic of the armament of the flagship," Smith said, after delivering a reproving glance. "And, I am sorry to say, some of the scientifics joined in the general ruckus." He paused, pouring coffee. "Happily, however," he finally went on, his voice muffled by the napkin he was dabbing at his mouth to catch up stray crumbs, "the condemnation of the role played by Thomas ap Catesby Jones was universal."

Wiki was struggling to make sense of this. "Why Thomas ap Catesby Jones?"

"Because he was the one who concluded to reduce the armament of the flagship, of course! To the detriment of our safety if the savages should attack!" said Lieutenant Smith roundly; but then, flushing as he abruptly recollected that Wiki was one of the so-called savages, covered up his lapse by plying the napkin again.

"I must admit there was some general approval of his choice of personal weapons," he allowed, after this tactful pause was over. "Personally, I do think the Elgin cutlass-pistol is a first-class weapon in such circumstances, and there were several voices raised in defense of the Hall breech-loading rifles that have been issued to the expedition. Though seemingly outdated, they are perfectly suited to the job, according to the experts. And so, in the end, quite a cheer was raised by the midshipmen for Commodore ap Catesby Jones."

"They cheered for Captain Wilkes's predecessor?" Wiki dryly inquired, thinking that Wilkes would not have been very pleased.

Then he frowned, struck by a sudden thought. Stanton was one of Wilkes's cronies; and yet, at the Newport News banquet, he had been loud in his praise of Thomas ap Catesby Jones—or so Rochester had reported. In view of this, it did not seem like a diplomatic stance. In fact, it was distinctly odd.

Having chosen not to answer, Lieutenant Smith had poured more coffee and was sipping with enjoyment. Then he said, in a reminiscent kind of voice, "That round of cheers for Thomas ap Catesby Jones led to a somewhat farcical moment."

"It did?"

"Yes. When the cheering had stopped, Astronomer Stanton called out, 'I have not yet *begun* to fight!'—for a toast."

And Lieutenant Smith let out a merry little giggle, along with quite a few crumbs.

Wiki froze. Then he said softly, "Astronomer *Stanton* called out the rallying cry of John Paul Jones when the cheer was up for Thomas ap Catesby Jones?"

"I knew you would see the joke," Lieutenant Smith said, with an approving smile. "There was some little embarrassment at the time, but I am sure it will be remembered in the future with a laugh. After all, he is only an astronomer and can't be expected to know any better."

Wiki said carefully, "But I was under the impression that Astronomer Stanton was an admirer of Thomas ap Catesby Jones."

"Oh no," said Lieutenant Smith, "you are confusing him with Astronomer Burroughs, who, bless his departed but misguided soul, was a devoted admirer of Thomas ap Catesby Jones. In fact, it is a testament to Captain Wilkes's tolerance of other loyalties that Astronomer Burroughs was allowed a place with the expedition."

Wiki said numbly, "Oh, my God." It was suddenly so clear.

He swung round to Forsythe, who was still leaning in the doorway, and exclaimed, "I was wrong!"

Forsythe blinked. Then he grinned sardonically and inquired, "Which time?"

"I was wrong when I said that Burroughs posed as Stanton to get into the house and collect Ophelia's corpse! Instead, he posed as Stanton at the *banquet!*"

Forsythe's grin slipped, his mouth hanging loose, his face completely uncomprehending.

Wiki said urgently, "Rochester told me that Stanton was in high spirits at the banquet—as if he had something to celebrate, which Burroughs did! All he had to do was pass as Astronomer Stanton at Newport News, and he would get a place with the expedition. I'm sure he didn't know that it was to give Tristram Stanton an alibi. He probably did not even stop to ask why Stanton wanted him to do it, because the reward was so irresistible!"

Wiki's thoughts were flying on, faster than he could tumble out the words. "And that's why Jim Powell was sent to Newport News! *Stanton* sent him! Powell's orders were to bring back a note from Burroughs—to let Stanton know whether the deception was working or not!"

No doubt just a brief message was all Tristram Stanton wanted—but, because of his ebullient mood, Burroughs had waxed eloquent. "That," said Wiki with a perfect sense of rightness, "was when Astronomer Burroughs wrote that ode—the same ode that Grimes found discarded in a box of equipment."

"Wrote an ode?" interrupted Lieutenant Smith sharply. "What ode, pray?"

Wiki merely glanced at him, thinking that the poem had probably irritated Tristram Stanton extremely, because the last line—*All's well, all's well, all's well*—was all that he needed, and without the repetition at that. "All's well" was all the assurance

Stanton needed that Burroughs's masquerade was working—that he now had an alibi for the night.

"It was Tristram Stanton," Wiki reiterated softly, looking at Forsythe, "who took a horse, went to the house, took your cousin to the pool, and set up the scene to look like an elaborate suicide. Not John Burroughs, but Tristram Stanton himself!"

Forsythe's mouth drooped open, but then, to Wiki's intense relief, he saw a spark of understanding in the dull eyes. "*Stanton* was the bastard what carried off her corpse?"

"His father might have been the man who poisoned her, but Tristram Stanton was the man who set it all up and disposed of the body."

Forsythe pursed his lips but then nodded. "That works," he said. "I couldn't believe it of that soft swab Burroughs, but Stanton surely has the guts for somethin' so cold-blooded."

Lieutenant Smith burst in, "I don't know what this is about—but it sounds to me like the disorderly kind of slander that should never occur in navy ships, and I am forced to protest!"

Wiki ignored him, keeping his eyes fixed on Forsythe. "It also accounts for why Stanton's clothes were so muddy—and why his boots were wet. He had to wade into the pool to punt the boat off."

"So why did he snap her bloody neck, if his father had already poisoned her? Just to have a little fun with her corpse?"

Wiki shook his head, remembering the rush of superstitious horror that had engulfed him on the high bank of the stream as he had looked down at where Ophelia had been dumped in the boat—the preternatural knowledge of the violence that had been done there and the shocking abruptness of the release of the woman's spirit.

"I think she regained consciousness while he was getting her off the horse at the top of the cliff overlooking the pool. There was a struggle—or maybe she fell. I'm sure her neck wasn't broken on purpose because Tristram Stanton didn't take any notice of it until some time after the boat had floated away. Then, perhaps remembering the way her head had lolled, he realized what had happened, panicked, and galloped back to the house for his rifle."

"I am tired of this insolent determination to carry on a conversation without your having the common politeness to explain," Smith said petulantly.

This time Wiki spared him a glance. He shrugged and said, "The man at the banquet in Newport News was the wrong man, that's all."

"That's odd," remarked Smith, suddenly looking quite animated, as if this obscure and slanderous conversation had some meaning after all. "That's exactly what Midshipman Keith reported hearing Passed Midshipman Rochester saying just before he disappeared."

"What?"

"According to Mr. Keith, Passed Midshipman Rochester muttered to himself, 'I have to tell Wiki it was the wrong man'— or 'not the same man,' or something like that. Then he asked Keith to get a boat and boat's crew so he could hasten to the *Swallow;* but when Keith came back, he had vanished. Mr. Keith was the last man to see him," Smith concluded complacently, leaving the word "alive" unsaid but hanging in the air.

"Oh, my God," said Wiki softly. His pulse was hammering with a new sense of crisis. "George had realized that the man at Wilkes's feast was a different man from the one at the Newport News banquet—and Tristram Stanton was watching him as he worked it out."

Knowing George as well as he did, Wiki was certain that his expressive face would have revealed every nuance of thought. Tristram Stanton would have realized at once that it was necessary to get him out of the way before he blurted out his suspicions, that it was just as urgent to get rid of George Rochester as it had been to get rid of . . . Jim Powell. Before Jim Powell told anyone the whole truth about that note.

Wiki said urgently to Smith, "Have they found Jim Powell's body yet?"

"Who?"

"Jim Powell—the seaman who was nearly strangled by the buntline."

Smith said petulantly, "Why do you ask at a time like this? Why is it important?"

"Because Tristram Stanton murdered him—just as he murdered Astronomer Burroughs. He broke Burroughs's neck after knocking him out with a blow to the head and then strung up his corpse to make it look as if he'd hanged himself, but he couldn't manage the same trick when he killed Powell. So, Lieutenant," Wiki said savagely, "I would be obliged if you would tell me if they've found Jim Powell's corpse yet."

Lieutenant Smith puffed out his chest and said with dignity, "They have not, but the matter is closed. Captain Wilkes's verdict was that Powell went overboard during the storm. There is no evidence of foul play whatsoever."

"Even if no one saw Jim go over—which I find very hard to believe—why was there no sighting of his body? Bodies float, Lieutenant, and there's a complement of more than two hundred on the *Vincennes!*"

"And there are sharks in the ocean, sir, sharks!"

Sharks. Wiki stilled utterly, lost in a ghostly memory of

phosphorescent trails cruising the expanse of sea between the flagship and the *Porpoise,* his mind reverberating with the long death chant of the Rotuman.

Sharks. It had been the night of the first live firing, Wiki remembered. Had the school of sharks been drawn by the concussion of cannon—or had there been blood in the water? He thought of the way the great predators had circled, and Rochester's lively description of the way the barrel had exploded into tiny fragments. *As every seaman knows, a handful of chips heaved overboard will float in all directions—in ever-widening circles. If there was blood or flesh in among those chips . . .*

Every muscle was tense, a past conversation with this pompous little red-faced man vividly in mind. Wiki said slowly, "When Captain Wilkes kept back a select few to drink port and madeira, was Astronomer Stanton included?"

"He had an invitation," Smith replied. His lips were pursed in a way that showed how much he disliked this cross-examination. "However, he rather rudely excused himself on account of the headache. He had drunk rather a lot of wine," he added, with more than a hint of disapproval.

Wiki took a deep breath. "So was it Astronomer Stanton who suggested today's exercise?"

"Why, yes!" Smith had been busily pouring himself more coffee, but now he looked around, his expression surprised. "How did you guess?"

"Did he also suggest that it should be a live exercise? With a barrel as a target?"

"Yes—just as before! And he offered to find the barrel, too."

Wiki whispered, "Oh, dear Jehovah," and sprinted up the stairs.

Far across the water, a boat was putting out from the flagship. As Wiki watched with urgent intensity, screwing his eyes up against the bright sun and the glitter on the sea, the boat pulled slowly but steadily until it was about two hundred yards from the *Vincennes*. His fists gripped the rail so hard the wood bit into them, and he was only vaguely aware of the two lieutenants arriving alongside him. The harsh light stung his eyes so piercingly that tears ran down his cheeks, but through the blur Wiki watched as the oarsmen stilled the boat, stirring the water with their long blades. A couple of others stood up, balanced themselves, and then manhandled a cask over the gunwale. Over it went, with a distant splash, to settle, bobbing, halfway to the surface. The boat's crew took up their oars again and sculled back to the flagship.

Wiki could just discern the open gunports and imagine the short muzzles of the carronades. The snout of the starboard chaser was poking over the rail at the quarter.

He spun round and exclaimed, "They mustn't fire—we have to stop the exercise!"

Lieutenant Smith went redder in the face than ever, his little eyes popping. "What's that?"

"We must stop them firing those guns—before someone is killed!" *Unless George is already dead*. Wiki thrust the thought away.

Forsythe's hoarse drawl inquired, "And how exactly, Mr. Deputy Coffin, are we going to manage to do that?"

"Signal them!"

"I doubt they'll take a single damn moment's notice of any signals we might fly."

"Lower a boat," Wiki said desperately. "Get the boat between the cannon and the target."

"You're insane, Mr. Coffin!" snapped Lieutenant Smith.

"You propose frustrating a naval exercise on the basis of a wild whim!"

"And who do you think will be brave enough to get between a loaded cannon and its target?" queried Forsythe, with unabated amusement, paying no attention whatsoever to his apoplectic second-in-command.

"Volunteers," Wiki looked around, sorting out names in his head. Sua and Jack Savvy would be with him, he was certain. Then he looked at Forsythe, and said, "Lower a boat. When Captain Wilkes holds an inquiry, I'll accept all the responsibility."

"You got a reason for this?" said the southerner, his expression cynically entertained. "Or are you jest tryin' to be a pain in Stanton's arse—seeing this exercise was all his idea?"

A drum was rattling out on the *Vincennes,* heard only in faint scraps at that distance, but still identifiable as a beating to quarters. All too vividly, Wiki could picture Captain Wilkes standing on the poop, his speaking trumpet at the ready.

He said desperately, "If that barrel is sunk, the only evidence that John Burroughs was the man at the Newport News banquet will be lost. Tristram Stanton's got rid of everyone else. He murdered Burroughs by snapping his neck, just as he snapped Ophelia's, except he managed to pass it off as suicide. Then he got rid of Powell by knocking him on the head and putting him in the target barrel! That's how he got rid of the corpse!"

"That's accusation without a shred of evidence!" shouted Lieutenant Smith. "It has been bad enough listening to the wild slanders you have made against Astronomer Stanton—which I will *certainly* report—but for a civilian to bear a hand in the affairs of the ship—"

"Why, what gives you that idea?" said Forsythe to Wiki, looking interested.

"The sharks! The sharks that came all about after the last exercise! Don't you remember them? They were drawn by the blood in the water!"

"I cannot allow this!" Lieutenant Smith cried. "Lieutenant Forsythe, order the bo'sun to take charge of this man!"

"You call me *captain* while you're on board my goddamned ship!" barked Forsythe. Then he looked at Wiki and nodded. "Lower a boat," he said. "Call for volunteers."

"Captain Forsythe, I protest most strenuously! If you value your career—"

"Oh, do shut up, you noisy little bugger," said Forsythe, and put a large hand in the middle of the taut little paunch and shoved. Lieutenant Smith staggered backward and sat down on the deck abruptly, but Forsythe was not even looking. Instead, he brushed his palms together, as if to get rid of dirt.

Wiki looked back at the distant *Vincennes*. To his horror he glimpsed activity behind one of the gunports as a carronade was run out. The exercise had commenced. He spun on his heel, shouting names.

Men seemed to take an age to listen and comprehend what was needed, but then all at once they were at the starboard rail and the boat was down. Even as it splashed, there was a distant concussion from the flagship. Wiki watched tensely, his breath held as the ball soared over the target and hit the water farther on. The barrel was bobbing hard, bouncing up and down as if some great fish was nudging it from beneath the surface.

Abruptly, then, Wiki realized that Forsythe was beside him—carrying a rifle. Not one of Stanton's, but his own favorite weapon. "I'm coming," the southerner said shortly. Wiki paused, but there was no time to argue. Then, on a sudden impulse, he dashed across the deck to the signal locker, grabbed a flag, ran back to the rail, and vaulted into the boat.

As the oarsmen hauled at their oars, another thudding explosion sounded from the *Vincennes*.

Twenty-six

*C*aptain Wilkes hollered, "Silence fore and aft!"
Midshipman Keith rubbed his palms down the sides of his trousers to wipe off the sweat. The preliminary orders to wet and sand the decks and cast loose the guns, after removing their tompions and muzzle bags, had been heard and followed long since. There had been five dumb practice exercises, and now the live show was about to commence.

Keith was determined that his gun crew—Passed Midshipman Rochester's gun crew—was not going to let the missing officer down. They had won the competition before, and they were going to hit that target again. His five tackle men had clapped onto the ropes and run the gun carriage inboard, and now they stared at him with resolute expressions that reflected how he felt. One of the scientifics, Astronomer Stanton, seemed to feel the same confidence, too, because he was standing close by, watching every preparation with narrow attention.

Midshipman Keith started to bawl out the next order, stopped when his voice threatened to squeak, and then said gruffly, "Chock your luff!"

The ship was barely moving on the flat calm of the sea, so the men at the tackles simply braced their shoulders to maintain tension on the carriage.

"Stop vent!"

The captain of the gun leaned over the breech and placed a piece of leather over the touch hole.

"Cartridge!"

The powder boy fished about in his leathern bucket, produced a cylindrical bag of gunpowder, and heaved it across to the loader, who swung it around and shoved it up the barrel.

"Wad and ram home!"

The rammer inserted a wad and pushed it up the maw of the cannon as far as it would go. The captain of the gun bent over again to poke his priming iron through the breech and wiggle it. Looking up at Midshipman Keith, he said gravely, "Home, sir!"

"Grape, I think—don't you?" asked Keith. A democratic fellow, he had decided on a program of building camaraderie by consulting with his men.

"Aye, sir, most certainly, sir! Let's blast that barrel to smithereens!"

"Then make it so," said Midshipman Keith, and watched the loader heave up the bag of grape and shove it down the barrel. "Ram home!" he cried, and the rammer leaped forward with his wad and rammer again.

"Man side-tackle falls, run out!" The two side-tackle men hauled mightily at the ropes, running the gun up to the rail and forcing out the snout as far as it would go. Squinting along the brute length of it, Midshipman Keith fixed his eye on the target—which was bobbing up and down in a highly uncooperative fashion, considering the flatness of the sea—and cried, "Crows and handspikes!"

During the exercises he had kept the muzzle of the cannon aimed at the surface about two hundred yards off, guessing that that was where the target would be, and so there was not a great deal of heaving and hauling necessary. The chaser, in fact, was primed and aimed for action in a satisfyingly short time. However, to the gun crew's intense irritation, the other chaser had the first shot. Midshipman Keith heard hurried footsteps as Astronomer Stanton went across with his spyglass to check their aim, followed by Captain Wilkes's shout, "Number six!"—followed by a great boom from the far side of the deck.

To the gun crew's satisfaction, however, the shot soared over the target and then bounced and sank. Astronomer Stanton arrived back at Midshipman Keith's side and said, "Quite a few degrees high. Do you think you should lower your sights, officer?"

"Sir, I think we are fine," said Keith firmly, disliking interference from a civilian, and wondering why he was taking such an active part.

Stanton's reply, if he made one, was muffled by Captain Wilkes's shout, "Number four!" A carronade hurled its charge, but, because the *Vincennes* ducked a sudden curtsey as a gust of wind came out of nowhere to slap the sails briefly full, the shot was well wide of the target.

Astronomer Stanton said sharply, "Bring your bearings round, Midshipman. Make allowance for the movement of the ship."

Midshipman Keith said coldly, "I beg your pardon, sir?"

"Don't you want to win? There's a gold guinea for each man of your gun crew if you blow that barrel to pieces."

"Number seven!" roared Captain Wilkes's amplified voice.

Keith's crew spat on their palms and braced their shoulders, enlivened still further by the prospect of a bounty. However, the midshipman was frowning, wondering about the astronomer's urgency.

"Take your time, my lads," he said.

"But you must take advantage of the lull!" Astronomer Stanton urged as the puff of wind died. "Tell your captain to cock the lock and prime the charge, sir! I will double the bounty if you smash it first shot!"

Keith stared at him, acutely aware that the gun crew was fidgeting with impatience, and that the whole ship was watching and waiting. Then, from beyond the astronomer's head, he glimpsed a movement, a half mile out.

"Hulloa," he said, going to the rail to see better. A boat was pulling out from the little brig *Swallow*, her men pulling at the oars with evident frenzy. Obviously, it was not part of the stated program, because Keith could see Captain Wilkes and the First Lieutenant conferring while they aimed their spyglasses, and hear stray bits of their conversation, which betrayed that they were as mystified as he was.

Astronomer Stanton said sharply, "The exercise has not been cancelled, Midshipman Keith. It is your turn to fire, and your captain expects you to do your duty."

He was right, Keith thought unwillingly. He turned to the gun captain and said, his voice reluctant, "Cock your lock, if you will."

The gun captain poured priming powder over the vent with the aid of a goose quill, but Keith's eyes kept on moving away from him and back to the boat. It had become evident that it was not steering for the *Vincennes*, as he had originally thought, but was making for the barrel target. Even more oddly, despite the fact that there was scarcely any breeze, one of the men in the boat was stepping the mast.

Click. It was a small sound, but loud enough to seize Keith's attention. When he looked back at the cannon the captain had pulled back the hammer. His eyes met Midshipman Keith's and held an attentive stare, his whole frame poised as he held the string of the firing lanyard in his hand, ready for the igniting pull.

"Blow your match," said Keith to the loader.

"You don't need the match," Astronomer Stanton exclaimed. "Give the order to pull!"

"Routine, sir, must be followed," said Midshipman Keith, carefully keeping reprimand out of his tone. While he watched the slow fuse smolder red as the loader blew gently, just in case the flintlock did not catch, his eyes kept on flickering over to the boat. The mast was up, and a bundle of brilliant fabric was being bent to it. It might as well have been a sail because no sooner was it attached than another gust of wind flicked up and the cloth billowed out.

It was a flag—the ensign of the United States! Everyone was staring in puzzlement, and Keith could hear muttered exclamations and queries from all about the deck.

"Fire!" exclaimed Astronomer Stanton—and Keith whirled round. For an instant he thought that the gun captain would obey the civilian, simply because of the authorative snap in his voice. But a loud cry from the quarterdeck distracted the gunner, so he looked around instead of yanking on the cord.

Captain Wilkes had an arm out, pointing at the main truck

of the brig *Swallow,* and all the heads on deck were turned to see what the agitation was about. A signal was being hoisted—a signal that Keith had never seen before, a blue triangle with a rectangular cutout in the middle of the hoist.

Captain Wilkes and the First Lieutenant were equally perplexed, it seemed, because the quartermaster was being summoned. Hurried footsteps rattled over the quarterdeck and books were being consulted.

Then, with a shock, Keith felt his upper arm gripped. He swung around to find Stanton's heavy, furious face close to his. The astronomer snapped, "When the hell are you going to order them to fire that goddamned gun?"

"Sir, I—"

Keith stopped. A voice echoed from the quarterdeck, saying, "The signal reads that the brig *Swallow* is endangered, sir—but from what cause, it is impossible to—"

Astronomer Stanton shouted in Midshipman Keith's ear, "Give the order to . . . FIRE!"

The last word was barked out like a command. Midshipman Keith swung around, again afraid that the gun captain had automatically obeyed. But, instead, he saw the gun captain staring at him questioningly, the firing lanyard in his hand.

Keith could see his fingers whitening as he got ready to pull. He shouted, "Belay that!"

Humiliatingly, his voice squeaked, but the gun captain had heard, and his instinctive movement had frozen. The next blur of motion came from a completely unexpected quarter. Astronomer Stanton sprung forward, knocked the slow match out of the loader's startled hand, and grabbed it up. Then he made a lunge at the breech of the gun.

Midshipman Keith broke out of a paralysis of disbelief and

threw himself at the burly form to grapple him away. He was young, tall, and strong, but Stanton had the strength of panic. Back and forth they struggled, and then unbelievable pain surged through Keith's shoulder as the astronomer gripped his upper arm and wrenched. Keith heard an appalling pop as the upper bone of his arm left the socket, and then all at once he was flying through the air and over the rail.

Flailing as he fell, Keith hit the water with a sickening crash. Down he sank, and the world turned bubbling and green.

Wiki was standing in the boat, one hand gripping the mast, while above his head the great flag alternately flapped and sagged, so that the twenty-six stars winked and twinkled and the seven brilliant red stripes seemed to wriggle with menace. He saw the distant figure tumble down to the sea, but his concentration was on the snout of the cannon that was aimed directly at them. Even at this distance, it seemed as huge as doom.

Then he saw Tristram Stanton at the rail. He saw him dip, as if to pick something up, and straighten with something in his hand, and turn as if to go to the gun. There was a distant spark, and a little whiff of smoke as the astronomer held his hand in front of his mouth, as if he was blowing a flame to life. *He had the slow match,* Wiki realized with horror, and the cannon was aimed to blow them all to hell—and all at once a brawny, tattooed arm snaked around his throat, cramming his right ear tight against the mast.

Something hard and narrow pressed across the top of his right shoulder, and the tip of a rifle barrel slid into the bottom half of his vision.

Forsythe's voice grated in his left ear, "Hold very still."

Wiki braced himself, feeling the warm wood of the mast hard against his cheek, the weight of the rifle barrel, and the intensity of Forsythe's concentration. The wind had dropped again, and the boat scarcely moved on the flat, calm sea. He could smell Forsythe's rank odor and hear the slow harsh intake of breath. The breath was sucked in, held—and there was an almighty explosion.

When Wiki gasped, "My God!" with shock, he was so deafened he could not hear his own voice—but Stanton's distant figure had disappeared, dropped to the deck by the shot. For the first time Wiki really and truly understood that the southerner was an outstanding marksman. Then he abruptly realized his shoulder had been scorched with the exploding gas from the breech, wrenched himself free, and dived over the side into the cool water.

His hearing came back as the burn eased. Wiki held on to the side of the boat, looking over to where Midshipman Keith was floundering, noting that sometime in the interval the *Swallow* had put down the second boat, because he could see it now, determinedly heading for the *Vincennes* with Lieutenant Smith in the stern sheets.

He looked at Sua, saying, "*E hoa*. The barrel—secure it, and bring it into the boat, handsomely, now—gently—and open it very carefully." Then he added in Samoan, "My friend is imprisoned inside." Sua nodded with complete understanding, and Wiki struck out to rescue the drowning midshipman.

Epilogue

*W*iki hoisted himself over the gangway to the deck of the Vincennes with the aid of a thrown rope and a number of helping hands, his white-faced, miserably gulping, but nevertheless deeply grateful piece of human flotsam heaved up in front of him. Then he straightened and looked about—at a scene of utter chaos. Red-coated marines rushed past in a rhythmic stamp of boots and rattle of arms, responding to an uproar of conflicting commands. Gun-carriage wheels grated and men cursed in panic-stricken shouts as cannon were run out and brought to bear on Forsythe's boat, now jerkily pulling toward the Vincennes and getting closer by the moment. Officers were screaming at their gun crews to hold their fire, as boats loaded with marines dropped down on the water.

Fifteen yards off, Forsythe's boat stilled. The southerner's stance was tense as he stood at the steering oar, waiting for the soldiers to come alongside. The wind that had reached them was stiffening, so that the brilliant flag blew out straight, revealing George Rochester sitting in the middle thwarts, slumped but indubitably alive. Wiki felt a rush of overwhelming relief. George looked up, as if he sensed Wiki's searching stare, and grinned and waved. Hunkered protectively at Rochester's shoulder, Sua looked up, too, and punched a triumphant fist in the air. Then Wiki abruptly became aware of a shrill commotion on the quarterdeck.

Captain Wilkes's voice was raised in one of the tirades that had become so unpleasantly familiar to every man in the fleet—save that this rant sounded unusually hysterical. The general uproar silenced as men who had been watching Forsythe and the boat's crew being apprehended turned from the rail to stare in puzzlement at their captain instead. The quartermaster and First Lieutenant standing to each side of Wilkes were extremely wooden faced. Captain Wilkes was white lipped, his forehead gleaming with sweat; he looked on the brink of vomiting or fainting. Wiki mused uneasily that it was a very bad omen that the commander of the expedition should suddenly go to pieces like this, when the great challenges of the Antarctic and the Pacific lay ahead.

Captain Wilkes was shaking a long, trembling finger at the starboard gun crew. The ten men were standing in a shocked semicircle, closely surrounded by marines, the corpse of the astronomer at their feet. "Give me the name of the son of a bitch who struck down Mr. Stanton!" he screamed at their numb faces. "Where is the bastard who murdered Astronomer Stanton? By God, I will hang him—I'll flay him and throttle him! Say a name!"

Not one of the gun crew attempted to answer. The eyes of

the loaders and rammers flickered toward their gun captain, but he merely stared straight ahead, his form absolutely rigid, while every manjack on deck and in the rigging watched and waited. So concentrated was their attention that everyone jumped with surprise when Lieutenant Smith hove into view at the gangway.

He did not seem to notice, instead trotting furiously along the deck and exclaiming, "Captain Wilkes! Why did I have to come to report an emergency? Why did no one respond? Did you not see my signal?"

Wiki saw Wilkes's hands clench as he turned to face the choleric little man. "Of course we saw your bloody signal!" he savagely snapped. "But you didn't bother to let us know what *kind* of goddamned emergency you referred to! Was it that the brig was on fire? On the verge of foundering? Caught in irons on a lee shore?" he went on with vicious sarcasm. "Outnumbered by the enemy? Boarded by pirates? Your signal was not at all *clear*, sir!"

"I signaled that I had a mutiny on board—mutiny," said Smith, completely unshaken by the verbal attack. "That's what that signal represents, and I am surprised and disappointed that no one knew it."

"Captain Wilkes, sir," the quartermaster protested. "It's absolutely the first I have ever heard of that blue flag with the hole in the hoist meaning mutiny. Here's my book, if you don't believe me."

"A gross disobedience of orders is what it means, sir," Smith snapped, "a severe interference in the orderly running of the ship. It was an insurrection inspired by Wiremu Coffin, who has betrayed the great confidence we placed in him when we appointed him to the position of expedition linguister. But Lieutenant Forsythe is equally guilty, if not more so. When I tried to resist, he manhandled me, sir, shoved me to the deck—I was overpowered, sir, in the course of my proper duty!"

"For God's sake!" Wilkes roared. "He was the one in charge of the ship! He had every right to shove you to the deck if you interfered with his command! And can't you see that we have emergency enough already? Our astronomer has been *murdered*, sir—foully cut down in the prime of his life!—and I am determined to search out the man responsible and see him dangling from the mainyard."

Wiki felt someone brush past him. It was Midshipman Keith, pale and painwracked but very determined, blurting, "Captain Wilkes, sir—"

"Oh, for God's sake!" exclaimed Wilkes. "What is it *now?*"

"It is my painful duty to report that Astronomer Stanton—" Keith's voice failed, and he had to cough and start again. "That he—he was determined to seize control of my gun and blow Mr. Coffin's boat out of the water, sir—it was an attack on the U.S. flag, Old Glory herself, sir! I tried my best to restrain him, but he bested me. I offer my sincere apologies. I wish I had done better, but he threw me over the rail after crippling my poor shoulder—which I have to confess is in awful agony, and I would thank the surgeon kindly for his attention. Personally, I think the man who felled Astronomer Stanton should get a medal," he candidly added.

"*What* did you say?" roared Wilkes—and at that moment Lieutenant Forsythe clambered up onto deck, closely followed by a string of marines.

Ignoring his escort, the southerner strode over to where Tristram Stanton's body was sprawled on the planks, oozing fluids from the hole in his skull. He hunkered down, had a brief look, and then rose to his feet again, his expression sour.

"Damn," he said into the riveted silence, his tone quite dispassionate. "I was aiming for a gut shot."

"Lieutenant—" Captain Wilkes said, and then stopped. His expression was stunned.

"My cousin was a silly bloody bitch, but I liked her." Forsythe turned to Wiki and executed a mock salute. "Now it's your turn, Mr. Deputy Coffin," he said, and then looked at Wilkes. "This remarkable sleuth here will explain it all to your entire satisfaction," he assured the expedition's commander. Then he folded his arms and, like everyone else, waited for Wiki to begin.

Wiki shifted, grimaced, braced himself—and was forestalled by a huge shout of *"Ship ahoy!"* from high above.

"Ship?" cried Captain Wilkes. "What ship?"

"The *Peacock!"* cried five lookouts at once, from all over the rigging. "And in a hell of a hurry," observed one, in a voice not meant to carry, but which did. "Wind two p'ints abaft her beam and she's flying like the devil's on her tail. And flying a dozen urgent signals, too!"

"Oh, bloody *hell!*" Captain Wilkes exclaimed. "*More* goddamned signals? What *else* has this dreadful day got in store?"

A Few Recommendations for Those Interested in the Saga of the Exploring Expedition

Erskine, Charles. *Twenty Years Before the Mast: with the more thrilling scenes and incidents while circumnavigating the globe under the command of the late Admiral Charles Wilkes 1838–1842*. Washington, D.C.: Smithsonian Institution, 1985.

Philbrick, Nathaniel. *Sea of Glory: America's Voyage of Discovery, the U.S. Exploring Expedition 1838–1842*. New York: Viking, 2003.

Reynolds, William. *Voyage to the Southern Ocean: The Letters of Lieutenant William Reynolds from the U.S. Exploring Expedition, 1838–1842*. Edited by Anne Hoffman Cleaver and E. Jeffrey Stann (and with an excellent introduction and epilogue by Herman J. Viola). Annapolis, Md.: Naval Institute Press, 1988.

Stanton, William. *The Great United States Exploring Expedition of 1838–1842.* Berkeley, Calif.: University of California Press, 1975.

Viola, Herman J., and Carolyn Margolis, eds. *Magnificent Voyagers: The U.S. Exploring Expedition, 1838–1842.* Washington, D.C.: Smithsonian Institution, 1985.

Wilkes, Charles. *Narrative of the United States Exploring Expedition.* 5 vols. 1844. Reprint, Upper Saddle River, N.J.: Gregg Press, 1970.